GRAPHIC
BETRAYAL

To Gwen,

Christmas 2007

Gloria

x

G.D. Brown

The characters depicted in Graphic Betrayal are purely fictitious and bear no resemblance whatsoever to any person or event.

Note for Librarians: A cataloguing record for this book is available from Library and Archives Canada at www.collectionscanada.ca/amicus/index-e.html
ISBN 1-4120-9530-1

Printed in Victoria, BC, Canada. Printed on paper with minimum 30% recycled fibre.
Trafford's print shop runs on "green energy" from solar, wind and other environmentally-friendly power sources.

TRAFFORD
PUBLISHING

Offices in Canada, USA, Ireland and UK

Book sales for North America and international:
Trafford Publishing, 6E–2333 Government St.,
Victoria, BC V8T 4P4 CANADA
phone 250 383 6864 (toll-free 1 888 232 4444)
fax 250 383 6804; email to orders@trafford.com
Book sales in Europe:
Trafford Publishing (UK) Limited, 9 Park End Street, 2nd Floor
Oxford, UK OX1 1HH UNITED KINGDOM
phone +44 (0)1865 722 113 (local rate 0845 230 9601)
facsimile +44 (0)1865 722 868; info.uk@trafford.com
Order online at:
trafford.com/06-1285

10 9 8 7 6 5 4

One

Mathew Weekes glanced up at the new digital wall clock. He had preferred the old one with the enormous white face and black hands that had hung there ever since he joined the firm. Instead of large Roman numerals, this one had red glowing digits. Mathew read the figures 'seventeen forty-seven' and translated the numbers into words. 'Nearly ten to six,' he said to himself, as the old clock would have instantly told him. He lowered his eyes to face his client who was seated directly under the clock on the opposite side of the desk. He was anxious to wrap this up and call it a day.

'I can hear what you're saying Mr. McCormack, but a jury won't buy it,' said Mathew, sternly, 'your barrister will agree with me, a jury just won't buy it.'

McCormack gazed across the desk at Mathew Weekes. A dull ache hit him in his stomach as the words of his solicitor echoed in his head and stuck hard.

'You don't believe me do you Mr. Weekes?' said McCormack childishly. He interlocked his fingers tightly and pressed his sweating palms together. He kept them clasped beneath the desk and out of sight of his adviser, and again muttered, 'you just don't believe me.' The legal opinion could not have been worse. He felt sick; looming ahead was another long stretch inside.

Mathew Weekes rose from where he had been sitting and, still facing his client, placed both hands on the desk in front of him. He leaned on them hard and bent forward to face McCormack squarely. 'It's not a matter of me not believing you is it?' said Mathew, 'these are very serious charges. There is so much evidence against you that it was delivered by van with enough boxes of paper to keep my secretary supplied for the rest of her working life.' Conscious that he was losing his patience and raising his voice, Mathew lifted his hands from the desk and stood upright. It wasn't his intention to intimidate his client, but he was exhausted. They were speaking the same language, but his client just wasn't listening. He glanced again at the clock just above McCormack's head and then walked towards the window of his office. His voice mellowed as he gazed out at the River Thames. 'All I mean is it's going to be a hell of a job to convince a jury that you knew so little.' He turned to face his client again. 'Fraud can send you away for many years, all I can do is try and minimise the length of time you serve; that's all I can do, just reduce the time. My advice is quite clear, you should plead guilty.'

McCormack had never been good at decisions, but now he felt that his choice of legal representative was the worst choice he'd ever made. He had decided to stick with Mathew Weekes simply because he had been there from the start, since the day of his arrest in fact. McCormack didn't want to get to know anyone else, or tell his tale to another single soul. It made sense to stick with the devil he knew, despite everything that he was now being told.

It all began when they met at Beconsbridge Police Station. Mathew Weekes was a duty solicitor; Martin McCormack a legally aided suspect arrested for fraud. From the outset, Mathew had not been convinced by McCormack's version of events that preceded his arrest, and McCormack had been as equally unimpressed with Mathew Weekes, who had simply been chosen by the police from the duty solicitor rota. If it had been another day, another time, he would have met a different lawyer who might have been more agreeable, but it was Mathew Weekes who was called to support him, to advise him and fight his corner. McCormack had doubted Mathew's ability to even get him out of Beconsbridge police station, let alone prevent him from being charged. He hadn't liked the advice, and he certainly hadn't taken it, particularly the warning to say nothing at all to the police. He just couldn't stay quiet, and Mathew had no choice but to sit and watch his client while he gave the police a full and embarrassing interview, which, as predicted, had tied McCormack in knots. When the interview was concluded Mathew used every trick in the book to persuade the police to let him go. It was only after every condition possible had been offered and attached to his bail that McCormack was eventually released. The bail conditions meant that he had to remain living at his present address and surrender his passport. He was forbidden to speak with any witnesses and had to remain outside of a three-mile radius of several named addresses. Of course, there were special exceptions to allow for medical and legal appointments, and appearances at court, but McCormack was not happy. He now had to observe a curfew from 9.00pm to 8.30am and report daily to Beconsbridge police station until the day of his trial. In addition, the police had asked for a surety to be taken up, but Mathew had argued that this was unreasonable, bearing in mind McCormack's circumstances; he had no one to offer a financial guarantee against absconding and he had no living family. The few acquaintances that he did have were workmates, many of whom were either witnesses or defendants themselves. Taking everything into account, Mathew thought he had secured a very good deal, but McCormack didn't think so. He was eventually charged with obtaining property by deception and conspiracy to defraud. The total value placed on the crimes ran into millions.

The meeting today did little to alter Mathew's earlier impression of McCormack, or to vary his advice to plead guilty; the convincing evidence demanded it. He didn't believe a single word his client had uttered since they first met at the police station, nor during the several months that had since passed, but Mathew reminded himself that it wasn't his job to be policeman, judge, or jury, and most certainly not all three. He was a facilitator of justice according to English law, and prided himself on his ability to remain strictly impartial. He would do everything by the book; give the best service he could provide, and nothing would deter him from securing his client's right to a fair trial, despite his own opinions. These were the lessons he had been taught, and the rules to which he had vowed to adhere; remaining impartial had been by far the hardest lesson of all. If McCormack went down for his crimes then it would be because justice had been done, and had been seen to be done, not because his advice was sloppy or his efforts half-hearted. However, there was nothing further he could say or do at this stage to make McCormack feel any easier.

Martin McCormack continued to stare at his solicitor as he walked back towards the desk where his client remained seated.

'But Mr. Weekes', said McCormack, 'you have to believe me ….' but before he could utter another word, Mathew stopped him in his tracks.

'I'm sorry,' he said abruptly, 'I'm late for a meeting.' He took the file containing details of McCormack's past, present, and likely future, and rested it on its edge on the desk between them. Mathew tapped its paper contents and glanced again at the clock above McCormack's head. 'Seventeen fifty-two … nearly six,' thought Mathew. The meeting had to end here and he was eager to see McCormack get the message and rise from his chair. McCormack got the message. He stood promptly and firmly shook his adviser's hand in an automatic gesture of gratitude, and said goodbye to his brief.

It wasn't until McCormack had reached the main doors leading from the office reception, and felt the first cold blast of street air attacking his senses, that he realised there was no reason at all for him to be grateful. As he descended the stone steps from Marshall Maplin & Weekes, he doubted whether his solicitor had the ability to minimise his stretch, let alone secure his freedom. He had wanted the chance to confide a lot more about his past life and history of offending, but his solicitor had appeared agitated and disinterested. McCormack felt he had been deprived of proper attention from his legal adviser. He hadn't liked the way the meeting had ended; his opinion of Mathew Weekes had definitely taken a turn for the worse.

He felt in his pocket for some small change and pulled out a few coins, along with an out of date bus pass. He would normally jump the bus and flash the pass quickly at the driver, but feeling as he did about the way his luck was running he settled at the prospect of a long walk home. It was a dry, bright evening, with a crisp coolness in the air; McCormack was in no hurry. He had nothing to do, no one to see, no one was waiting for him. He decided on the longer route home so that he could catch a glimpse of the river on the way; he wanted to live and feel his freedom for as long as possible.

Despite having several acquaintances, McCormack had made few friends in his forty-three years of life. His skills were few; he was virtually illiterate, surviving the best part of his life through the pickings of petty crime. He was a known face to the police, and notorious within his own fraternity. He had been in and out of prison since he was old enough to go there, but there was nobody close to him, and no one he could confide in; his solicitor was his only hope. Since his last stretch inside, he had tried to resist all the temptations that came his way that offered him a chance to earn some easy money; he had been doing everything right, or so he thought, but he was now firmly of the opinion that despite all his efforts to keep straight and stay away from crime, those efforts hadn't paid off. Crime always had a way of finding him, and combined with his own lack of judgement, he was now in a deep and complicated mess.

At his meeting with Mathew Weekes he had tried, unsuccessfully, to convince his solicitor of the part played by Bernie Cullum. If only he could be traced, Cullum would be able to back up everything he had said about his role in the businesses, but despite extensive efforts by himself and the police, they had not found him. Cullum's very existence was therefore in question; the search for him was no longer being taken seriously. After today's meeting, McCormack felt that it was not just the prosecution who accused him of inventing fictitious characters, but his own lawyer too.

He reached the river's edge and stopped to lean on the rail and gaze out at its flow. There were many commuters taking a breath of air before facing the journey home; one or two of them stared at McCormack, who was only too aware of his shabby clothes in contrast to theirs. He felt as inferior as he had done when he shook his solicitor's hand while at the same time being told to prepare for a stretch inside. McCormack had readily accepted that his story was unbelievable and had even thanked his adviser for telling him so. He felt stupid. He clenched his fists hard at the thought of how he really should have reacted, what he really should have said and done.

He looked down over the rail on which he was leaning and to his horror, he glimpsed the dirt beneath his fingernails and the frayed edges of his grubby shirt cuffs. McCormack had intended to wash all his clothes before going to Marshall Maplin & Weekes so as to give his solicitor a good impression, to come across as an honest, clean living person. Only clean, tidy people tell the truth; he knew that. That was how society worked. People who couldn't afford a suit, a new shirt or shoes, poor people, unlucky people, they tell lies. His appearance was therefore important, but with no electricity for the past fortnight, he had barely been able to bathe himself, let alone wash his clothes. He knew his brief had noticed; this was probably the reason he had failed to convince him. He glanced at the working people surrounding him; all were dressed in immaculate suits and clean, crisp shirts, some holding quality woollen coats and rainmacs over their arms, or draped around their shoulders. Others carried leather cases that contained important paperwork that McCormack would never understand. He knew very well the gulf that separated him from all of them; he lived and breathed the differences daily. It was natural, and understandable, that they should look down on him; that's the way it goes. That's how it's always been. He quickly pulled his fingers away from the rail so that the couple standing next to him would not catch sight of his hands and dirty cuffs. As he put his hands to his face, he felt the stubble of the last few days' growth around his chin. He straightened himself up quickly and the girl turned and glanced at him, then quickly turned towards her partner who wrapped an arm around her shoulder, and pulled her towards him. McCormack saw his protective gesture. He wondered if the girl really did need protecting from people like him - a scruffy illiterate with no hot water.

He turned his back on both of them, and stared out at the river. He could jump and it would all end there. He was a poor swimmer; no one would attempt to save him. It could be the most dramatic thing he had ever done. McCormack only dreamed of such heroics, but he did nothing. He headed away from the river passively accepting his position, as always. All he could look forward to that evening was the stroll home and the hope that he had something to eat on his return to the flat. In his earlier hurry to keep his appointment, he had missed his usual routine at the shops in his own locality. When the schools closed, the stores would fill with excited hungry school kids and the staff would watch them carefully, in preference to watching McCormack. If he timed it right, he would normally come away with enough for a reasonable meal; today he might have to go hungry.

The hour-long walk had tired McCormack; he was physically and mentally exhausted. He reached the grounds to the estate and looked up towards the window of his flat situated on the eighth floor of Banners Court. He entered the lift and smelt the stench of the life he had chosen to lead. He pressed the appropriate button to take him to floor eight and began to reflect on the day's events, his solicitor and his forthcoming conference with his barrister, and how he could possibly escape custody. But more than anything else, his mind was firmly fixed on Bernie Cullum.

Two

Philip Davidson thought life was brilliant; by the end of the day, he knew he would be even richer still. He was coming up to his fifty-fourth birthday; if he wanted to, he could retire tomorrow. As he turned in his silk sheets, he could feel the lithe body of Natalie lying next to him. He knew she would be feeling rough from the night before, but thought little of it. If it wasn't for him, he thought, she would still be entertaining desperate punters in sleazy clubs. He had saved her from all of that; she no longer had to drink too much or dance for anyone, and was happy to be living in the luxury of his penthouse overlooking the Thames. He looked at her lying asleep, her hair blending with the sheen of the cream silk pillow. She looked about seventeen, but Natalie had convinced him that she was in her twenties, not that he minded how old she was; she belonged to him like everything else he considered bought and paid for, like a penthouse, or a Jaguar car, or a fleet of motorbikes. He had worked hard for his money, and it was his money that could get him what he wanted, when he wanted it. Morality played no part. Natalie was still oblivious to the world, thanks to all the double vodkas, and the effect of yesterday's alcohol on her mood somehow put him off. It wasn't that he felt bad about taking advantage of her; he just didn't like women who drank too much. He decided to let her sleep.

He slipped out of bed and put on his pure white towelling robe with the letter "P" embroidered in blue silk on the top left pocket, and opened the French doors to the roof garden. The sun peaked occasionally through the clouds leaving an explosion of sparkling diamonds across the water. He watched while a ferry loaded with tourists made its way slowly up river. Faces gazed up towards his penthouse in what he considered to be pure unadulterated envy. He could just about hear the commentary from the tour guide, who was picking out the places of historical interest and the homes of the rich and famous who had also chosen, like Philip, to live on the River Thames. 'The whole world knows the River Thames, and I live on it,' mumbled

Philip. 'Bloody marvellous.'

While watching the ferry trundle past him cutting through the sunlit water, he wondered how much more pleasant and viable it would be for his courier service business to expand to the river. He fixed himself a strong black coffee and returned to the balcony where he sat and pondered on the business prospects for several minutes. His fleet of bikes needed regular servicing and were a constant source of aggravation. With a ferry, he could carry so much more and employ fewer staff; but he had to think of speed. He dismissed the thought from his head almost as quickly as it had entered; safe in the knowledge that everything he had done so far had been a huge success. 'Why change it?' he thought. As he remained gazing out over the river that was now coming alive with boats and distant voices, he remembered his father and his love of the Thames that came second only to his greatest passion of all - Jaguar cars. 'A Jaguar,' his father would say 'is like a temperamental woman. You think you're giving her what she needs, but you could be wrong. Never try to fix her unless you're sure she's broken.' His father always considered a Jaguar as a female. He always talked in terms of 'she'. He would say 'she's gorgeous; she's running smooth.' Philip thought of his father and smiled smugly to himself. Everything was running smoothly; nothing was broken; nothing needed fixing. He'd stick to running his business in the same way as he always had, except for the new little extra outlet he was trying to get off the ground, which he anticipated would more than pay for itself.

Philip finished his second cup of coffee and walked back into the bedroom to see Natalie still lying there asleep. He wondered how different his life would have been if his wife had not discovered his many affairs, and he had stayed married, had kids. He doubted that he could ever have been completely content with one partner, except perhaps for one person, but she was beyond his reach. He often justified his actions. In other cultures, having multiple wives is expected. These regular checks on his behaviour frequently, and easily, absolved himself of any wrong doing in thought, word or deed, if he were ever in any doubt. Philip Davidson thought all women were marvellous, and like other great pleasures, a classic Mk 2 or an XK120, an E-Type or an XJ6, once bought and paid for they could be expensive to run, and tricky to understand, but so long as they were happy, and running smoothly, nothing could be finer.

He and his brother had enjoyed a comfortable upbringing, and his father was proud of him when he set up a business of his own. In contrast, his brother Robert had made a bad decision; he was messing about in art school, and would get nowhere in life, according to his father. Out of the two of them, Philip knew he had always been the favourite. Despite Robert's success as a graphic artist, it had never impressed the old man who had himself stayed all his life in the civil service, paid to predict the amount of office space required for future supplies and staff. It was a mystery to Philip how he and his brother could share the same father; at least he had inherited his father's passion for Jaguar cars and the finer things in life, but so far as Robert was concerned, he could think of nothing relevant at all. Nothing, that is, except perhaps his happy marriage; Robert's lasting relationship with Jennifer was about the only thing that followed in his father's footsteps, but Philip tried not to dwell on any thoughts of his brother's relationship, it always conjured up feelings of jealousy. Predictably, Philip's envious thoughts overwhelmed him, as they often did, exacerbated by watching Natalie lying there. For all his wealth, perhaps his brother was the richer man. Natalie's un-stirring and meaningless presence annoyed him more and more, and he began to think that maybe it was time for an additional distraction; he had to have something to keep him going, not so much a replacement, but more an addition to his collectable pleasures. His thoughts went instantly to the new receptionist at Graphic Solutions, his brother's place of work. Philip was confident that his charm had worked wonders and that she had taken to him instantly. She was a little older than his usual conquests but would still be a pushover. Sometimes he would drink coffee with the girls while sorting out orders for his private sideline, a sideline of which Robert was completely ignorant. Philip benefited greatly from his brother's position within the firm because it supplied his company with

12

regular business. It was mainly because of Robert's senior position at Graphic Solutions that Philip's company, Parcels and Courier Express, held a contract for a large slice of the delivery of orders undertaken by the firm. But Philip also benefited in other ways. Apart from the continuous courier work that boosted his empire, he was able to use the facilities that Graphic Solutions had to offer, such as printing and photo graphics in particular, and this was a huge bonus. He was looking forward to visiting the receptionist, knowing that his charm was irresistible. At the same time, he could get some business done.

He went to the bathroom and took a shower. For a man of his age he was in good shape. He had a long close look at himself in the mirror of the medicine cabinet, and acknowledged his good looks. His grey side-burns were distinctive and did not age him in the slightest. He sleeked his hair backwards with a steel comb, and gelled the sides above his side-burns so that the hair parted in small wet grooves. He was confident he could get almost any woman he wanted, and now was the time to increase his collection; essential to achieve some more goals. Philip did a swift self-check of his behaviour, particularly his loyalty to Natalie, but as usual, he quickly exonerated himself from any wrongdoing; all he was doing was putting his ideas into action, and ideas bring fortunes. It didn't matter too much that his family might not approve, he'd cross that bridge when he came to it.

Three

Mathew was trying hard to get away from the office, and had dismissed his last client abruptly. He wanted desperately to see his father who had been in St. John's Hospice for a year, and was waiting to die. All that could be done had been done, and it was now just a matter of passing the time away as peacefully and pain-free as possible. Since the death of Mathew's mother, George Weekes had given up on life, and Mathew could not come to terms with this. Seeing his father always saddened him, not only because he was terminally ill, but also because Mathew felt he had lost him many years before. He was angry at the wasted years George had devoted to grieving for his wife; he thought it was out of all proportion. Any happy memories of childhood that he might have had were destroyed by the death of his mother; everything suddenly changed. With a father who had hardly noticed him, having a sister had been a lifeline. Had it not been for Jennifer and Robert, he would have been left to live with his father alone, and likely he'd have sunk, just like him.

Mathew read through his last brief quickly. The case was one where his client's version of events had not convinced him, and his proposed defence was on shaky ground. He was anxious to get a second opinion on the advice he had already given. His client was insisting on defending several counts but he thought the case didn't stand a chance. On behalf of the accused, Mathew had instructed Queen's Counsel, Jonathan Bowers, of Kings Bench House, to advise Martin McCormack in conference; the brief was now ready to go. He could rely on Sarah to have typed it accurately with all enclosures correctly attached. He didn't have to check it. Sarah had worked as his personal secretary for nine years during which time she had proved to be invaluable. They had enormous respect for each other, and their close relationship remained on a purely professional working basis. She was an attractive woman in an efficient sort of way, but Mathew was not physically attracted to her. He was comfortable in the knowledge that she was not physically drawn to him either, and this helped to keep the running of his criminal department in perfect working order. Sarah's clothes were sharply pressed and tailored in impeccable taste and classic style. His father would have referred to her as 'well turned out'. She wore a respectable amount of make-up, with a slight shadow on the lid of her eyes and just a hint of pencil liner. Her light brown hair had a permanent shine and turned under on immediate contact with her collar. When she spoke, she did so with such confidence that any advice offered to Mathew never failed to get noticed. Personal lives were rarely discussed apart from the odd occasion when advice may be sought for a birthday present, although somehow they each knew of the other's circumstances without discussion or announcement. He could not wish for a better secretary.

Mathew scribbled at his post and passed it to Sarah.

'You get off now,' said Sarah as she gathered up the papers in front of him, 'don't be late for your father.' Mathew was convinced, as always, that everything was in her safe hands. There was no need for him to stay any later. He took hold of his case and fled from his office. Sarah was standing clutching the evening's post close to her chest.

'Page me if there's anything urgent,' said Mathew as he left, though he knew he didn't need to say a word.

'Of course. Goodnight Mathew,' she replied.

He found himself on the street hailing a cab. He had meant to go home to the flat first to see Susan, his long-term girlfriend, but decided to go straight to the hospice and call her from there. The cab pulled harshly into the kerbside and Mathew stepped back quickly trying to avoid the splash from the water trapped in the gutter from the morning's shower. It annoyed Mathew that some of the old kerbsides were still so deep in that part of London; any Victorian drains that couldn't cope with the unexpected downpours left deep streams of water at the edge of the road. Mathew addressed the driver sharply as he opened the back door of the cab.

'St. John's please.'

'St. John's? Is that the hospice?'

'Yes.'

'Sad place to be going sir. Still, we all have to go. I'd rather be in a place like that than left on a trolley in Bradley General.'

'Yes. I suppose so,' said Mathew.

'Do you know, my neighbour had to go in there as an emergency,' the driver continued enthusiastically, 'he got took by an ambulance with a suspected burst ulcer, or something like that. He was left for ages on a trolley, in agony for all to see.'

'That's pretty awful,' said Mathew, hoping the conversation would end there. It did not.

'His wife reckoned he was on that trolley stuck in the corridor for more than two hours, until some young nurse had a look at him and went off for the doctor. The doctor didn't get to him until it was nearly too late, so he got rushed into the theatre just at the last knockings apparently, according to his wife that is. I've only been in Bradley General once, and that was ...'

Mathew closed his eyes in the back seat of the taxi and let the driver spill it all out for the remainder of the journey. Why not? Talking rubbish was something everybody seemed to be doing just lately. Mathew said nothing more until the hospice was in sight.

'Just here will do. How much do I owe you?' said Mathew. The cabbie stated the fare, continued to talk about how he'd like his last days to be spent in a place like St. John's Hospice, then wished Mathew 'all the best.' Mathew handed the driver a ten-pound note and told him to keep the change. Next time he might just walk.

St. John's looked splendid. As a house for the dying, it was beautiful, and he was glad his father would have his last days here and not on a trolley in Bradley General. He walked through the revolving door and into a surround of polished timber. It smelt like heaven. He was saddened at the thought that one had to be dying to live in such glorious surroundings, but that was the price to pay to earn calm like this. He absorbed the peace about him, breathing it deeply into his body; he needed this tranquillity most days of his life. He sucked in the lavender fragrance that emitted from the newly polished timbers, and other sweet perfumes that caught hold of him as he passed bouquet after bouquet of the most beautiful flowers he had ever seen. He imagined occupying a room here for just one or two nights a week, and would pay generously for a modest room in such a heavenly place. He wondered if there were any spare, or if he could dare to ask, since a vacant room would only exist at the expense of someone's sorrow. These thoughts quickly disappeared as he walked towards his father.

'Dad? You awake dad?'

'Mat? Is that you? I was dozing that's all.'

Mathew could see the anguish in his father. It had always been there but now it seemed to have worsened. He was sure he could see some tears.

'Dad? Shall I get a nurse or someone?'

'What good is that? What can they do? No son, I'm thinking of your mother. I'm wanting to get to your mother now - to be by her side.'

'Come on dad, it's all so long ago. You haven't been dredging it all up again have you? It won't do you any good to be dwelling on it all.'

'I couldn't help her son. I reached for her and I held her hand so tight - too tight maybe so that she couldn't grip me. I wasn't thinking. I did what I thought was best. I should have got something. I should have shouted for someone, but I was struck dumb. I didn't think; that's what killed her. All the trust she had for me; it all drained from her when she knew she was slipping from my grasp. I could see it in her eyes; those beautiful big eyes, looking at me in disbelief. I've never forgotten it - the way she stared. She looked at me for what seemed like an hour that day when she slipped; but it was only a matter of seconds. I could see in her eyes she thought I'd failed her. That was my job, to keep her safe. My Josie, I failed her bad, son. She trusted me and I failed her bad.'

'No dad, you didn't fail her. You did all you could.'

'But I didn't. They told me not to go in, but I should have gone after her. She just slid between the quay and the fender; just enough room for her to slide down. She wasn't fat, but she wasn't thin either. She was just right, your mother.'

'I know she was. Don't upset yourself. Do you want to have a look at the racing pages?' asked Mathew, trying to divert his father's thoughts.

'They told me she'd gone right under the boat; they were looking for her to come out the other side,' George Weekes continued. 'I let them wait those precious moments for her to slide under and out the other side; and she did. She slid out but she was gone; all the pulling and dragging at her; her clothes all astray, showing to everyone. Your mother was always well turned out; she wouldn't have liked it. There she was with her straps all showing and her dress all up and clinging to her. I couldn't think of her being dead, only that all those boat people were looking at her. I threw myself on her when they put her on the quay, and I covered her up. She'd have died if she'd seen herself; I know she would. Huh! What am I saying? She'd have died!' The old man gave a gruff gurgle deep in his throat. 'Mustn't chuckle in here, son. They'll think there's been a miracle and send me a priest, but Josie would have smiled at what I've just said, she'd have laughed, wouldn't she?'

'Yes, dad. Yes, she would.'

Mathew watched his father close his eyes, still with a slight grin amidst the anguished background of his face, and he drifted off to sleep. There might still come a day, Mathew thought, when his father might ask after him; perhaps ask how his day has been. He may give him a chance, a small moment or two to speak about his work, his clients, his relationship with Susan, and his financial affairs. He never had any of this type of interest from his father; at least not since Josie's death, yet there had been times when he had really needed it. 'Just ask about me,' whispered Mathew as he leaned closer to his father's face. 'Don't go dad, not yet,' he continued softly 'ask me how my day has been. Just once.'

After what seemed like hours, his father woke suddenly. His eyes were wide and staring. He reached for Mathew's hand and spoke excitedly.

'Pass the paper, son. I'd nearly forgotten. There's been a whisper from one of the nurses for Doncaster tomorrow. A three-year-old called "Heaven's Above". Heaven's Above! That's just where I'm heading, I hope. I thought the nurse was having a laugh. Sort me an each-way, son.'

Four

It was a Monday morning and the avenue in the Essex suburb came suddenly alive with the roar of Toby's motorbike.

'Has war been declared or is that our son going to work?' mumbled Jennifer Davidson as she turned in her bed, and buried her head further into the pillow. 'What time is it? Feels like the crack of dawn.'

'That's music to my ears' said Robert proudly. 'Our son is not only up at six o'clock and on his way to a paid job, but he has just turned over a Kawasaki GT 750. What's more, he has no alcohol or drug dependency, and he hasn't got his girlfriend pregnant. Don't knock it,' said Robert as he left the warmth of his bed and pulled on his dressing gown.

'Shouldn't he start it up down the road or make it quieter somehow? He must have woken the whole neighbourhood,' said Jennifer.

Robert looked from the bedroom window to see Toby pull away. His brother's company, Parcels and Courier Express, owned the Kawasaki. The letters P.A.C.E. were boldly displayed in bright green lettering along each pannier, and Robert could just make this out in the dawn light. He watched his son ride off, the roar of the bike becoming only slightly fainter as Toby disappeared from sight. Robert had fond memories of the days he rode his own bike. The sixties were packed with long hot summer days, and his 750cc Harley had been a beast to ride; but he would give anything to travel back in time to re-live the trips to Brighton and Hastings and feel how it was to ride without a helmet in the scorching sun. Things were different now. No scooter boys. No Battle of Hastings. No mods and rockers. But he knew the pleasure his son must be feeling riding off into the quiet dark morning on a mission, despite the volume of traffic, speed humps and cameras. How pleased he used to be to have a family name of Davidson. He had wanted to call his first-born Harley, but Jennifer would not agree. He stood by the window until the sound of the Kawasaki was completely gone, then slowly turned away and gazed at the same woman who had ridden pillion with him, and shared the same passion, all those years ago. A lot had changed since then.

'Of course you can't make it start quieter,' said Robert as he climbed back into bed, 'it's supposed to sound like that; sounded very sweet to me.'

'Did you say it was six o'clock? He's leaving earlier every day,' said Jennifer as she turned and pulled the duvet even higher so that only the top of her head was visible.

'Philip has some regular early deliveries over the next month or two; special audit work or something. There's a whole bunch of accountants working through the night. Anyway, don't complain. My brother is employing our son, and our son is enjoying his work; it doesn't get better than that. He gets a pretty good wage too, so everyone's happy, eh?' said Robert as he manoeuvred himself next to his wife and under the warmth of the duvet.

'I suppose so,' said Jennifer. 'Actually, Philip is very generous.'

'But not as generous as me.'

Robert rolled towards his wife; she was sleepy. Their other two children were still fast asleep in the adjoining bedrooms, so they had an hour before they would be getting up for school. Robert buried his head in his wife's thick dark hair and kissed her neck where it had parted.

Robert remained like that for only a minute, then turned to look at the clock again. Jennifer remained motionless, momentarily feeling distanced from her husband; an insensitivity that she could not quite grasp, or was it her own state of mind playing tricks again. Whatever it was, it disturbed her for a second or two. Jennifer reached for her husband who turned towards her again, and Jennifer lay with her head in the crook of his arm. The feeling passed; it was just her imagination; her insecurities had got the upper hand, again. She closed her eyes, happy in the knowledge that Robert still loved her as much as he had always done. They fell asleep for the remainder of the hour until the shrill voice of their daughter Lucy was heard by their bedroom door. It was nothing unusual. Lucy and Luke, her fourteen-year-old brother, were arguing. It was something to do with using the bathroom, but it didn't matter what it was, they would always find something to quarrel about. Of the two children, Robert quite openly favoured his daughter; he made no excuses for it. Preference would always be given to Lucy, no matter what; she had first say on everything. This was the only subject that caused argument between Jennifer and her husband, but she was so conscious of her failings in Lucy's early years that she tended to let Robert off the hook more often than not.

Robert propped himself up on one elbow and shouted loudly towards the direction of his youngest son. Robert's anger was not disguised. He swung himself out of bed, grabbed his gown and headed for the bathroom door. As always, Jennifer was uneasy, but said nothing.

The house regained its quietness as Robert re-appeared in the bedroom, still tying his dressing gown.

'I know what your thinking, so don't say it,' said Robert as he leaned towards his wife to place a kiss on her forehead, 'Lucy is my only daughter,' he said, 'her brothers should care for her, treat her gently; she's very precious.'

'They're all precious,' said Jennifer, 'but Luke needs to feel important too, he's not going to if you never listen to what he has to say. You can't keep letting her get away with everything she does, without even questioning her. I don't think it's right. Being fourteen is difficult, and he's had little chance at being the baby of the family. I really worry that you're being too harsh on him.'

'Harsh on him? How can you say that? Harsh on him?' said Robert with some astonishment. 'Toby and I devoted ourselves to him after you had Lucy, when you couldn't cope. How do you think I felt then? A beautiful baby girl, and you wanted nothing to do with her. If you're talking about harsh and what's right, then that's not right is it? He's had his share of being the baby, don't you worry about that. He's had his special moments, and lots of them. For heaven's sake Jen, give it a rest.'

'I just think you should give him more attention; make him feel a bit more important, that's all. In any case, I want you to stop spoiling Lucy like you do. It's not going to do her any good.'

'What would you know about spoiling her?' said Robert.

Jennifer wasn't going to continue this dialogue. It couldn't be rectified and she couldn't go back in time. She reached from her bed to the small cabinet by her side, and checked her watch. 'I'm getting breakfast,' she said, 'if only Toby hadn't woken me with that bike.'

Luke appeared at the bedroom door and slowly walked towards his mother. As he sat on the edge of the bed, Jennifer took his head in her hands and pulled her son towards her neck as she lay with her head still on the pillow.

'It's not fair,' he mumbled.

'I know,' Jennifer said apologetically.

Robert ignored his son's remarks and continued walking to and from the landing and the bedroom door. He spoke to his wife with an air of authority, more for Luke's benefit than anything else, but he was calm. Robert was always calm.

'You stay in bed - I'll sort these two. I want to get in early today,' said Robert. 'There's a big job coming in from National Heritage; plenty of castles and stately homes to be produced before the day is out. Not the most exciting of assignments, but it's good to get the work.' Robert looked at Luke. 'Leave your mother to rest,' he said abruptly, and ushered his son out of the bedroom, closing the door behind them.

Jennifer shut her eyes. She daydreamed as she lay there, half asleep. She had wanted to do so much today, including visiting her father. She hoped that her brother had managed to find time to escape from his criminal clients to fit in a visit to the hospice. Mathew found it hard to find time for anything lately, so she wouldn't be too harsh on him, but he did have a way of brightening George's mood, usually by looking at the racing papers.

Jennifer sunk deeply into the luxury of her pillow, enjoying the quiet solitude of her bedroom; she dozed for an hour or so. When she woke, her thoughts were immediately on her boys; Luke, the middle child, often feeling neither the least nor the most important, neither the grown up, nor the baby; Toby, the eldest, a success as Robert had reminded her. He had a job, a steady girlfriend who wasn't pregnant, and he wasn't a junkie. If this was how successful parenting is measured, then she had to agree that Toby was a credit to her.

The telephone rang by the side of her bed; she was delighted to hear her brother's voice.

'Mathew. Did you see dad?' she asked.

'Yes. Last night,' said Mathew hurriedly. 'He's very morbid. He's dwelling back on the past about mum's death and how it was his fault. He seems to be regressing. It's like he's gone back years.'

'Oh, Mathew...'

'I think we should meet and have a chat. He was going on about not waiting much longer to see Josie - to be by her side. He's had enough. The only thing that brought him out of it was a bet on the horses. I promised I'd put one on for him today, but I'm just so busy. How are you - and the kids?'

'Toby's still riding that death machine for his uncle Philip, but he loves it. I'm sure he woke the whole neighbourhood this morning. Luke and Lucy are arguing as usual.'

'I don't know how Robert can let his son work for that man, even if it is his brother. He's always up to something unsavoury. He's a nasty piece of work'.

'Mathew!' shouted Jennifer disapprovingly. 'Don't speak like that. I know you've got little time for him, but he's not all bad. He's my husband's flesh and blood and he's here to stay, so it's high time you swallowed your differences. I can't cope with all this arguing.'

'Yeah, alright, but he's one family member I could do without. I'm not going to argue with him, I just don't want to see him. Oh dear, Sarah is standing next to me; I need to get off the phone. I'm getting the feeling it's something important so I really must say goodbye. Sorry it's such a quick call, but you know how it is. I'll phone again soon, we need to meet up, maybe get to see dad together.'

Jennifer said goodbye to her brother, got out of bed, and headed for the bathroom for a long hot shower. Her husband

and her brother always brought up family matters that would get stuck in her head for the rest of the day, 'poor dad,' she thought.

She climbed in the shower and looked down at her body. Her stomach was protruding only slightly, and at forty-five, she was a good match for any woman half her age. She had borne three healthy children, but only she knew why she had felt such coldness towards her baby daughter.

She finished her shower and walked to the bedroom dressing table. As she stood before the mirror, she remembered the pain, the burden of it all. Her feelings for Lucy had never been right; Robert got out of bed each and every night in order to feed her. When Jennifer heard her, wailing and demanding, she had no reason to get up; Robert was always there. Within seconds, the crying would stop and she would hear her husband talking softly. Without any hesitation or complaining, he would cradle Lucy, carry her out to the kitchen where he would warm her feed, and tell their daughter his each and every action. Jennifer would cry secretly in her pillow; she had desperately wanted a daughter, and there she was, in the kitchen with Robert, and ignored by her. Eventually he would return to bed, and whisper that Lucy was o.k. This happened night after night, and each night felt worse than the last. She knew that her feelings were wrong; it was not the baby's fault, and she would never harm her, but she resented her presence, she did not belong in her house as the rest of the family did. She was an outsider, a visitor that wouldn't go home. She was amazed that Robert coped with this apparent madness, and the juggling of his affections, but somehow he did; he took it all in his stride, was always there.

As she stood before the mirror some thirteen years later, she remembered all this as if it happened yesterday. The babies hadn't spoilt her looks and this was important to her; she blamed all her insecurities on how she looked, how she felt about herself, but the sad truth was, most days she didn't like herself at all. The more years that passed, the more the pain faded; but her fear, and the burden of the secrets she carried, felt worse.

She moved away from the mirror and went to the wardrobe

where she pulled a pair of Levi jeans from the shelf. From a drawer she took a clean white T-shirt and placed the items on the bed where she now sat. She wished she didn't have these moments, it saddened her to dwell on those past times, but these thoughts were occurring more regularly lately. She tried hard not to allow her guilt to surface, it would only make her cry, but the memories of betrayal, abandonment, her mother, were in a train of thought that was running wild now; it would not stop. The tears were rolling down her face; though she wiped them quickly, there were plenty more still to come. She hadn't told the truth, she had rejected her baby, she was a bad mother, a bad wife. She tortured herself in these reflections, but there was nothing she could do to stop them happening, the secrets were getting harder to keep inside.

Jennifer could see herself as she once was, the eighteen-year-old whose mother had drowned in a freak accident. Josie Weekes had missed her footing while climbing onto a boat on a family day out. She had been told that her mother had slipped into the water next to the quayside, squashed between the quay and the rubber fenders of the boat. In her panic to stay above the water, she had struggled to grab the quayside wall, but could not reach it. Her father had wanted to get into the water, but onlookers told him he would only make things worse. As George Weekes was screaming at his wife to hold onto his hand that he held outstretched down the quayside wall, she suddenly slipped away and out of sight. When they pulled her from the water minutes later, she was already dead.

Robert offered to step into the household to help care for her father, and young brother Mathew; Jennifer readily agreed. Everyone was devastated by Josie's death, and the tragic way in which she died made it all the harder to forget. Nothing ever felt secure without Robert around, and it still felt like that now; she would be lost without him. Mathew was eleven years old, and felt safe with Robert in the house; he brought normality. There was little support from George Weekes, he was in a permanent state of grief, but Robert never failed him, despite his own father's efforts to pressurise him to get a proper job, or go into business like his brother, Philip, instead of wasting time at art school. Robert helped to pull the family back into shape, with countless nights working with Mathew; encouraging the type of study that would eventually get him to University. They remained living with George in the family home until Mathew had achieved some qualifications that would lead him to an independent future, away from his father's misery.

Mathew became a successful lawyer, and was now a partner in the firm of Marshall, Maplin & Weekes. His success was mostly due to Robert's unfailing commitment, and Mathew had never forgotten it. It was hoped that George Weekes might one day re-marry, but he wanted no one, perpetually blaming himself for Josie's death. As a consequence, he continued to deteriorate, both mentally and physically. Only his flutters with horseracing brought him any relief from his self-persecution, but as the years passed and he became weaker, his visits to the bookmakers became more infrequent, until eventually, he hardly left the house at all. It was almost inevitable that a serious illness would move in on George, as his will to carry on living moved out. Even the diagnosis of cancer was greeted fatalistically, there was going to be no fight against it, just acceptance, and surrender to a punishment that he felt he deserved. Now he was a resident at St. John's Hospice where he was content to play a waiting game, until the day he would be reunited with his wife. George had hardly noticed when Mathew went to University to study law, and had shown little interest in his son's chosen career, but Jennifer was proud of her brother's achievements, due in large to all the support her husband had given him. She married Robert at the age of twenty-four and their first son, Toby, was born within the year.

Jennifer knew she could achieve nothing through these reflections, and though her life appeared more settled, she carried many burdens inside, well hidden, for the sake of her family's happiness. She hated these moments. She dried her eyes, applied some light make-up, and went downstairs to make a large mug of tea. When she had these moods, the only cure was a long drive with her favourite companion, her Mk 2 Jaguar three-point-four saloon. She sipped her tea as she walked from the kitchen to the lounge, and looked out of the window onto the gravel driveway. There 'she' was, her adorable sanctuary, its shiny chrome mascot with its large front paws turned under, in a mid air leap of strength; the car was calling her, eager to take her to a better place, an altogether better state of mind.

Five

Mathew had just said goodbye to his sister when the telephone immediately rang again. Sarah was still standing by his side waiting to speak to him.

'I need to talk to you,' Sarah said, 'I need to fix a conference for Martin McCormack.'

'Hang on; let me get rid of this call. I'll be quick,' said Mathew as he picked up the receiver.

'Remember me?' said Susan from the other end of the line, 'you and I live together. We share the same flat; the same bed sometimes. I've got short brown hair, green eyes ...'

'Susan, I'm sorry,' said Mathew. 'I went straight to see my father last night. He wasn't good, and it really churned me up; I had a beer afterwards, and I didn't realise how late it was. You were fast asleep when I got in. I would have woken you this morning but it was so early, you wouldn't have been very pleased.'

'How do you know that?' she said crossly, 'just tell me you'll be straight home tonight; we hardly see each other.'

'Well ... I need to attend a conference in town. It shouldn't take longer than a couple of hours, and I could be home by nine.'

'If you don't have to have a beer that is,' said Susan sarcastically.

Mathew turned to Sarah, who was still waiting patiently. She would only leave his office if Mathew signalled for her to do so, but he had not.

'Hold on a minute,' he said to his girlfriend, loosely cupping his hand over the telephone mouthpiece, 'Sarah,what time is that conference tonight?'

'I thought six-thirty would suit you. Shall I book it?'

'Yes, please do. Six-thirty then. That's fine.'

'I'll phone chambers to confirm. I'm making some coffee, shall I bring you one up?' said Sarah.

'Yes please, that would be great; and a biscuit too if there are some,' said Mathew boyishly.

Susan could hear the conversation her partner was having with his secretary, and although she knew she was completely unreasonable to feel resentful, nevertheless she was.

'Forget it Mathew. You have coffee and biscuits with your secretary and come home when you like. I might not be there...'

'Susan please ...'

The line was dead. Mathew listened to the purring tone for a few seconds before replacing the receiver reluctantly. He was exhausted. Why didn't she understand? He had more work than he knew what to do with since becoming a partner at Marshall Maplin & Weekes. Maybe he should have stayed a salaried defence lawyer dealing with the run-of-the-mill files. There would be less pressure on him to secure new clients, less pressure to earn money for the partnership, and he could still have holidays in the sun, sick days when he felt ill. But it was all too late for regrets. He was a partner with responsibilities to the firm, and there was no getting off the hook now.

It was twelve noon, Susan must have made the call in her lunch break, he thought. He pictured her on playground duty, angry, sulking. Hopefully the children were not taking the brunt of her mood.

Perhaps he should cancel the McCormack conference, or maybe send a clerk in his place. It was a case that he was particularly concerned about, and he had been a little abrupt with his client the day before. It was a difficult case; McCormack had been charged with a complicated fraud involving twenty-seven bogus companies, which he had allegedly helped to set up with his associates. There were many debtors, and even some of these were bogus; the debts totalled millions of pounds. There were seven co-defendants, all were separately represented, and many had used aliases for various transactions; current accounts, deposit accounts, overseas investments, property deals, credit cards, directorships; you name it and they had tried it. Mathew was representing just one of the defendants, but when the case papers had arrived at his office they were delivered by van; fourteen boxes in all. He had spent the last month ploughing through the evidence and taking meticulous notes. The idea of sending a clerk on this conference was out of the question, and his client would be extremely nervous without him. He had to go himself, and Susan would have to understand. This was the career he had chosen, and nothing was going to stop him doing the job he was paid to do. His office door opened and Sarah walked in with a large cup of coffee and a plate of chocolate digestives.

'Having a hard time?' said Sarah in a motherly tone, 'perhaps a coffee will do the trick.'

'Thanks, that's lovely,' said Mathew as he took a sip of the white froth from the top of the cup. 'I need a couple of hours to myself, no more calls,' he said. Sarah acknowledged his request, closed the office door behind her, and disappeared until such time as she was needed again.

He lifted his briefcase from the floor and placed it on his desk on top of the paperwork that he had decided could wait until tomorrow, burying the McCormack papers, which had been placed prominently by Sarah in the hope he would refresh himself on the prosecution evidence before attending the conference she had now booked. Instead, he opened the case and took out a small scrap of paper. He had a very important call to make.

'Hello. Account number four three double zero six; the three-thirty at Doncaster. Ten pounds each way please on number four. Yes, that's right, "Heavens Above".'

Six

The school playground was exceptionally noisy. There seemed to be more children than usual, and all of them appeared to be running. Susan Bishop could not see one child standing still. Her colleague, Patrick Myers, was in the midst of a cluster of children. Each of them was shouting loudly so as to try to be heard above the others. She hated playground duties, but thankfully, this one was her last for the next two weeks. She had little concern for any of the small bodies racing around her, knowing that they would all be loved and cared for at the end of the day, as soon as they got home. Even Patrick, tall, gawky, bespectacled and balding, had a woman waiting for him with open arms, but Susan felt she had nothing like this. At the end of her day she would return to the flat she shared with Mathew, and will undoubtedly spend the night alone. He told her he'd be home at nine, but in her head, she knew this would be more like eleven. He will come in tired; and by eleven o'clock, she would be tired too.

Patrick had now sorted out the squabble of children, and seemed to be making a beeline for her.

'Susan! Can you take my information technology class tonight? I know it's short notice, but can we do a swap, I'll take yours tomorrow. Claire wants us to go out and celebrate our three years of blissful married life!'

'And has it been? Blissful I mean?'

'Oh yes. I couldn't think of anyone else who'd put up with me. I've got no regrets marrying Claire. Can you keep a secret?'

Susan nodded at him with raised eyebrows, encouraging him to continue.

'I think I'm going to be a dad. Claire gets her result this evening after work; if it is bad news, and she's not pregnant, then a good night out and a romantic meal will cheer her up. Of course, if it's good news…well…we'll still have a night out and a romantic meal, but we'll just go steady on the plonk. Can you swap? Would it put you out at all?'

Susan had nothing to lose by staying late and taking his I.T. class. It was probably preferable than going home to an empty flat. She liked Patrick, and had worked alongside him for many years, but there was something enviable about his relationship with Claire that painfully highlighted the failings in her own relationship. She desperately wanted a child, but Mathew had point blank refused to become a father. As far as Mathew was concerned there was to be no discussion about it, and in all fairness, he had told her this from the very beginning. Foolishly, she thought he would change his mind, but so far, he had not. It wasn't as if he hated children, on the contrary, he quite liked them, and doted on his sister's kids, but he didn't want the responsibility or heartache that he knew a child would bring. Mathew had noticed through his dealings with troubled teenagers, that not all of them had parents who were irresponsible, or with a criminal history. It was Mathew's opinion that all the good parenting in the world couldn't protect a child from the worst influences. He just wasn't prepared to take that chance; he had seen too much. Mathew didn't think his reasoning was selfish; instead, he considered it a sacrifice not to bring a child into the world; it was full of uncertainty, and where would he find the time to devote to such a responsibility.

She found Patrick staring at her, waiting for a reply.

'Susan? Will it be o.k.? Have you got something else planned for tonight, because if so ….'

'No Patrick, it'll be fine.' said Susan. 'I've got nothing planned for tonight. Isn't Lucy Davidson in your class? I think Mathew's sister mentioned that she was.'

'Yes she is, but she hasn't turned up for the past month or so. It's not compulsory, as you know, but the class is full and there are others waiting who could do with some help. I've been meaning to have a word with her form teacher, I'd like to know what's going on.'

'I'll have a word with Mathew, when I see him that is. I don't know why she isn't attending, but it's likely that her dad just lets her skip it. According to Mathew, Lucy is one spoilt little girl. If she turns up tonight, I'll have a word with her.'

'Thanks Susan.'

'I sincerely hope that congratulations will be in order in the morning. Enjoy your night out.'

The bell for end of break resounded loudly across the tarmac, but still had to compete fiercely with the sound of screeching children coming to a halt and arranging themselves in different groups. Susan and Patrick controlled half each; leading them back into school through separate doorways. She had quite an easy afternoon ahead of her; one double physical education session, followed by a film on road safety.

It wasn't long before she began to regret her offer to take Patrick's lesson. It was a bigger class than she was used to but she knew all the children by sight, and they were delighted to see her. She settled the children at the computers and looked to see if she could see Lucy. She wasn't there. She called the register and the children responded in turn, with the exception of Lucy. The pupils were quick to inform her that Lucy Davidson had not attended Mr. Myer's class 'for ages', they said.

Susan completed the register with only one name missing. It may not be anything to worry about, but she made a mental note to ask about Lucy as soon as she got the chance.

Seven

Martin McCormack had done conferences before, and he couldn't believe he was back doing them all over again. His past had been full of lawyers and barristers discussing his future; he had thought he had left all that behind.

It was early evening when he arrived at Temple underground station and he had spent the previous few hours making sure his clothes were the cleanest they could be. He had shaved twice, and his chin was still tender. His hair was cut close to his head; too short to be styled. He wore a charcoal grey suit over a white shirt of good quality, which he matched with a patterned tie consisting of bottle green and light grey squares. His whole outfit, including his black laced highly polished brogues, had been bought that morning from the Banners Street charity shop in aid of the elderly. He had been surprised at the quality of clothing on offer, and the generosity, or wastefulness, of those who had donated them. He felt a lot better than he had done when he attended Marshall, Maplin & Weekes, but he wasn't entirely at ease with his masquerade. He felt uncomfortable, but was prepared to put up with a little discomfort; it would help him to stand a better chance of being believed by his barrister, at least more chance than he had with Mathew Weekes.

His tall, slim build could have given him the agile appearance of a much younger man, but a slight stoop around the shoulders and the swagger in his walk made him look as though he had not only seen life, but had fought his way through it. To his amazement, and delight, no one was noticing him as he walked along Victoria Embankment alongside the Thames. He blended in well. There were hundreds of people scurrying around. He passed thick queues waiting to board the floating restaurants and bars; dozens of tourists huddled in groups, people looking at maps, all chatting and laughing. The place was alive with busy people, and he was a part of it.

He wasn't late for his appointment with Mathew Weekes and Jonathan Bowers, QC, so he decided to visit the small bar on the corner opposite the station, for a quick Scotch; it would steady his nerves. The bar was noisy and crowded, but the atmosphere was placid compared to the drinking establishments he was used to. He manoeuvred through the layers of people and eventually stood behind a young man who had just finished being served and was putting some change into his pocket. McCormack stretched his arm around him and rested his hand on the bar counter, holding a five pound note for the barmaid to see.

'Single malt, no ice. When you're ready love,' said McCormack confidently.

The young man, who McCormack had been leaning over, turned abruptly away from the bar. He was holding two full pints of lager that hit McCormack suddenly, the glasses knocking straight into his chest. In a matter of seconds, his white shirt, grey jacket, checked tie, were all soaked, and splashes of the drink were now dripping onto his suit trousers. McCormack's reaction came much too late as he tried to jump backwards while flicking the liquid from his clothes.

'Sorry mate,' said the young man quickly, still holding the two glasses and unable to help McCormack at all, 'really sorry.'

'You will be,' snapped McCormack, angrily, 'look what you've done!'

'It'll come out in the dry clean, I've done it myself,' said the young man, 'I'll pay for it. No worries. It'll be good as new tomorrow.'

'Tomorrow's too late,' said McCormack solemnly. 'It's too late. You don't understand what you've done.'

McCormack moved away from the bar and the young man, before he had a chance to do anything that might lead him to more trouble. He made his way through the crowded bar and found himself back on the street, wet, dishevelled, and angry. His efforts had all been for nothing and he was agitated as he left the Embankment and headed for Inner Temple. As he walked, his jacket and shirt were slowly drying in the evening air, but there was little he could do about the lager stains rapidly appearing, most noticeably on his best white shirt. By the time he reached Kings Bench House, where he had an appointment fixed with his legal advisers, he felt as out of place as he always had. His confidence was gone. Now he was never going to be believed.

He pushed the large doors and followed the sign to the reception. Mathew Weekes was already seated and reading a bundle of papers, which he had pulled from the file of Martin McCormack. He saw his client walk in, tucked the papers back inside the folder, and stood up.

'My client is here now,' he said to the receptionist, 'shall we go up?'

'Yes, second door on the right,' she replied.

'Come on Mr. McCormack,' said Mathew, gently guiding his client towards the staircase that would lead them to Jonathan Bowers, QC. 'Let's get this over with,' he said, as they climbed side by side up the wide, carpeted staircase.

'Do come in,' said Mr. Bowers as Mathew tapped softly on the dark oak door.

Mathew entered the room first, and greeted the barrister enthusiastically before introducing his client, Martin McCormack. Mr. Bowers then made a further introduction; a young clerk who was sitting at the far end of the oval, polished table, too far from them to shake hands conveniently, so he stood briefly and simply said 'how do you do?'

'This is Michael. He's here to make sure I don't leave anything unsaid, or forget anything that needs to be discussed,' said Mr. Bowers directly at McCormack, (who was sure that the barrister was staring at his shirt). 'Do sit down.'

'Well, Mr. McCormack,' the QC began, 'what are we going to do with you?'

'What do you mean?' replied McCormack.

'You're clearly in a lot of trouble.'

'Oh yeah. I know that alright,' said McCormack without hesitation.

'I understand you are prepared to plead guilty to only a few of these counts. Is that right?'

'Well I'm not owning up to setting up companies that never existed, if that's what you mean.'

'And what's all this about a Mr. Bernie Cullum?' the barrister continued, 'is he real?'

'Of course he is,' said McCormack, giving a sideways glance at Mathew, who was seated next to him.

'But why can't he be traced? Why is there no record of him at all?' asked Mr. Bowers.

'Can't answer that.'

'Well you're setting me a difficult task,' said the QC, 'it's going to be very hard to progress if you stick to this line of defence.'

'But it is my defence, Mr. Bowers,' said McCormack. 'It's my defence because it's the truth.' McCormack saw his barrister and solicitor exchange a knowing glance. He knew this was going to happen. What was the point of telling his solicitor all that went on, only to tell someone else who shared exactly the same opinion; that there was no such person as Bernie Cullum.

The conversation with Jonathan Bowers, QC, travelled along the same lines for several hours, and the clerk had taken a bundle of notes. There was little more to be said by anyone, and McCormack's stance hadn't altered.

'Have another think about it, Mr. McCormack,' said the barrister as he brought the conference to a close. 'You know my advice, but if you want me to proceed with a defence that relies on incriminating a third party, who no one can trace, then so be it. I've explained the risks and I can do no more. Have another chat with Mr. Weekes and be certain in your own mind that this is the route you want to go down.' Mr. Bowers looked at Mathew for confirmation.

'I'll have another good read of the papers,' said Mathew. 'I'll be in touch as soon as we get a trial date. If my client's instructions change before then, I'll get the case listed before the court and we can go from there.'

'Fine,' said Mr. Bowers.

The clerk stood up and said goodbye to the solicitor and his client. Jonathan Bowers walked to the door, gave each of them a firm handshake, and returned to his desk.

'What do you make of that, Michael?' he said to his clerk.

'Nothing unusual. Not that different to the standard defence of "I met some bloke in a pub". It's the same meat, just different gravy.'

'You don't believe him then.'

'Not at all. And I doubt if a jury will,' said Michael.

'Have you got a note of the enquiries made by the police to find the mysterious Bernie Cullum? Perhaps I should have a closer look,' said Jonathan Bowers.

'It's all here. It was unused material, but now the prosecution have served it as evidence,' said Michael, as he leafed his way through a bundle of papers. 'Here it is; no known addresses for him, no criminal record, no National Insurance number, no National Health number, no vehicles registered at DVLA, he's never worked, has never paid tax, and has never borrowed a single penny from anyone. He's never been married, and he hasn't died. We can only assume that he's never been born.'

'I find it hard to believe that Mathew Weekes would take a client down this road of defence if he didn't think he had a chance. He's very astute. Maybe he'll get him to change his plea; I'm not looking forward to defending this one.'

'All I know is, if I had a meeting with Queen's Counsel, I'd at least put on a clean shirt,' said Michael, despairingly.

'Quite,' said Jonathan Bowers, QC.

Martin McCormack and Mathew Weekes looked at each other as the oak doors closed behind them

'Do you think he noticed?' said McCormack.

'Noticed what?'

'My shirt, my jacket, the drink stains.'

'Oh. I don't think so,' said Mathew kindly.

'I bet he did,' said McCormack, as he followed his solicitor down the staircase, past reception, and through the large swing doors at the exit of Kings Bench House. 'That's why he didn't believe me,' continued McCormack as they headed back towards the Embankment and Temple underground station.

'I really don't think he did,' said Mathew, unconvincingly. 'I'm going to get a cab. Can I drop you somewhere?' Mathew asked.

'No, I'm ok,' replied McCormack, despondently. 'The Underground will do me fine.'

Mathew walked to the edge of the pavement, placed one foot in the road, and waived an arm at a black cab that was travelling in the opposite direction. The taxi driver spun his vehicle around in an uninterrupted perfect "horseshoe", and pulled up at the kerb where Mathew climbed aboard. Once seated, he pulled the window down and called to McCormack who was already on his way.

'My secretary will phone you - we'll have another chat,' he said. He wasn't sure if his client had heard him as he watched him disappear down the steps leading to the Underground where he would catch his train home.

Eight

The conference had taken longer than expected, and it had been a long hard slog to get clear instructions from his client. Mathew Weekes was reflecting on the evening's event in the back of the taxi, disappointed that his client had been prepared to plead guilty to no more than a handful of counts on his Indictment. He would now have to prepare what was probably the most complicated defence he had ever encountered.

Counsel, Jonathan Bowers, QC, had agreed to advise on the offences that McCormack had admitted in conference but where his version of events differed with his co-defendants. He would also prepare for trial on the remainder of the counts that he denied, and awaited further instructions from Mathew as to which course the defence would take. Out of the twenty-seven bogus companies that had been fraudulently set up, McCormack was implicated in nine. Counsel was of the opinion that the prosecution could easily prove his involvement in at least five of these, but McCormack would plead to only three offences of deception. He had readily admitted to assisting his colleagues when they obtained huge bank loans for three of the companies, and McCormack had allowed them to use his name when setting up the Directorships. There was no way out of this as the admission had already been made in police interview; McCormack had been asked if he had been aware of the use to which his name was to be put. Mathew had advised him to say nothing at all, there was so much evidence against his client that there had been little point in giving the police any more, but McCormack could not keep quiet and spoke spontaneously in reply to all questions asked. Mathew could clearly remember cringing in disbelief when his client responded by saying, 'I thought at the time that it might be a bit iffy.' His comment was disastrous; Mathew had no alternative but to advise him to plead guilty to these three offences. If he'd taken the legal advice on offer, things might have been different, but admitting he thought his co-defendants might be acting illegally by using his name to secure bank loans, was nothing short of suicidal; there was no hope of a defence, just mitigation based on stupidity, though he wouldn't tell his client this in such blatant terms.

Mathew still had his work cut out defending him on the other six counts on the Indictment. Defences had to be prepared concerning his dealings with six fraudulent companies and the thousands of transactions that were made involving two fake printing firms, three fake stationery suppliers, and one office furniture manufacturers. Most of the prosecution evidence consisted of invoices, orders, and delivery notes bearing the name or signature of his client, which had passed through two specific printing companies; Masterprints and Expressive Prints Express. Neither company actually existed, just like the stationery suppliers and furniture manufacturers, but McCormack insisted that he did not put his name to any document. He truly believed that the directors of these printing firms, which were managed by Bernie Cullum, had properly employed him; he thought he was a bona fide employee, paying his tax, his National Insurance, and even a pension contribution to the firm's scheme.

As things now stood, all the directors were co-defendants, and Bernie Cullum had not been traced. McCormack insisted that Cullum would have all the answers, and that he should be made to testify so as to prove his innocence. During the conference, he had confirmed what he had already told Mathew; Bernie Cullum was responsible for the whole running of the printing companies, appearing from time to time to look at the books and the general running of things. Mathew had doubts as to Cullum's existence, but McCormack stuck to his story throughout. Apart from the printing companies, he stated he knew nothing about any stationery or office furniture business; if it was his signature or name on anything connected with them, then his signature must have been cleverly copied. Mathew told him that this could be proved, and McCormack remained unabashed.

Finding Bernie Cullum was not going to be easy. Mathew noticed that he had been implicated by at least two other co-defendants for using their identification on various fraudulent transactions, invoices, etc. Despite this, there was a risk to his client going down this line of defence; if the existence of Bernie Cullum was eventually proved to be a complete fabrication, he could face further charges of conspiring with these two co-defendants, who could have plotted together and invented 'Bernie Cullum' in an attempt to exonerate them all. These two co-defendants happened to be represented by Dominic Sabastas-Grant, a defence solicitor who had point blank refused to reveal any of his clients' defences to Mathew. There was to be no agreeing any proofs, or sharing any evidence with him - that was for certain. Mathew remembered him from his trainee days when they would meet on various law courses, or as representatives at police stations. Sabastas-Grant would take no chances when it came to taking a client's instructions. Self preservation and the safeguarding of his own career were always top priority for Sabastas-Grant, and of course the meticulous calculation of costs. 'Self first, client last,' he would say quite shamelessly; without any pretence of social conscience. He meant it. Mathew had always considered him to be an exceptionally pompous character, and his arrogance had no justification, or place, amongst the working class clientele that he often represented. However, Dominic Sabastas-Grant was acting for two defendants who, between them, were facing seventeen counts on Indictment, while Mathew was acting for McCormack who faced only six. McCormack was hardly a big-time villain, unlike the co-defendants represented by Sabastas-Grant, but this didn't make proving his innocence any easier.

Mathew couldn't accept all that his client was saying, but nevertheless, he considered McCormack to be little more than a stool pigeon; a pawn in the big game. Now that his barrister had advised McCormack that if he were to be found guilty he would go to prison for several years, Mathew and Jonathan Bowers, QC, had a hard job ahead of them to keep him from a custodial sentence; meanwhile, finding Bernie Cullum was turning into an obsession for Martin McCormack.

His client's alleged involvement in choosing the printing, stationery and office furniture companies needed to set up the frauds, was not immediately apparent to Mathew. The amount of invoices, statements, and order sheets containing thousands of minor items was unnecessarily complicated, carrying a high risk of becoming unstuck. It came as no surprise at all to Mathew that the banks launched an investigation. Bankruptcy could have been a way out for all those involved, and probably would have provided the only option enabling a return to normal life. To keep the scam going any longer, they would have had to be mathematical geniuses not to get caught. Once the ball got rolling and the banks had come up with the money, and one company was ordering from another, the paperwork had to keep flowing. The value added tax alone must have caused some serious headaches, and the more successful the companies appeared to get, the more the paperwork grew, and this had to be dealt with. McCormack did not look like a paperwork person; he had enormous difficulty reading his own Indictment.

Mathew pulled the conference notes from his case for a last quick look before the taxi stopped. It would only make his home life worse if he read them in the flat with Susan around. He looked at the Indictment again and slowly began to mark off each count according to whether they were to be guilty, or not guilty, pleas. He got to count four, and his eyes were immediately fixed on what he was reading. Although he had read the Indictment many times before, something extra, and worrying, was now registering. He gazed at count four, and to the bogus printing company named within the wording of the Particulars of Offence: Expressive Prints Express. He had seen this name before, but for the moment could not remember where; Expressive Prints Express, a terrible use of English, and a clumsy name for a company. While he continued to stare at it, he remembered he had seen this at his sister's house. Why hadn't it registered sooner? He was certain that the company name was one of Robert's assignments; he could see it now, on the desk in his study. Robert had been asked to design a logo and letterhead for Expressive Prints Express, and he remembered Jennifer had found it very amusing; of all the difficult and intricate work that Robert produced for a living, this job had caused him a lot of problems. Robert had been struggling for weeks to come up with an idea for a logo because there was nothing in the company name that caught his imagination; it had got him completely stumped and he had made a real fuss about it; becoming moody, Jennifer had said. It was all flooding back; he too remembered Robert's irritation at the time. Mathew had to think carefully; why hadn't he noticed it earlier, why hadn't he read the papers more scrupulously, before getting so involved in the case.

'Here all right sir?' said the taxi driver suddenly.

'Oh, thank you,' said Mathew vaguely. 'Sorry. Would you mind very much if we went around the block a few times?'

The taxi driver readily obliged. Mathew's heartbeat was quickening as he stared again at count four on the Indictment; Expressive Prints Express. A bogus company fraudulently set up so as to obtain fraudulent investment and income. He suddenly felt hot; he must speak to Robert before the case goes any further. There was always a chance there was more than one company with the same name, but as soon as he thought of this excuse, he realised how unlikely it would be. He will ask Robert where the work came from; who requested it. He remembered it was a very small job compared with the standard of assignment he usually undertook, and more likely to have been a one off favour for someone with very little reward, maybe no payment at all. Robert had often produced work for his family or friends, more for the pleasure of doing it than anything else. He offered his artistic talents on many occasions; Susan's school had once got him to design a whole backdrop for a drama class production of 'A Midsummer Night's Dream' and Robert had refused to take any payment at all, not even for materials. Maybe this is what had happened here, thought Mathew. He prayed it was a favour with no reward.

Mathew got the taxi to stop, having circled his block several times. His London home was a flat in a converted Victorian house in Hackney, East London, originally built for a large nineteenth century family together with their servants. Mathew and Susan occupied the ground floor two-bedroom conversion, with garden.

Susan was already in bed when Mathew entered the flat, but

she was not asleep. Their bedroom was at the end of the hallway, and he could see that the door was slightly open.

'Have you been in long?' said Mathew as he entered the bedroom.

'About an hour,' said Susan sleepily. 'I took Patrick's class tonight so that he'll do mine tomorrow. He thinks he may become a father; he's very excited.'

Susan could tell that Mathew had his thoughts firmly fixed elsewhere.

'Are you listening to me? Perhaps we can have an evening together tomorrow. I swapped with Patrick.'

'I think I've stumbled across something that I wish I hadn't,' said Mathew as he slumped on the edge of the bed with his case at his feet.

'What do you mean?' said Susan curiously as she leaned on one elbow, twisting her head towards him.

Mathew pulled some papers from his briefcase and continued to stare at the Indictment.

'I don't know if I'll be home tomorrow. I have to go and see someone.'

'Who? Who do you have to see?'

'I have to go and see Robert.'

'What's the urgency, you can see him any time,' said Susan.

'Like I said, I've come across something, but I'm unsure. I can't tell you about it right now, but I won't have time to take you out tomorrow night so there was no point swapping with Patrick on my account. Going out is the last thing on my mind; the least of my priorities. I'm sorry, but this involves my family.'

'Right, o.k. So I'm not family? Do you know why I took Patrick's class tonight? So that he could take his wife out for a romantic meal to celebrate their three years of being together. Do you hear me Mathew? And if Claire is pregnant, he'll be over the moon.'

'Please don't get on the subject of kids right now. Please.'

Susan turned away from Mathew and closed her eyes. She

was angry and very hurt. She could still hear him shuffling his paperwork as he moved around the bedroom. She knew she would not be communicating her feelings tonight.

'Forget it, I'm going to sleep. Who'd want kids with someone who's never around and never talks even when he is,' she said coldly, 'and if it's not too much trouble,' she continued sarcastically, 'would you mind asking Jennifer why Lucy isn't attending I.T. classes. Not too menial a task for you is it, bearing in mind that nobody's liberty is at stake? Will you remember to ask, or shall I phone her myself?'

'I'll remember,' said Mathew, ignoring Susan's remarks.

'Thanks. Oh, and a nurse phoned from St. John's with a message from your father. She said to tell you "Heavens Above" finished up front at fifty-to-one.'

'Brilliant. That's the best news I've had all day.'

Nine

Lucy looked out of her bedroom window and could see her uncle walking briskly up the path. The doorbell rang.

'I'll go - it's uncle Mathew,' Lucy shouted as she ran down the stairs to the hallway, heading for the street door.

Mathew stood nervously on the doorstep, feeling anxious about how he would approach Robert. The last thing he wanted was for him to be connected to a criminal investigation, no matter how remote his involvement might be. Better to get straight to the point, thought Mathew to himself; Robert wouldn't like any dithering, just tell him what you know and the rest is up to him. Probably nothing, he thought. His contemplations were suddenly halted at the sight of Lucy, who was now grinning at him from behind the opened door.

Mathew looked straight past his niece and along the hallway that separated the dining room and lounge. Jennifer was rushing backwards and forwards across the passageway, carrying various items from one room to another. She stopped when she saw Mathew standing at the doorway, and smiled as he approached his sister to place a gentle kiss on her cheek.

'Robert's in the study, so just go right in,' she said, 'he's drawing castles! Great eh? Forty-nine years old and he's getting paid for drawing castles. Go on in. I'll get you some coffee.'

Mathew tentatively put his head around the study door. He could see Robert bent over his drawing board with an array of pens and spiteful looking instruments strewn over his desk. Robert was aware of Mathew's presence, but didn't immediately look up. Instead, he continued to work with his face close to a large white board; his nose remained almost touching the paper's surface. He was engrossed in his work, and spoke quietly.

'The thing about castles,' said Robert, 'is that they're very repetitive. Each brick or slab, or whatever they were made of, each look-out hole, each turret; everything has to be individually drawn, and this one I'm doing here has bloody thousands.'

Robert turned his head sideways and looked towards Mathew who was standing staring at the intricate lines on which

Robert had spent hours of his time. Robert was almost relieved that Mathew had supplied a reason for him to stop. He lifted his face further back from his drawing board and placed several instruments firmly on the desk.

'Sorry Mathew,' said Robert who was now sitting upright and stretching his arms up high above his head. He gave a loud yawn. 'How are you? Come and sit down.'

He gestured to Mathew to sit near to him, but Mathew began speaking before he was seated.

'I'll come straight to the point, and Jennifer doesn't have to know if you don't want her to. I'm very concerned.'

'What do you mean?' said Robert. 'What's this about?'

Robert pulled a chair towards his desk and again beckoned to his brother-in-law to sit down. Mathew quickly seated himself and shuffled the seat closer to Robert. He rested his folded arms in a formal fashion, as he would when interviewing a client. He spoke softly, just in case Jennifer might overhear.

'A peculiar thing has happened. It might just be a coincidence. I'm a bit worried about something I've come across. It involves a client's case.'

'Your client's case? Something you've come across? What do you mean?' said Robert anxiously.

'Let me explain,' said Mathew, trying not to excite Robert any more than he had to, and certainly not enough to bring Jennifer running into the room asking questions that he couldn't answer. He wasn't finding it easy to get straight to the point, not as he had hoped; and Robert was looking truly worried. 'I've got this client who's charged with fraud,' he continued, 'there were a lot of companies set up, and most were bogus, but the companies raised millions by all sorts of deceptive means. I only represent one defendant, although there are six of them charged. My client's involvement is relatively minor on the face of it. That's putting the case very simply.'

'Why are you telling me all this? Spit it out Mathew!' said Robert impatiently.

Mathew took a deep breath and continued as calmly as he could.

'One of the bogus companies is called Expressive Prints Express. Does that mean anything to you?'

Robert took a sharp intake of breath.

'Good God.'

'So you do remember the name?' said Mathew quickly, not wanting to delay any response from his brother-in-law.

'Yes, of course I do,' said Robert sternly, 'of course I do.'

Just as Mathew was about to get the answer he wanted, Jennifer arrived in the study. She was carrying a tray with two large cups full of hot coffee. Her daughter, who was holding a plate of mixed biscuits and two slices of cake, accompanied her. Lucy offered the plate to Mathew expecting him to take a few chocolate biscuits, his favourites, but he did not respond; so she manoeuvred the plate onto her father's desk, avoiding the inks, pens, and instruments, and tried to draw her uncle's attention to the treats on offer. Jennifer similarly lifted the two coffees from the tray and placed them carefully on the desk, beside the two men.

'Are you staying for tea?' said Lucy.

Mathew wasn't listening to his niece, or looking at the cakes and biscuits; instead, he sat staring at Robert, impatient to hear his explanation. He had no intention of speaking at all while his sister was present, unless of course Robert spoke first; but both were eager for Jennifer and Lucy to disappear from the room.

'Can you excuse us?' said Robert to his wife. 'Mathew and I have some business to discuss. Lucy, go and help your mother, or get on with some homework.'

Robert picked up one of the coffee cups and took a sip. He did not look at his wife but kept his eyes down towards his work of art. Jennifer looked at her husband, then at her brother.

'Is everything alright? What's going on? What business?'

Robert turned to his wife and spoke abruptly.

'Jennifer please. Get Lucy out of here too.'

Jennifer was taken by surprise; how could something be so important that she wasn't to know about it? Her husband was deliberately excluding her, and it involved her own brother. How could he? Her imagination began to run riot, once more.

Perhaps they'd gambled everything on the horses; they would have to sell their home and all their worldly possessions; their father had deteriorated further; her children were in trouble. As Jennifer left the study, ushering Lucy in front of her, she pushed angrily at the door, which swung wide open and bounced noisily against the wall. Mathew was about to ask Robert to get her back into the room, to tell her everything at the same time; he didn't like secrets between him and his sister, and she looked very hurt, but Robert spoke quickly.

'Close the door Mathew. I don't want to worry Jennifer, not right now, but that printing company, Expressive Prints Express. I did a favour for a friend. I designed a logo and letterhead, but I didn't take anything for it. It should have been a real quick job so I said I'd do it as a favour; in fact, it took me ages. How can anyone be creative working with a name like that, Expressive Prints Express - it's terrible.'

'You're going to have to tell me a bit more about it,' said Mathew.

'Are you saying that I might be in some sort of trouble?'

'I hope not, I just want to know who asked you to do it. If it's someone I know, or maybe even one of the co-defendants, I'm going to be in a really compromising position, and it could easily come out at the trial. Just suppose if one of the defendants decides to name the person who got the letterhead and logo organised, and it turns out that I, the defence lawyer, actually know them. Imagine the trouble that could cause. Do you think I know them?'

Robert thought carefully as he spoke.

'The person who asked me to do it was not actually the person who wanted it done. He said it was for someone else; he owed them a favour,' said Robert cautiously.

'Do you know the name of the person who the design was for?'

'No. He didn't tell me his name.'

'Who was the person who contacted you?'

'Mathew, this is very difficult and I don't know if I should say.'

'Have you ever heard the name Bernie Cullum?'

'No. Never.'

'Are you sure?'

'Positive.'

'Well you must tell me who contacted you, at least. What is there to lose? Who was it?'

'I just don't know if I should do this. What a mess.'

'At least tell me if I know them.'

'Yes, oh yes. You know him.'

'Who was it? You must tell me.'

'If I say anything at all, you must swear to me that this goes no further. You didn't hear it from me. O.k?'

'Of course not. You have my word,' said Mathew reassuringly.

Robert hesitated, gave a deep sigh, and said, 'Philip. My brother, Philip.'

'Well, well, well. Now why doesn't that surprise me,' said Mathew quietly, almost to himself.

'What?'

'I said, your brother's up to no good and it doesn't surprise me; and right on your doorstep too.'

'You don't know that,' snapped Robert.

'Well I'm going to find out.'

'So long as you leave me out of it,' said Robert, 'you shouldn't jump to any conclusions; you should know that. It's a big world out there and he knows a lot of people. It could be anybody; any one of thousands.'

Mathew said no more. He knew he wasn't about to hear Robert pulverise his own brother, so there was no more to be said. He walked towards the study door, turning to say goodbye to Robert before opening it. Robert had returned to his original seated position, the one he was in before he had been disturbed; his head was bent over, his nose almost touching the white board that displayed the half finished castle. Robert said nothing, and Mathew left without another word.

Ten

Marshall Maplin & Weekes had a welcoming feel early in the morning; before the staff arrived. Mathew worked at his best before the onslaught of the morning's post. Before settling down to examine yesterday's conference notes on The Queen - v- McCormack and Others, he knew that he had to speak with Philip. It was eight o'clock and Philip Davidson would be at his pretentious riverside penthouse. Mathew dialled the number anxiously; it rang several times before a soft voice answered him.

'Hello.'

'Could I speak with Philip please. Tell him it's Mathew.'

'He's not up yet. We're ...'

'Well get him up,' said Mathew curtly. 'Just pass him the phone - it's urgent.'

Mathew heard a muffled conversation between Philip and the girl who answered the phone, before the receiver was presumably snatched from her.

'Mathew? You creep,' shouted Philip angrily, 'do you know what the time is? You might not have a sex life yourself but for God's sake - give a guy a break.'

'It won't take a minute,' said Mathew ignoring his tone, 'I'll come straight to the point. Do you know someone by the name of Bernie Cullum?'

'What?' said Philip in astonishment. 'What is this? Is this some kind of sick joke? What's the matter with you, it's the crack of dawn.'

Mathew made no apology at all for the time of day.

'Actually it's eight o'clock. Could you just answer the question.'

'Bernie who?' said Philip, reluctantly.

'Bernie Cullum.'

'No. Never heard of him. Now go away.'

Mathew couldn't lose this opportunity. He spoke quickiy so Philip would stay on the line.

'Didn't you ask Robert to design a letterhead and iogo for

Bernie Cullum's company called Expressive Prints Express?'

'Did Robert tell you that?'

'No, not exactly.'

'Well fuck off and don't bother me with your stupid questions at this time of day,' shouted Philip.

Mathew's resolve persisted. He'd be unlikely to get another chance.

'I'm asking you again, nicely,' he said calmly, 'who asked you to get a design done for Expressive Prints Express?'

'None of your bloody business; and what's it to you?'

'Fraud. It's to do with a fraud, that's all I can say.'

'Oh, I see. It's o.k. for me to be cross-questioned first thing in the morning, but you're saying nothing. You can't even tell me what it's about.'

'No. I can't. I'd be breaching a confidence. Can't you help me here; forget our differences. It's really important to this guy's defence. Whatever you can tell me might be just what I need to keep him from going down.'

'Well I couldn't give a toss about your client or his defence, and what about me having some confidentiality,' said Philip sarcastically. 'You don't have the monopoly on it you know. No comment o.k.? Ha! How do you like being on the receiving end? No bloody comment! Now why don't you just piss off!'

Mathew's anger was bubbling, but he refused to let it show. He became conscious of the thick dark scribbles he had made on the outside cover of a client's file. Philip was getting to him, like he always did. He felt sick at the thought of having to ask him for anything, but this information was needed for the sake of McCormack's defence. In fact, he needed to know for everyone's sake, particularly to safeguard Robert's position; he didn't know what the implications might be, if and when he discovered the truth. It was a stab in the dark that Philip was linked to Bernie Cullum, if Cullum existed at all, but right now he needed to know more about the logo business, for other reasons.

He tried hard to keep control of himself no matter how demeaning it was going to be. He put down the felt tipped pen, which stopped him doing any more scribbling, switched the telephone to hands free speaker mode, and walked to the window of his office where the sight of the river always had a soothing effect. Mathew persisted with his line of questioning.

'Are you certain you've never heard the name Bernie Cullum? How about if you talked to me about it and I took the risk of deciding what to do? No one would know where the information came from. You have my word.'

'I've never heard of Bernie Cullum and if Robert says I have then he's lying. I've never heard the name in my life. I've given you my answer; now don't ask me any more. Are you working for the police now or something? That wouldn't surprise me. You always were a cocky little shit Mathew; you and your law degree, your hypocritical right-on lifestyle. You put me down at the first opportunity, accuse me of exploiting people and using unfortunates for my own gain. Well let me tell you something lad, I've earned every penny I've got. If I ever got rich from criminality, at least I was in the firing line. You remove yourself one step from your client and his nasty activities, get fucking rich in the process of defending him, and then consider yourself holier than me because you didn't get your hands dirty. Well in my book, you're the nasty villain; the villain without the bottle. You've got no fucking guts of your own so you get off by mingling with those who have, only from a nice clean safe distance. You're the one who's feeding off the suckers you slimy little creep, and you're not getting any help from me. Got it? Now I mean it - piss off and get a life!'

He heard Philip shouting for some coffee before the receiver went down with a crash. If nothing else, he had spoilt his morning.

Mathew didn't know what could be done to make him talk; a police investigation would be certain to involve Robert, and so far as speaking to his sister was concerned, Robert had already silenced him. Jennifer was not to be involved, and that was that. He had given Robert his word not to disclose the information he had confided, and it would serve little purpose for his sister to know, but he was convinced that Philip recognised the name of Bernie Cullum; he probably even knew his whereabouts. His silence meant that he would be helping McCormack go down for a very long time, but this meant nothing at all to Philip Davidson.

Mathew's dislike of him grew even stronger. The thought that he was withholding vital information was infuriating; Philip would be confident that he would not involve the police, no matter how far he was pushed. Jennifer's fondness for her brother-in-law, and his popularity with her children, was no secret. Mathew would do nothing that risked creating a gulf between them, making his situation immensely irritating; his anger was building up all the more as he thought of his family's affection for Philip. Why didn't anyone see him as he did? He longed for him to come unstuck, but for the time being he had no choices; he had to let it go.

He returned to his desk and switched off the phone, which was still whining from the discontinued call. He didn't feel like working. He picked up the felt tipped pen and this time began to make incomprehensible shapes on a note pad. The shapes got deeper and thicker as his anger rose. He sat at his desk like this for some considerable time, until his thoughts were interrupted by the appearance of Sarah at his office door.

'Morning,' said Sarah cheerfully.

Mathew seemed almost surprised to see her. He looked up at the clock and the bright red numbers, eight, five, six. 'Nearly nine o'clock,' thought Mathew, silently.

'Everything ok? You look worried,' said Sarah inquisitively. She walked towards the desk and picked up the pad containing the thick black shapes that covered almost an entire page. 'What's all this? Thinking of changing careers? A few clients would have something to say about you becoming an artist,' said Sarah jokingly.

Mathew didn't respond, and Sarah said no more. She removed the top page of the note pad, and then the second sheet where the thick ink had also seeped through, and gently replaced the pad on the desk with a clean sheet uppermost. She put the black felt tipped pen into a pot, and took out a blue ballpoint, which she laid across the pad. She neatly shuffled the

McCormack papers together, and then piled them high, placing them directly in front of Mathew. The conference notes had to be read, and the trial of McCormack had to be carefully prepared; no stone was to be left unturned, and the sooner he got started on the case, the better it would be for everyone. She placed several other clients' folders to the side of his desk, removing many other loose sheets of paperwork that had not yet found their way to their respective files. Mathew looked up at his secretary; his desk had been transformed in less than a minute.

'Thanks,' said Mathew softly, 'how do you do that?'

'Years of practice,' said Sarah.

'I'd better get started hadn't I?'

'Yes, I think you better had,' replied Sarah. 'Coffee and biscuits are on their way'. She left his office still holding the scrapped sheets of Mathew's doodles. It was going to be another very long day, for everyone.

Eleven

Mathew had not slept well; a rushed meal from the microwave was all he could manage last night before he fell into bed next to Susan, who was already asleep when he got home. Despite his tiredness, he couldn't stop thinking about Bernie Culum, Expressive Prints Express, the letterhead, McCormack; they all churned through his brain one by one, and he couldn't cut them off. Today was going to be no different.

The clock said six thirty; he was already up and almost on his way. Susan could hear the sound of water coming from the bathroom and he heard her voice as he stepped from the shower and hurriedly dried himself.

'Mathew this can't go on,' she yelled from the bedroom. 'I hardly ever see you; it's like living with a ghost. It was the same yesterday; all that's happening is I'm woken up to the sound of the front door slamming. We're never in bed together; consciously that is. Please slow down and talk to me, what's going on with Robert and Jennifer? Did you ask about Lucy?'

Mathew emerged from the bathroom hurrying as if his life depended on getting the next flight out. Without looking at Susan, he sat on the edge of the bed and lifted one foot after the other; pulling his socks over each foot in a matter of seconds. He didn't have any time to spare to talk about school kids.

'Sorry, I completely forgot to ask. There's a lot been happening. I saw Lucy at the house only the other day; she seemed fine.'

Susan ignored him as she got out of bed, brushing past him to reach her gown. She made her way to the bathroom where Mathew, who had been so anxious to leave the flat, had left his razor and shaving foam balanced on the edge of the bath. She picked these up and threw them into the corner, where they landed silently on top of his used towel. She wanted them to make a cracking sound against the tiles so that Mathew would come to her, hold her, and ask her what was wrong. This didn't happen. She bent over the bath and turned each tap on full so that the noise of the fiercely running water reduced her desire to scream.

She walked back to the bedroom to confront Mathew again, but instead she heard the sound of the front door slamming, and Mathew shouting goodbye. If she had been decently dressed, she would have ran out after him; screamed at him, until he could feel what she was feeling inside. Instead, she sat at her dressing table and stared into her eyes that were now beginning to glaze over. Her reflection gave no answers to her dilemma. Should she stay with him, living in a single-handed, endless effort to keep their relationship in tact, or should she plan her future without him; with or without children.

The running water began to sound quieter. She rushed to the bathroom to see a mountain of foam waiting to comfort and surround her. She stepped into it and lay back with a sigh; it felt good. She felt her stomach, trim and flat; not as she wanted it. She thought of Patrick, and his delight at the thought of becoming a father. She dreaded him updating her with the size of Claire's girth and the next anti-natal visit. Susan was thirty years old, and if she remained with Mathew there was no chance of motherhood for years yet; if at all. Her body clock was ticking, and Mathew controlled it; her only alternative was to give up on him and look for love elsewhere. Her mind slowly drifted to thoughts of the oncoming day; her classes; last night's marked exercise books; her information technology class where she was going to introduce spread-sheets; and Lucy. She mustn't forget to speak to Lucy.

The foam had stopped making the small bursting noises around her neck and ears. The water was cool and the bubbles had gone. She opened her eyes sharply and, realising she had overdone it, leapt out of the bath and grabbed the same wet towel Mathew had left behind. His razor and shaving foam now made the very noise she'd hoped for earlier, as she lifted the towel and shook them off in anger, causing them to hit hard against the tiled floor. She dressed quickly and rushed from the flat.

It was a cold, damp morning outside. Although it was just a short walk to the Underground, it seemed to take her longer than usual. She felt exhausted even though the day had just begun, but she forced herself to walk briskly, taking the moist air deep into her lungs. The station platform was already full and she didn't have the energy, or the will, to push forward and claim a space on the tube train that had just pulled into the platform. She decided to wait for the next one; she couldn't have coped with being crushed any more than she had been already. She wanted space, freedom, happiness, laughter. None of these things were on offer today. The next train was only a little less full, but she got on it. She stood just in front of the seated passengers; reaching upwards to hold onto the bar to stop herself falling on to them. There was a young woman sitting in front of where Susan was standing. She watched the woman laugh gently as she read a letter, presumably from some-one very close. Because of the crowds pushing at her from all sides, Susan was forced to face her way, and she couldn't help but look downwards and read the beginning of the letter. It be-gan, "My Darling Katie". Susan envied her; she would be happy to hear words like that. Just an acknowledgement of Mathew's affection would be enough for now. She didn't want to read any more of the young woman's letter, it wasn't her business, but she could hardly move for the crush of passengers around her. She looked upwards at the oblong cardboard advertisements, read one about cheap telephone calls abroad, another for car insur-ance specifically for women, and another for hotel city breaks. This last ad looked very appealing. She glanced down again as the woman held the last sheet of her letter openly on view, as though she wanted everyone to see. The page was full of crosses, circles, and hearts, and the final words read "Love you always". The young woman looked up to try to see what station they were approaching next, while the tube train slowed a little. The sign on the tunnel approach read Beresford Street. The woman quickly folded the letter and tried to stand up, but couldn't quite do so because of the volume of people. She gave a sweet smile to Susan, who smiled back, and she remained seated until the train came to a stop where the young woman, and Susan, made their way to the open doors and pushed their way through the crowded platform. Susan decided to climb the escalators in order to save some time, and caught a final glimpse of the young woman again; walking past her as she stood on the right hand side of the escalator, without a care in the world, re-reading her love letter all over again.

Susan rushed from the station. After the heat of the train journey, she almost welcomed the cold dampness of the London air. She felt a little more awake as she entered the grounds of Beresford High School and hurried to the staff room to grab a quick cup of coffee before the start of her English literature class. She saw Mrs. Brampton, Lucy's form teacher, who got up from the only easy chair in the room, and placed a cup on the table next to where she had been sitting.

'Susan - you're a bit late for coffee,' she said apologetically.

'I stayed too long in the bath,' replied Susan. 'I was dreaming of better things.'

'I know the feeling - there goes the bell.'

Mrs. Brampton was about to leave the staff room when Susan took her opportunity; there was no use waiting for Mathew.

'Can I ask you about Lucy Davidson,' she said, 'I haven't seen her for a while and I wondered if you knew why she wasn't attending I.T. after school. Patrick wanted to know, but I could give her some extra help at home if she needs it.'

'Oh? You do surprise me,' said Mrs. Brampton, 'I'd have thought you would have known.'

'Known what exactly?'

'Well, you're right her attendance has been poor. She hasn't been in school at all for the past few days, but she always has a note. I know she had one yesterday excusing her from I.T. It said there were family problems.'

'Family problems?'

'That's what it says. I thought you would know all about it, seeing as she's Mathew's niece.'

'Can I see the notes?'

'They'll be in the office in her file; the most recent one is in my desk, I haven't had a chance to file it. I'll get it for you break-time.'

Mrs. Brampton hurried towards the staff room door and Susan reluctantly followed. They each went in their separate directions once outside, and Susan could hear Mrs. Brampton's dominating tones resound throughout the school as she shouted to a pupil.

'Don't run in the corridor. I said don't run, you wretched boy!'

She only had to raise her voice and the whole school seemed to stand still. Susan envied her control over the children, who still respected and liked Mrs. Brampton, regardless of her no nonsense tone. She wondered what the children made of her. Did they respect Miss Bishop? Did they even like her? She was feeling so unnoticed and worthless that the children might not even notice if she wasn't there at all, and Mathew had made her feel this way.

She could see her class hanging around the doorway and gathering in small clusters in the corridor. Mrs. Brampton's class would be settled down by now; paying strict attention to her every word. Susan's class looked a terrifying sight and she was in no mood to deal with them. If she did get pregnant, she thought, it would only eventually grow into one of these uncontrollable beings. Maybe Mathew was right. She approached the children and lethargically ushered them into the classroom. They responded like reluctant sheep, herded by an unenthusiastic collie.

'Right you lot,' said Susan, about to give her class the brunt of her temperament. 'I'm not in a very good mood today. "To Kill a Mockingbird". Does anyone have the slightest idea what we were discussing in the last lesson? Take out your books and don't speak to me, or each other, until you have explained in your own words how Miss Maudie's attitude to the trial differs from that of the Maycomb population in general. What does it say about her sympathy for Tom Robinson, and her sensitivity towards others? You can contrast this with the attitude of Miss Crawford and how she embodies the worst aspects of Maycomb people. You have until break-time, and I want your best hand-writing.'

A lone gasp of astonishment was heard from just one of the children; the others remained still, and quietly open-mouthed.

'There's to be no talking, so get on with it. Don't just sit there, looking gormless, you're wasting time.'

Wasting time; was that what she was doing? Susan sat at her desk, puzzling over her relationship with Mathew. Then her thoughts went to Lucy. Family problems? What family problems? Why didn't Mathew speak to her about it; why doesn't she feel like part of his family, or just lately even part of his life.

Break-time took an age to arrive.

'Pass your sheets to the front please,' said Susan to her class. She could see by the amount of paper being handed in that the children had made some effort; they had taken her seriously. She wondered if she should adopt the same approach with Mathew.

As she left the classroom, she saw Mrs. Brampton again, marching a child to the head teacher's office in military style. She called to her just before she reached the door.

'Yes, Susan? Oh, I've got that note for you; it's quite legit,' said Mrs. Brampton.

She handed her a folded sheet of quality notepaper. It read
" Lucy is unable to attend Information Technology
after school due to family problems."
The note was signed: "R. Davidson"

'Can I keep this?' Susan said.

'Take a copy and let me have it back. Just for the file.'

The note disturbed Susan; there was something going on and it was being kept from her. Mathew had told her that Lucy seemed o.k. But what was the urgency to see Robert, and why couldn't he talk to her about it? Her curiosity wouldn't wait; she would have to speak to him about it at lunchtime.

She struggled through the rest of the morning, anxious to talk to Mathew. She used the telephone in the staff office. Mrs. Brampton and Patrick were talking to a new trainee in the kitchen area just far enough to be out of hearing. She dialled Mathew's direct line. A familiar voice answered.

'Hello Sarah,' said Susan, 'is Mathew in the office?'

'Yes, he is, but he's with clients; he won't take any calls.'

'Tell him I've phoned. I suppose it will have to wait until tonight.'

'His last appointment this afternoon is going to make him late getting away, so don't expect him home too early,' Sarah replied.

Susan hated the way she protected him; Sarah knew more about his life than she did. She spent twice as many hours with him and knew his every move. So far as Susan was aware, they hardly ever disagreed on anything; she knew that Mathew would be lost without her. Everyone had a large piece of Mathew, except for her. Jennifer, Robert, his father, his criminal clients, his spoilt niece, they all had a big chunk of him, not to mention his perfect secretary, and at the moment, Susan felt that Sarah had the biggest share.

'Don't worry Sarah, I never expect him home. We are but ships passing in the night.'

'Oh dear,' said Sarah, detecting a rift between them, 'well he's had a very busy week; I can assure you that he's working very hard.'

'Yes, I'm sure he is.'

'Maybe he'll get a peaceful weekend.'

'Yes. Maybe.'

The rest of the day dragged painfully slowly for Susan; her class becoming restless as she failed to show her own enthusiasm for the reasoning behind the attitude of the Maycomb population.

'You can do whatever you want for the last hour, provided it's something quiet, very quiet,' she announced to her class.

The children were delighted, and amazed. Susan watched the oversized clock move its second hand until the minutes and the last hour of her working day had passed; she couldn't wait to get home to find out more.

She could sense that Mathew was already home as she turned the key in the front door lock.

'In the kitchen,' Mathew shouted, as he heard her close the door behind her, 'want some tea?'

'You're home! I can't believe it. Were you evacuated from

the office by a bomb scare?'

'Don't spoil it. Sarah told me you had phoned, so I've made a special effort to be home early; the new trainee, Jason Collymore, is seeing my last client, and I've also foolishly sent him to City Road police station, though heaven knows how he'll get on, and Sarah is signing all my post. I've organised things so that we could spend some time together, so don't let's get off to a bad start. Sit down, have some tea, and take your shoes off. If you want me to spoil you then here's your chance.'

'Why? Why do you want to spoil me? There's something wrong isn't there; what's going on?'

'Nothing; nothing to be concerned about. Can't I be nice to you without the Spanish Inquisition?'

Mathew coaxed Susan over to the sofa where she allowed him to remove her shoes and place her feet up onto the cushions. She loved Mathew in this mood and had forgotten how attentive he could be. She gazed at him lovingly, but could see the troubles of the day, the week, still buried in his brow. She wasn't going to be distracted from the subject; she just couldn't drop it. Something was terribly wrong and she had to know or she would burst.

'Is there something wrong with Lucy?' she asked.

'Lucy?'

'Robert has excused her from lessons dozens of times; there's a note in my bag saying there are family problems. Didn't he say anything to you?'

'I told you; I forgot to ask. I couldn't see anything wrong with Lucy; Lucy is not the problem.'

'But the note says there are problems. Family problems.'

'If there are family problems, no one has told me.'

'What is it then? What's bothering you? Can't I help?'

'No, it's just client stuff; you wouldn't want to know, honest. I'll ask about Lucy next time I'm there.'

Susan shut her eyes; her feet resting in Mathew's hands. The stresses of the day suddenly lifted from her; within a very short while, they were curled together in each other's arms, closer than they had been for some considerable time. Susan could feel his affection; it was probably always there, whether or not he had time to show it. She forgot all about school, forgot all about Patrick and his pregnant wife, and forgot all about Mrs. Brampton and Lucy's notes. Any other thoughts, such as packing her things and leaving Mathew, completely drifted away.

Twelve

Lucy was looking at herself in the hall mirror, and Jennifer was watching her. Lucy had re-arranged the fringe around her face, and pulled her ponytail higher, so that small spikes of hair leapt out in all directions around the band. She turned sideways, each side in turn, and adjusted the collar of her school shirt before moving closer to the mirror to inspect the final details of her skin, teeth and eyes. Jennifer could see that her daughter was growing fast, but the older Lucy got, the nearer her secret became. She just couldn't, or wouldn't, allow herself to get any closer to her daughter; Lucy wasn't bothered, and never had been. She was used to her mother's aloofness; attaching herself completely to her father, who in turn adored her. As she watched her getting ready for school, she could see nothing of herself in Lucy; the long fair hair, that had not so much as a kink in it, was nothing like hers. She had a small neat nose, and a broad, charming smile; it would win any heart.

'I'll be late home tonight,' said Lucy as she finished the final inspection of her appearance. 'Tell dad for me,' she said casually.

'Is it I.T tonight?'

'Yes. Then I'm going to Fiona's. Her brother will bring me home about half past ten.'

'I think that's a bit late.'

'Dad says it's o.k. I've already asked him.'

Jennifer reluctantly accepted the arrangements; obviously already agreed between Lucy and her father. She called upstairs to her youngest son.

'We'll be waiting in the car; get a move on Luke.'

She walked out of the house to see her prize possession waiting in the roadside, her maroon 1963 three-point-four Jaguar, with overdrive. She turned the key in the lock, slid inside, across the leather grooves, and closed the door with a heavy thud. She pressed the ignition button; not many things made her happier than driving this car. At least she was in control of something, if not her daughter. She loved the smell of the leather that hit her each time she unlocked the door; the force of the steering wheel and the effort on her arm muscles that it took with each turn. It struggled against her to some extent, offering a slight resistance on just about everything; even the doors weighed a ton. The steering wheel was oversized and heavy; the clutch too firm; the foot brake an enormous pad, and the gear stick would crunch on occasions, particularly if it was plunged into first gear without due care. Anyone unaccustomed to this car would always grate first gear; guaranteed. She loved it all the more because it wasn't easy, but it was powerful, and perfect for her. It was Philip's gift to her on her fortieth birthday and it had taken some getting used to. Mathew had thought that it was a typical gangster's car, advising his sister not to accept it; warning her that the gift from Philip might easily have originally been two cars welded into one, with both owners still searching for each part. Jennifer had not welcomed her brother's advice, or his accusations; she was confident that Philip would never allow her to drive anything that was not completely legitimate and safe. Robert had also dismissed his remarks as just another opportunity to criticise Philip and his lifestyle. In fact, Robert felt rather proud to see his wife handle the three-point-four Mk 2 with no power steering, and he felt that his children were very safe within the sheer weight of it.

Lucy got into the back seat and she and her mother waited for Luke.

'So what's this about Fiona's brother walking you home?'

'Dad doesn't mind so why do you?'

'Because I think ten-thirty is a bit late, that's all.'

'You'd let Luke stay out.'

'Luke is fourteen, and he's a boy.'

'So what? He's not that innocent anyway; you don't know what he gets up to.'

'What do you mean, not that innocent?'

'Nothing. Forget it.'

Just as Jennifer was about to challenge her daughter further, Luke scrambled into the back seat alongside his sister. He caught the tail end of the conversation, and could see his mother looking at him through the driver's mirror. He glared at his sister.

'What's going on?'

'Nothing.'

Jennifer lightened the conversation before another argument broke out, avoiding any confrontations until later; a full-scale quarrel on route to school was the last thing she wanted.

'Lucy doesn't think that you're perfect Luke. At least not as innocent as you look,' said Jennifer.

Luke stared at his sister as Jennifer pushed the gear stick into first, pulled away, and quickly pushed it downwards into second. If there was one thing she didn't like about the Mk 2, it was first gear. No one liked first gear, Philip had told her, but the rest of the car would make up for it. And it did. Lucy stared back at Luke and whispered harshly.

'I haven't said anything.'

'You'd better not.'

'Or what?' said Lucy menacingly.

'You'd just better not. One word to mum and you're for it. You're not so perfect yourself. You'd be in big trouble if she knew what you were up to.'

'And you'd be in big trouble with dad.'

'Could I ask what's going on in the back; don't you ever stop squabbling? Do you do this in school?' said Jennifer as she swung the car fiercely into a right hand turn.

'I try not to bump into her if I can help it,' said Luke.

Lucy stretched across the leather armrest that separated them both. Jennifer had always joked that Jaguar had purposely designed the fat leather armrest with Luke and Lucy in mind, to keep them apart. Nevertheless, Lucy still managed to lean across it and land her brother a punch.

The journey came to an end outside Beresford High School. Jennifer had reached top gear for only a few minutes out of the fifteen-minute ride, and the overdrive had been completely redundant. She desperately wanted to get on an empty open road and drive for hours, to nowhere in particular, so long as her car was allowed to stay in overdrive with no interruption, no squabbling kids, and with the promise of an ocean at the end of the journey. She missed the years when she would go biking with Robert on the empty roads in the long summer heat. The roads were so much busier now. Her thoughts were suddenly broken with the thud of each back passenger door and the sight of both her children walking through the school gates separately, as though they were complete strangers to each other. She knew Luke and Lucy had their secrets, but Lucy's behaviour, she thought, was getting worse.

Thirteen

'Graphic Solutions. Good morning.'

'Could I speak to Robert Davidson please. It's Mathew Weekes.'

'One moment sir.'

Mathew held on the line for several minutes, waiting for his call to be answered. Robert had been experiencing some problems at work; he hadn't confided in anyone, especially not Jennifer. His work just recently had not been up to standard for the brochures for National Heritage; one of Graphic Solutions' biggest clients. His artistic skills and fine line drawings were being superseded by computerised graphics and much younger people, particularly those who had graduated in computer art and technology in preference to more traditional forms of artwork. Robert had a serious problem with one person in particular, twenty years his junior, and an expert in the field of computerised art. His name was Mark Daniels, and his knowledge of photographic applications was vast, as was his artistic talents in general. He was good-looking, impeccably dressed, and confident in both his ability to do his job exceedingly well, and be popular with the management. On one occasion, when Robert's work had been returned to him for alteration and improvement, Mark Daniels had seized the opportunity to show his superiors his true worth in the hope that he would be given the chance of such assignments himself. Within a few hours of discovering that Robert Davidson's work had been returned, he had scanned Robert's meticulous drawings and copied them into his own computer, where he proceeded on screen to make the necessary alterations and improvements required by National Heritage; producing a completely fresh alternative to the original design and layout, using his knowledge of computer applications and artistry to the full. Robert had to admit that the finished product was very good, but if he had allowed Daniels to show them to management he could have risked losing the assignments altogether, probably clearing the path for Mark Daniels to be given first choice on all future orders from National Heritage. Up until now, these were always automatically Robert's referrals. He saw Daniels as a great threat; on that occasion, he had erased the work his rival had copied from him while Daniels was at a meeting with top managers discussing his future and opportunities for promotion. On his return, there had been a huge argument between them, and Daniels had threatened to expose Robert's jealous actions to the directors. Daniels said it would be easy to convince them that Robert's line of work was now antiquated, and had no place in the future development of graphic design. If he wasn't careful, Daniels could ruin all his financial prospects.

Robert had been employed by Graphic Solutions for almost all his working life, and had produced excellent work, but he could not muster the enthusiasm required to get to grips with new, more advanced graphic technology, and he was worried that his position in the company would suffer. The presence of Daniels exacerbated Robert's depressive mood, making his working life that much harder. Jennifer knew nothing of this, nor of the precarious thread on which his employment, and financial security, was balanced.

Robert's particular expertise was fine line drawing, and the company, up until now, had considered him to be their most talented and senior artist. His knowledge of computerised graphics was limited and although he had been capable of producing one or two fine pieces of work by that process, he had a lot to learn. There was no comparison with his talents and those of Mark Daniels in the field of computerised art. Robert had now worked alongside him for almost nine months, and the atmosphere between them worsened by the day. Robert had decided to keep watch on him and his work, and this meant regularly working through lunch hours and arriving early in the mornings. Daniels also stayed late on many occasions and Robert was finding it difficult to keep up with the same long hours. He had a feeling that he was not just after his job as senior artist, but that he was using the equipment in work time to produce his own publications for outside marketing. He had seen Daniels working in the offices of other departments, well after normal working hours. If he could prove this to the management by providing some evidence, then he could be sure that the directors would dismiss him on the spot.

Robert was trying to look at Daniel's latest piece of work on screen when, inconveniently, the telephone rang at his desk. He was surprised to hear Mathew's voice as he rarely had time for a telephone conversation during working hours.

'Mathew! Everything o.k?'

'No, not exactly. Your brother won't give me any information on that letterhead business, and I need it. I know he's got something on Bernie Cullum but I just couldn't get anywhere with him, I'm the last person on earth he'd ever want to help. Do you think you could have a word? It would be a great help to me, and this case I'm battling with.'

'I don't think I can,' said Robert, dismissively, 'you know what he's like. I've never interfered with any of his business and I really don't want to start now. If he's hiding something then I'd prefer to be kept out of it. I've already told you that; it's nothing to do with me. I was asked to do a design and I did it; end of story. He's probably got very good reasons not to tell you anything more. Sorry Mat. I'd like to help but I don't want to be in the middle of it. You shouldn't have approached him; you gave me the impression that you wouldn't, and I'm beginning to wish I hadn't told you anything at all. Just leave me out of it. You haven't said anything to Jen have you?'

'No, no I haven't.'

'Best way. She'll worry over it and it will do no good. No one can get anything out of Philip if he doesn't want to give it, he'll just dig his heels in. If Philip won't tell you who asked for the letterhead and logo then that's the end of it and there'll be no budging him, especially if it's going to help you, or your client I should say. Expressive Prints Express; it was trouble right from the start, and it's still haunting me. Do you know how many hours I spent on that? I don't really want to hear about it any more if that's o.k. If the police turn something up then that's a different matter, but I'm not going all out to investigate my brother.'

'Fair enough. Thanks.'

Mathew thought he had replaced the receiver a little too

abruptly on reflection. Perhaps Robert was right. Why should he want to get involved? McCormack's fate meant nothing to him, and who would want to implicate their own brother? If he had a brother he would probably do the same to keep things under wraps, but if it was a brother like Philip Davidson, who knows. Mathew needed to think some more about whether to speak to Jennifer. If anyone could get a result from Philip it would be her, but Robert would never forgive him.

Mathew checked his watch. He had an hour before he was due at Beconsbridge Police Station for Johnnie Raybourne, one of his regular clients, arrested last night for a residential burglary. He had been woken by the custody sergeant at two o'clock this morning, and had advised his client by telephone. At the time, Mathew had thought that there was no need for Raybourne to have spoken to him at all since he was very experienced at conducting himself at a police station without his help; he wouldn't say anything to the police until they were ready for a formal interview. Mathew thought that Raybourne wanted simply to kill some time by having a chat in the early hours of the morning; also letting the police know that his brief was on their case. Susan was furious. Raybourne had been responsible for causing her many sleepless nights when Mathew would have to leave the flat in order to get him bailed. Raybourne had caused havoc with various social events, infrequent as they were; Susan being abandoned for a burglar who made relentless demands on Mathew's attention, and took priority over her. She had never met Raybourne, but she thought he should be locked up for good. Mathew knew not to argue with her on the subject of Johnnie Raybourne. It was impossible to get the message across that because he had been convicted of dozens of burglaries, it didn't mean he was committing every single one in the vicinity; the police did sometimes get it wrong. Mathew had allowed Susan to have her half hour of rage at two o'clock, without uttering even one word in Raybourne's defence; this was the only way for them both to get back to sleep.

'Remember you're due at Beconsbridge Police Station at eleven thirty,' said Sarah as she put her head around the door, 'do you want to look at this now?'

Sarah was holding the morning's post, clasping it closely, suggesting it was not that urgent. Mathew loved Sarah for her ability to sift through his workload, presenting it to him in order of priority and immediacy; he didn't have to think about it. Did she know how valuable she was?

'The only thing you may like to see is regarding McCormack and Others,' said Sarah. 'The prosecution have sent us the transcript of the police interview of one of the co-defendants; it was missing from the original bundle, what was his name, Spike something? They've also attached a copy of McCormack's previous convictions. Other than that, I think you can leave the rest until you come back from sorting out Raybourne. Shall we go through it together after lunch say?'

'Yes Sarah. Thankyou. Just give me what you have on McCormack.'

Sarah passed him a few A4 sheets for him to look at, and left the room. Mathew looked at McCormack's previous convictions; it included one conviction for possessing pornographic literature, two for assaulting police officers, five for theft of motor vehicles and two non-residential burglaries. He had received one juvenile caution for attempted theft of a motorbike. Mathew thought that he was probably guilty of a few more offences, but had simply escaped conviction. McCormack had told Mathew of all his previous convictions, save for the possession of pornographic literature. Maybe this embarrassed McCormack; or maybe he thought it irrelevant. Mathew couldn't see that this particular conviction had any relevance to the present offences McCormack was facing, but he didn't like anything to be kept from him. He would discuss this with McCormack the next time they meet.

He turned to the transcript of the taped interview of the co-defendant known as Spike. His real name was Mfgwe Olebedogayani; Mathew was more than happy that he was referred to as Spike. The first part of the transcript was as Mathew had expected, and Spike was playing down his part in the two businesses, Expressive Prints Express and Masterprints. He stated the nature of his employment, his qualifications in the printing field, which somehow did not ring true, and the responsibilities given to him at his place of work. At first glance, there was little in the police interview to affect McCormack's position, until Mathew read the end of the transcript. DC Bowden had specifically questioned Spike about McCormack; whether he knew if he had ever used an alias name. Mathew was horrified as he read the last part of Spike's interview, beginning with Spike's reply:

" *'McCormack did call himself Cullum sometimes. Bernie Cullum.'*

'Why would he do that?'

'Because that was the name he used to set up the printing businesses. First there was Masterprints and then Expressive Prints Express.'

'Are you saying that Bernie Cullum is McCormack's alias? That there is no such person as Bernie Cullum?'

'If there is I've never met him.'

'Who signed the cheques?'

'We all did. Except McCormack didn't like to.'

'Why not?'

'Search me. His signature was authorised though. He could also sign as Cullum but he didn't like to deal with the cheques. Mostly Dave and me dealt with the banking. McCormack kept a low profile coming in when he felt like it, placing orders, receiving orders, doing all the hustling if you know what I mean. Didn't do much of the paperwork.'

'For the record, the person you refer to as Dave is your co-accused, David Black.'

'That's right.'

'Did you ever see McCormack sign his name as Cullum?'

'Yeah, once or twice. What's Dave told you?'

'I'm not at liberty to tell you that.'

'Well I'm not saying any more. Ask McCormack yourself, or Dave, or one of the others. I've said enough.' "

Mathew jumped up from his desk and called along the corridor to Sarah, as he walked towards her door. He quickly entered his secretary's room.

'Get McCormack to my office. I've got one or two questions to ask him. I don't think he's been entirely straight with me!'

'Well it wouldn't be a first would it. I'll get him on the phone and fix him an appointment. Will tomorrow be o.k?'

'The sooner the better. I'm off to Beconsbridge Police Station now. Raybourne will be a piece of cake in comparison. If I'm not careful, McCormack's going to make me look a complete idiot. Bernie Cullum indeed, the lying creep,' shouted Mathew as he walked briskly back to his office, pulled his overcoat from the back of the door, and hurried to meet his next client.

Despite his mind not being entirely focused on the job, Mathew's attendance at Beconsbridge Police Station was a successful one; he was in a no-nonsense mood. He got Johnnie Raybourne out of police custody, charged only with a Public Order offence; it could have been a lot worse, and his client was more than pleased with the result. When Mathew returned, McCormack was already waiting in the office reception. He was sitting looking as though he was reading an article in last week's Sunday colour supplement, which Sarah never failed to supply first thing Monday morning; Mathew suspected he was probably just looking at the pictures. He looked up as Mathew entered the reception from the street, but was disappointed when his solicitor failed to supply his usual welcome.

'I'll be with you shortly,' snapped Mathew as he hurried past him through reception, and up the back staircase leading to his office; Sarah met him at the top of the stairs.

'You're a bit later than I thought you'd be - McCormack's been waiting for about half an hour.'

'Well he can wait. Is there any coffee? Raybourne's been charged and bailed, make sure you've got a note of the date he's up at court. I had a hard time getting him out, but we got there in the end. He got of lightly, that kid must have nine lives; they're getting sick of him down there.'

'I'm not surprised. Still, he's good for business isn't he? His files take up half the cabinet from L to R. We'd be close to unemployment if it wasn't for him,' said Sarah laughing.

Sarah's comment made him feel uncomfortable, particularly in view of Philip's earlier verbal attack. It was unfortunately very true; people like Raybourne were good for business, and where would he be without them? Perhaps he was the true villain after all; the villain without the bottle; the lover of criminality without the dirty hands. Worse than that, he was making a good living out of their criminal existence. Philip's words were still painfully present; was he courageous enough to commit a burglary, a theft, or a massive fraud. He needed people like Raybourne and McCormack so that he could earn a decent living; perhaps he shouldn't go too hard on them, perhaps Raybourne and McCormack were the braver men, but they still did things that society could do without. It wasn't his fault that his clients were as they were; he only represented them in law. That was all he did, and everyone deserved to be heard.

'You may as well send him up now Sarah.'

Within a few minutes, McCormack was seated opposite Mathew who had pulled out various sheets of paper from his file.

'Is there something wrong Mr. Weekes? Has anything happened?'

'I'm going to ask you some questions and I want you to answer me truthfully. I cannot continue to act for you unless you allow me to help you. There are a few matters that have come to light; basically, I want some straight answers, ok?'

'Fire away Mr. Weekes. I want to tell you all I can. I haven't never told you a lie.'

'Whose job was it to organise the logo, letterhead and general display and design for the company Masterprints?'

'Bernie Cullum. I've told you this.'

'And for Expressive Prints Express?'

'Bernie Cullum. I had no dealings with any designers, artists, sign writers, or anything like that. I just dealt with orders and ...'

'Hold it! I'm asking the questions and you're giving me answers. Who was your immediate boss?'

'Dave, Spike, all of them really.'

'So where did Cullum fit into it all? Tell me again.'

That could be for a very long time. There's no purpose served in approaching him. You can see what he's said to the police, it's here in black and white, you have no need to speak to him at all. Trust me, there is nothing to be gained. Just stay away from all of them or you'll just make matters worse. I'll do my best to get to the bottom of it, provided you are telling me the truth.'

'I am Mr. Weekes. I am.'

'Then I have to act on what you say. There's just one other thing I need to ask. Your previous convictions include one for possession of pornographic material. Why didn't you tell me about this?'

'I don't know, I should have I suppose. It's a few years ago now and it's a long story; these days I probably wouldn't have even got arrested, let alone charged and convicted. To tell you the truth, I'm a bit embarrassed about that one; it's another thing I got stitched up for. I had the photos on me, but they weren't mine. I was asked to hold on to a package for a couple of days; I didn't know what was in it, didn't want to know, didn't even get to see them until I was arrested and the police showed me, but no one would believe that would they? I was going down for some burglaries anyway, so I took the rap for someone else and they saw me right when I came out. I was a fool to do it, and I wish I never had. I'm not into that stuff; honest I'm not. What are we going to do now Mr. Weekes?'

'I'm going to prepare your defence,' said Mathew firmly, 'that's what I'm going to do. And you're going to tell me the truth and answer every single question I ask you. Is that agreed?'

'Agreed, Mr. Weekes. Agreed.'

'Good. Then I'll get started.'

McCormack got up and shook Mathew's hand before saying goodbye. This time he had every reason to be grateful.

Fourteen

Mathew took up his favourite position by the window of his second floor office, which overlooked the River Thames in one of the less appreciated spots in East London, but still just a few minutes' walk to the city. There was always something new to watch, and the river altered by the moment. It was hard to believe the changes that had taken place over recent years; he had been strongly opposed to the redevelopment, the flattening of old historic buildings, the dismantling of dockyards, the disintegration of local community groups, boat clubs and the like. But now he could see something different finally emerging from the builder's rubble; new buildings, new offices, and new luxury flats created from disused warehouses. The area looked richer and more prosperous than it had when he was growing up, but he remained very conscious of the people who had truly benefited; not people like Martin McCormack, who was still stuck eight floors up on a run down housing estate, but people like Philip Davidson, whose penthouse suite was only a stone's throw away. The view of the water from Mathew's office always managed to calm him enough to allow for some clear thinking, and McCormack was in need of some proper attention.

Bernie Cullum's identity had to be discovered, and quickly, and his brother-in-law was a good place to start. Convinced that he knew about Cullum, and his whereabouts, he focused more on Philip's suspicious reaction when he called him; he had refused to divulge anything at all. He did have another avenue he could explore in order to get the information he wanted, but he was not happy at using his sister in that way. Philip was very fond of Jennifer; Mathew had always suspected that his feelings might go further than that, as much as Philip's feelings were able to grow for anyone. There had even been a time when he thought Philip and his sister were having an affair, but the very thought had sickened him so much that he dismissed it altogether. Philip employed Toby as a courier rider, with the Kawasaki thrown in, taxed, insured, maintained, for him to use whenever he pleased, and he spoilt Lucy with all the affection of a doting uncle. There was no reason at all for Jennifer to have any complaints about her brother-in-law, or co-operate with any investigation of him. On her fortieth birthday, Philip had given Jennifer one of his beloved Mk 2 Jaguars, saying that no one was more deserving. 'A beautiful motor for a beautiful woman', he had said; it had made Mathew nauseous, but although he doubted the authenticity of the car, this was more than he had ever given anyone. There were times when Mathew could sense Philip's envy of Robert's marriage, he was sure he'd like to be in Robert's shoes. Mathew appreciated his sister was attractive, with a great sense of fun, intelligence, and sensitivity, but it was the boyishness that Mathew had always loved about her, and this was the kind of woman that Philip longed to be with. Instead, Philip had convinced himself that he could get along nicely by doing without the commitment; surrounding himself with money, fast cars, and women half his age, but it was small compensation for what he really desired.

Mathew focused on Philip's soft spot for Jennifer; he was very tempted to use this for his own means, or rather for his client, McCormack. Despite Robert's warnings, this was his sister and his client; justice was waiting to be done, and it wasn't for Robert to determine the outcome by stopping him discovering more, no matter how this was achieved. He was going to approach Jennifer, and persuade her to get whatever she could on the mysterious Mr. Cullum. If Philip was going to open up to anyone, that person would be Jennifer, no one else would even get close.

Sarah had seen that Mathew was deep in thought and had left him gazing out at the Thames, as he frequently did. She had been sifting through a pile of paperwork on his desk.

'Have you finished with these McCormack papers?' Sarah asked as she tried to make some space to place a bulky pile of correspondence and a bundle of police tape cassettes of clients' interviews.

'No. No, I haven't,' said Mathew as he walked back towards his desk. 'This case is going to be difficult,' he said as he sat and rotated the large leather chair to face the pile of paperwork. 'I've got a plan - but I'm not entirely happy about carrying it out.'

'Oh? Sounds ominous.'

'Close the door Sarah. I need to tell you about it. Come and sit with me for a bit.'

Sarah noticed Mathew's usual look of seriousness had been replaced with a look of immense anxiety.

'Are you sure you want to speak to me about it?'

'Yes. I need to speak to someone, and not a member of my family.'

'Oh? Now you're worrying me.'

Sarah seated herself at Mathew's desk, as a client would do. She sat opposite and waited patiently for him to tell her more.

' I want to confide something very serious, which may have implications for my family.'

Sarah wasn't sure if she wanted to be involved in his family problem, that wasn't the arrangement that they had; she liked things as they were, at a respectful distance.

'Why don't you talk it over with Susan?'

'I don't want to involve her; she's had enough of my work and life-style just lately, and if I begin to tell her I would have to tell her the whole lot, and I don't want to do that. I can't do that. Anyway, she's sick of my clients and their cases.'

'Are you telling me that your family is involved with a case? A case from this office? Involved with one of your clients?' Sarah said in amazement.

'Yes, possibly.'

'Which client? Not Raybourne, please don't tell me it's Raybourne!'

'No. Not Raybourne,' said Mathew reassuringly, 'in a way, I suppose it's worse. It's Martin McCormack. My family is involved with "The Queen versus McCormack and Others". Quite astonishing, isn't it? It just goes to show, anyone can get involved, consciously or not. What a game it is, all the family can join in,' said Mathew, cynically.

Sarah looked at him in disbelief.

'McCormack? Are you sure that I should know any more? Think carefully before you tell me Mathew; remember I have contact with all your family.'

'I want to tell you; I need to tell someone. It's actually to do with Jennifer and Robert. It's Robert's brother who's more involved, you know, the wide-boy who lives on the Thames? Rides around in Jaguars mostly, has a whole collection of them. A whole collection of women too, or girls I should say.'

'Do you mean Philip? Robert's brother, Philip? Is he connected with McCormack? He can't be.'

'I don't know for sure, that's what I need to find out.'

'He runs a courier firm doesn't he?'

'Yes. It's called PACE.'

'PACE? After the Police and Criminal Evidence Act?' Sarah said, looking astonished.

'Parcels and Courier Express,' said Mathew, 'but you're right; it's deliberate, and typical Philip Davidson bravado. Anybody else and I'd find it amusing.'

'Do you think his courier firm is connected in some way?'

'Possibly. I just don't know. One of the bogus companies in McCormack's Indictment is called Expressive Prints Express, which you might recall. Philip asked Robert to design a logo for that company, on behalf of one of his pals; probably the guy responsible for setting up Expressive Prints Express. I suspect that whoever that was is the missing Bernie Cullum, and Philip is protecting his identity. Why wouldn't he tell me anything, unless he was involved?'

'But didn't you suspect that McCormack himself was Bernie Cullum?'

'Yes, I did. In interview, the co-defendant, Spike, told the police that McCormack used the name of Bernie Cullum quite often, but what Spike says can't be relied on one little bit.'

'But didn't you think McCormack was lying to you?'

'I did at first, but now I'm not so sure. I just don't know. McCormack denies ever using the name of Cullum.'

'Well he would, wouldn't he,' said Sarah dismissively, 'you be careful how you choose which people to believe. It's happened before, hasn't it, having the wool pulled over your eyes.'

'I know, don't remind me,' said Mathew as he thought instantly of Johnnie Raybourne, 'but he seemed genuinely surprised when I told him what Spike had said. He also said that Spike was indebted to Cullum, that he was almost controlled by him, blackmailed even. It could be that Spike was lying to save Cullum's real identity coming out. The fact is, I think Philip knows who Cullum is, but I don't know how to get him to talk. My sister is really close to him; he's been very generous to her and the children over the years, but it's all for show, just to impress her and keep her sweet. Luke seems to be the only one he doesn't spoil, but then Luke is his own person, you can't get round him very easily; we share a lot of things in common, neither of us are fond of Philip.'

'Mathew, get to the point. What are you going to do? Are you thinking of involving the police?'

'I've thought about it, but I dare not do it. If McCormack is hiding stuff, it will make it worse, and if Philip is up to something with Bernie Cullum, I'll be to blame for landing him in it; Jennifer would never forgive me, and neither would Robert and the children. I don't like the man, but he's in the middle of my family. I don't know how far I should go to look out for McCormack at the risk of splitting my family to bits. I should really remove myself from McCormack; perhaps refer him elsewhere. Then again, what am I going to tell him? "Oh, I can't act for you any more because I think my brother-in-law is connected to your case. Oh yeah, and the police don't know it yet." It's a volcano waiting to blow. Anyway, I have a personal interest in Philip Davidson. I want to find out what he's up to.'

'Are you asking for my opinion, or did you just want to get it off your chest. Do you want me to advise you, is that why you're telling me?'

'I know this isn't fair. You're my secretary for heaven's sake. I'm the solicitor, I make the decisions.'

Mathew was clearly angry with himself; disappointed at his own weakness. Having to share his dilemma with his secretary was embarrassing. This was his client, his problem, and his family. Usually a difficult situation could be referred to Counsel for advice, but not this one; Jonathan Bowers, QC, would be of no help here.

Sarah got up, walked to the doorway, and stood there with her arms firmly folded in front of her. She was sad at Mathew's situation, and wanted more than anything for his family not to be involved in a criminal case, particularly not this one. She knew a lot about him; his love for his sister, the suffering they endured following the loss of their mother, his affection for Susan and his inability to give her the love that she deserved, partly through the pressures of his job. She knew that his father was dying, and there was nothing Mathew could do. Now she knew of his intense dislike of his brother-in-law, Philip Davidson. He had given her too much information about his family, but she had to help him.

'You haven't answered me,' said Sarah, her folded arms giving the impression that whatever she was about to say she would genuinely feel was right. 'You haven't said that you wanted my advice, but I'll give it anyway. You don't have to take it, but it's what I would do in your position.'

Mathew pulled his hands slowly away from his brow and looked up at Sarah as she spoke.

'Speak to Jennifer,' she said firmly, 'speak to your sister. Just take a deep breath and do it. Never mind how close she is to Philip; blood's thicker than water, always has been and always will be. Jennifer thinks the world of you. Speak to her, she'll know what you should do.'

Sarah quietly closed the door and returned to her room along the corridor. She had given Mathew her best advice and now it was up to him. He was on his own on this one.

Fifteen

Mathew took a deep breath and dialled his sister's number. Sarah was right. He had no choice but to confide in her, but he was going to go further than that. He was going to recruit her as his agent; to get the truth from Philip Davidson. Lucy answered the phone.

'Uncle Mathew,' she said cheerfully, 'if you want mum she's in the street sorting out the car. She's under the bonnet fixing something. She's in a bit of a mess, shall I go and get her?'

'Lucy? Why are you at home?'

'Dad said I didn't have to go in today because uncle Philip is taking me out on the boat with Natalie. We have to leave early because of the tide.'

'Natalie? Who's Natalie? Oh, don't bother telling me, I can guess. But what about school? Doesn't your mother mind you missing school?'

'Yeah. Of course she does. She always minds, but dad said its o.k. Luke has loads of days off and mum doesn't say a word, but whatever I do she goes crazy. Anyway, Natalie's really nice.'

'I'm sure she is,' said Mathew, unable to express his true opinions to his young niece, 'but Susan tells me you have a lot of time off school. She says you don't study information technology any more. I thought you loved I.T.'

'Did she say that? Well it's not true.'

'I'm sure she's not making it up,' said Mathew, 'she says you hand in notes all the time that your dad has written.'

'So?'

'So,' said Mathew patiently, 'that means that she's not making it up doesn't it? If you're taking notes in to excuse you, then you must be missing something, otherwise you wouldn't need a note, would you? It means you're missing lessons doesn't it?' Mathew waited for a reply. 'Doesn't it? Lucy?' There was no response.

'Mathew. I was under the bonnet fixing a hose,' said Jennifer breathlessly.

'When did you take up car mechanics?'

'It's just a hose, but awkward to get to and the clips were really old and rusty. But I managed it, with the help of Philip. He talked me through it on the phone. It felt like one of those medical emergencies where someone has to perform an operation with the equipment in their handbag. You know, steel comb, nail file. Robert has all the tools with him so I had nothing but a kitchen knife and a screwdriver, and there was Philip with all the patience in the world on the other end of the line. He was brilliant.'

'Yeah, if you say so,' said Mathew.

'Anyway, we'll soon see if I've done the job properly. I've got to drop Lucy off at Philip's flat. They're all going out on the boat for the day.'

'So I gather. You know my feelings about Philip, but I'll try to keep it under wraps.'

'Yes, please do.'

'Lucy's off school again then?'

'Yes she is. I don't like it and she knows so. This is all Robert's fault. She gets away with whatever she wants just lately. Still, so long as it's only a day here and there.'

'Susan told me Lucy's had a lot of time off recently. I just tried to ask her about it, but she disappeared off the phone, and a bit too quickly if you ask me.'

'What do you mean a lot of time off?'

'Well, for starters she hasn't been going to those information technology classes that she was so keen to go to; Susan's colleague was asking about her, Patrick, I think. Apparently it turns out she's missed whole days of regular school too. Maybe she's skipping off to see a boyfriend; they start young these days. But she's your kid, you should know.'

'I don't know what you mean,' said Jennifer seriously, 'Lucy has been going to I.T. I think Susan must be mistaken.'

'I don't think so. She did see a note signed by Robert.'

'A note signed by Robert? When did she see that?'

'Just the other day, she asked her form teacher. The note said something about problems in the family, but I told Susan there were no problems. I assumed Lucy was skipping lessons with your blessing. Are there any problems?'

'No more than usual; Robert seems to be more worried about work than usual these days, he seems very pre-occupied, but it doesn't stop him spoiling Lucy like he does. I don't know anything about her having time off, but I'm going to speak with Lucy about it, and with Robert. This just isn't on; she's getting worse. Now her father is writing notes without even telling me. I'm very cross about this, and you can thank Susan for her concern.'

'I actually phoned for a completely different reason.'

'Oh? Don't tell me, Luke's been skipping school and you've been writing the notes.'

'I'm sure if Luke was bunking off he'd have the balls to write the notes himself, not recruit me as his partner in crime.'

'True enough.'

'I want to speak to you about something, in person, not on the phone. It's a bit sensitive.'

'Sensitive? Well you could come round later. I don't like the sound of this, should I start worrying now?'

'I don't want you to worry at all. I just need your advice, that's all. Nothing to worry about.'

'I'm seeing dad at about six o'clock - do you want to come? We could meet at St. John's, see dad, and then go for a drink. How does that sound?'

'Fine. I'll be there about six-thirty. Tell Lucy I didn't mean to snitch on her; I hope she has a nice day out, despite the company. Tell her to be careful of the water.'

'I will. See you later, provided my mechanics have done the trick.'

Mathew's heart was pounding. Was he doing the right thing or was this going to prove to be one big mistake. He would soon have the answer, one way or the other.

Sixteen

It was nearly seven o'clock when Mathew pulled up outside the hospice. He could see his sister's car perfectly reversed into a bay reserved for doctors and consultants. The chrome Jaguar mascot was leaping forward open-mouthed towards him, as he took the bay next to the Mk 2. They were regulars here, so he knew they would be approached if the parking space was needed, but emergency consultants were rarely called to St. John's, other than sadly to deal with paperwork.

He walked along the corridors, making his way towards his father's room. He had the same sensation that he had last week, the stillness, the silence, and the perfume; it was all so inviting. He would give anything for this peace and tranquillity for at least a week, if not longer. He was still fantasising about renting a room as he walked past some that were now empty. He approached his father's bed where his sister was already seated; they seemed to be deep in conversation, and Jennifer appeared to be very disturbed. She looked round as Mathew approached.

'Mathew - I'm so glad you're here,' she said to her brother, 'he's getting worse. He's rambling on about Josie and the water. Won't he ever stop? Mathew, talk to him. For God's sake, someone get him to stop!'

Jennifer moved to one side so that Mathew could sit close to his father.

'Dad. It's me. Dad?'

His father opened his eyes and looked at him. He recognised his son, but all he wanted to do, all he had ever wanted to do, was let him know the pain he felt. It had never left him; he had never even tried to disguise it, not even for the sake of his children. His father would be of no help with the family matter Mathew now faced; he had never been of any help at all. Mathew looked at his father, who was all wrapped up in his own thoughts, his selfish guilt. For a moment, Mathew resented him. Jennifer simply stared at her father, thinking similar thoughts, wishing he had been there to help her when she had needed it. She had finally confided in her father; told him her darkest secrets. But now she wasn't sure if he had even heard her, let alone listened, or remembered what she had said. George Weekes stared deep into Mathew's eyes.

'I couldn't save her. She slipped between the boat and the quay and I held her hand. I tried so hard to pull her - my Josie - but she slipped and they told me to wait. We all waited. They said she'd gone under and would come out the other side. She did come out the other side didn't she? All her clothes pulled up and clinging, and I couldn't bear those people to see her like that.'

'Dad, don't.'

His father closed his eyes; slowly his ramblings came to a stop, and he fell into a deep sleep.'

'Shall we wait for him to wake Jen?'

'I'd like to get out of here. I need a drink. Let's go for a while, we can come back later. Let's discuss that problem you have. I can't think what it's about that you couldn't tell me on the phone, but anything's better than listening to dad's ramblings any longer.'

Jennifer looked so unhappy that Mathew half wished that he hadn't mentioned anything at all to her, but it was too late now. He took her jacket from the back of the chair and held it for her while she slipped her arms into each sleeve in turn, and then he headed for the door. Jennifer kissed her father on his forehead and whispered goodbye, while Mathew paced up and down in the corridor, waiting for his sister.

'What's the hurry Mathew? What's bothering you?'

'Let's get seated somewhere first. I need to ask you a favour. A big favour, and I don't think you're going to like it.'

They walked in silence to The Walnut Tree, just a few hundred yards from the hospice. Jennifer chose a table in the corner of the pub, by a window, and ordered a white wine with soda. While Mathew waited at the bar for his Guinness to be poured to perfection, he contemplated how he was going to approach his sister; this wasn't going to be easy. When he returned to the table with the drinks in hand, Jennifer wasted no time.

'So what's all this about?'

'It's about Philip,' Mathew said, as he pulled a chair nearer to the table and clasped both hands around his glass. 'I need you to find out something for me. I've asked him myself but he won't give me anything. You're my only hope.'

'Great. That's all I need right now,' said Jennifer as she picked up her drink and took a large mouthful. 'So, spill the beans,' she said impatiently.

Mathew took a huge gulp of his thick black drink, and manoeuvred his lips together so as to remove some of the white froth, delaying matters only for a moment or two. He took a deep breath in.

'It concerns one of my clients,' Mathew began, cautiously. 'Philip has some information that is essential to his defence.'

'What information? Mathew, what are you talking about?'

'Do you remember that day I came to the house when Robert asked you and Lucy to leave us alone?'

'Yes. He never would tell me what that was about.'

'Do you remember that awful job he had to do for Expressive Prints Express and how he hated doing it? How he couldn't find anything in the terrible title to spark his imagination?'

'Expressive Prints Express,' pondered Jennifer. 'Yes, I remember. It took him ages to think up a logo. He was really moody.'

'Do you know the person who ordered the letterhead? Did anyone come to the house concerning it?'

'Not as I remember. At the time I thought it had something to do with Philip.'

'Your damn right it did. Philip asked Robert to design the letterhead and logo for someone, and I want to know who that someone is. I have a client called McCormack who's charged with fraud. Without loading you with too much detail, he insists that someone by the name of Bernie Cullum ran various bogus companies, and used him as a stool pigeon. No one has ever been able to trace Cullum, but I'll discover his identity if I can find out who ordered the letterhead and logo. Cullum dealt with all that side of the businesses, or so my client tells me. Whoever asked Philip to get the job done could be Bernie

Cullum himself; Expressive Prints Express was not the only bogus company that he was involved with, there were many others, and the whole scam runs into millions. Do you know enough?'

'What do you want me to do?'

'I want you to find out who asked Philip to get the letterhead and logo for Expressive Prints Express. That's all.'

'That's all? And how on earth am I going to do that? You don't suspect Philip is involved do you? I know what you think about him, you're always criticising his lifestyle, but I'm very fond of him.'

'I know you are.'

'He's been incredibly good to me, and the children.'

'Yes, I know.'

'Look at Toby for instance, and Lucy is out on the boat with him right now. He's so generous.'

'So you say.'

'Do you know what? I sometimes suspect you're just jealous of his success.'

'You have to be kidding.'

'No, I'm not kidding. I know you don't like him and his penthouse on the Thames and all that goes with it, but he's earned what he's got, and I've got a lot to thank him for.'

'So you keep telling me.'

'If what your asking me to do will get him into any kind of trouble, then I don't want to be doing it. Do you hear me Mathew? I don't want any part of it.'

Mathew knew his sister had a mind of her own, and her affection for their brother-in-law annoyed him; Philip was a flashy, arrogant womaniser, who didn't deserve his wealth, and he certainly didn't deserve his sister's friendship. Jennifer didn't share these views; getting her on board was going to be tricky.

Sarah's advice was still ringing in his ears as he went to the bar to order another dry white wine and soda. He could see that his sister was deep in thought. She was unconsciously trying to achieve a perfectly balanced beer mat on its edge, on the rim of the table. It was clear to Mathew that he had only succeeded in making her anxious, and he was sorry for that. She had a lot to deal with, several people to care about, and on top of all her own problems, here he was, loading her with information she wished she hadn't been given. He was asking her to investigate some-one she was extremely fond of, and he weighed this up against McCormack's future; he owed McCormack only as much as his occupation expected from him, and no more, yet there was a burning desire in him to get justice for McCormack, and an un-easy, but exciting prospect of revenge against his brother-in-law if the information on Bernie Cullum could be secured. If only he could get this, he would be very satisfied indeed.

All was not yet lost. He approached his sister gently and placed another glass of white wine and soda carefully on the table, at a distance from where she had now successfully bal-anced the beer mat. As he put the glass down, she flicked the mat aggressively across the table towards him; she was angry that she had no choice, she had to put her brother first. He was her flesh and blood; they had been through too much together, she couldn't let him down.

'O.k. Mathew, tell me what you want me to do,' Jennifer said reluctantly, 'but I don't like it. I don't like it one bit.'

Sarah was right, thought Mathew with some relief. Blood is thicker than anything.

Seventeen

There were only a handful of people working through the night at Graphic Solutions; this made his task that much easier. He had instantly seen the opportunity to multiply his income, and it was not to be missed. He had high hopes of a wealthy, early retirement, but access to the material he needed had been out of his reach up until now.

He had become a changed person since discovering the horrible truth; he could hardly recognise himself. The life he had thought was his had been nothing but a trick, and he was now like a chameleon in waiting, longing for the moment he could make his escape and create a new identity. He would build a new life where no one would find him, but he needed to be rich, very rich.

His charming nature had earned him the respect that he needed right now; but most importantly, he was trusted. By successfully winning over the staff in reception, he had managed to sift through the new orders, picking out the images most suitable to his needs, and copying them, before returning them to their original place. The receptionists had paid little interest to what he was doing; when he needed to distract them from his illegal actions, he had succeeded every time. Once the selected material had been copied, and altered to his satisfaction, he would complete an order sheet in an alias name before sending the images to the photographic department for final enhancement. Then they could be delivered to the printers of his choice. The lads in the photographic department had seen it all before, and were not easily shocked. They were all experienced, and their street credibility had taught them there was no accounting for taste, or its diversity. Most of them were young and underpaid, especially those still in training, so the extra income that this sideline generated was very welcome, they considered it a perk of the job. The photographs and images held little interest; at the most, these illicit assignments only caused slight amusement, just typical banter. On this occasion, however, he had some very special photographs lined up for them, perfect for his new line of business. He was sure he could trust them with the project. He could finally envisage the inevitable day, and it was drawing closer; the day he would carry out his ultimate revenge on his tormentors. He had been inflicted with such unbearable pain that it had destroyed his very soul, but situations like these helped him through the darkness, enabling him to visualise some light in the tunnel. The day of reckoning was coming; and for his persecutors, what a dreadful day that will be.

Tonight he disregarded all security procedures in the building; the guards on duty greeted him as a familiar and respected face. He showed no cards, signed no papers, and just walked right in. He wandered the corridors of the first floor, avoiding those rooms where he could see even a glimmer of light. He chose a room to the far end of the building that contained all the equipment he was likely to need, including the most up to date scanner that Graphic Solutions possessed. He tried various computers, until he accessed one that contained low security information, and did not require a password. One by one, he proceeded to scan each photograph until they were loaded onto the hard disk. He viewed the oversized images on the screen before him, trying various applications until he was completely satisfied, and then applied the best one for the job. He proceeded to get down to some serious work. He introduced images over existing ones, deleting, adding, and building up each picture until the final products were perfected to the satisfaction of potential customers. He finished the whole job earlier than expected, and was feeling quite content. After producing one transparency of each image, he methodically deleted the evening's work. He was meticulous; ensuring no trace of his actions would be left behind. He carefully unplugged and replaced all the equipment he had used; making sure that not even a pen would appear to have been disturbed. He was becoming a master at this.

He left the room carrying just one envelope, but this had the potential of making him thousands; more importantly, the contents of this envelope would destroy the people who had stolen his life, and he became more and more excited at the very thought. With the envelope tucked under his arm, he casually walked past the security guards; nobody said a word. Tomorrow he will complete his order sheets, and pass them through the company in the usual way. The boys in photographic will recognise the fictitious name and, as instructed, make the deliberate mistake of forgetting to mark the docket. It was nothing unusual, unmarked dockets were received all the time, so it was no big deal, but it meant that the photographic processor responsible for re-touching the original order could not be traced. The processor will then return the perfected, finished product to reception, marked for delivery to Colourways, a well-established and reliable printing firm frequently used by the company. The receptionist will then arrange for collection by their regular courier firm, Parcels and Courier Express, who were very familiar with the run. It was as easy as that. Once it got to Colourways he would be on hand to oversee the final prints for himself; no one else would see the finished products, and no one would ever know that they were his. It was a simple plan, and he was confident that he would never be detected; a perfect, evil procedure, for use in the perfect, evil revenge, which was getting nearer by the day.

Eighteen

Toby mounted his Kawasaki with the confidence of an experienced rider. At twenty years of age, he could not wish for a better life or occupation. He was more than grateful to his uncle, who had now given him the bike, fully insured and regularly maintained, to use whenever he wished. It was Friday, and he was looking forward to finishing his deliveries early and spending the weekend with Rachael. As Jennifer's son, Philip naturally favoured him above his other employees. Most of the other riders would work right up to the end of the day, and later if need be; Friday or not. This would sometimes embarrass Toby, but Philip's response was that he was family, and it was normal that he should benefit from being employed in a family business. Toby never argued too strenuously; he liked the perks. He couldn't have a better employer, and Philip considered Toby to be a reliable, sensible young man, perfect for the job as his special delivery courier.

Toby checked the packages were safely encased in the pannier. He turned the ignition key and the bike immediately started up. While his left hand controlled the clutch and his foot was busy pushing into first gear, he simultaneously opened the throttle and sped off, working through the gears to the sound that he lived for. He weaved his way through the heavy morning traffic, taking bends and passing juggernauts with ease. The collection from Graphic Solutions and delivery to Colourways was a journey he had frequently completed. He knew exactly where to go, and the quickest route to get him there. This was his favourite run. He loved the wide, sweeping bend towards the end of the dual carriageway, which he could take at considerable speed. He had done this run many times, and he hadn't been stopped yet. The packages from his father's place of work were rarely heavy, allowing him to go at speed without any problems caused by weighty panniers. It was a bonus that Colourways was also on route to Rachael's flat; he could be finished by lunchtime, and then spend the rest of the afternoon with his girlfriend, who had hopefully skipped her Friday afternoon lectures, as arranged. He had the best job in the world.

He positioned in the outside lane of the dual carriageway and opened the throttle wide. The bike flew. Toby was the master of its destination, and he felt good. Without a thought to the speed he was travelling, he overtook every vehicle he came across; one by one he sped past them, each giving the short sharp sound of a buzzing insect as they were left behind, in the distance; each blurred car, van, lorry, gave their own variation of the split-second sound. He was in his element, with only Rachael on his mind.

Then he heard something very different. There was a wailing, high-pitched noise, and he became distracted from the mesmerising rhythms of the passing traffic. The sound was accompanied by blue flashing lights, which bounced off the highly glossed tanks of the Kawasaki. Reluctantly, he closed the throttle gradually to slow himself down, and manoeuvred to the left hand lane where he came to a halt on a gravelled area, just off the road. The traffic sounded different now as he removed his helmet and waited for the police. They had stopped several yards in front, and now turned back to approach him. He sat astride the bike and watched nervously as one officer slowly began the walk towards him. As he was walking, the officer took a notebook from his top pocket.

'Could you dismount please sir, and remove the key from the ignition.'

Toby got off the bike and rested it on its stand.

'What's your name?' asked the officer, as Toby offered him the keys.

'Toby Davidson.'

'This your bike?'

'No, Well...yes. It's sort of mine. I use it for work. It's my uncle's bike really but he gave it to me. I suppose it is mine. It's not registered in my name though. At least I don't think it is.'

'Shall we start again?' said the officer, breathing out with an impatient sigh. 'Is this your bike?'

'No.' Toby said, more confidently.

'Who does it belong to?'

'My uncle's company, Parcels and Courier Express. It says the company name on the side there - PACE - and that's their address,' said Toby, pointing to the smaller sign writing under the company name, in an effort to assist the officer. 'I'm working as a courier,' he continued, 'and I'm just making a delivery.'

'Where to?'

'A printing firm called Colourways.'

'Do you have their address?'

'It's on the packets, in my pannier.'

'Could you show me please.'

Toby unlocked the pannier and pulled out the packets, which he handed to the officer.

'Do you know how fast you were going?' said the officer as he looked down at the addresses written on the large brown envelopes.

'A bit too fast?' asked Toby, knowing he was probably doing double the limit.

'You're right there son; a bit too fast is one way of putting it. In fact, you won't be surprised to know that we clocked you at eighty-seven mph at one point back there. In a hurry are we?'

'No, not really,' said Toby.

'So you always ride at that speed, do you?'

'No,' said Toby, nervously.

'Just wait here a moment while my colleague brings the car nearer. We're going to have to do a check on the bike, seeing as you're not sure whether or not it's yours.'

Toby hoped his uncle had kept his paperwork up to date. He stood by the road and watched as the second officer, who had remained seated in the car, brought the vehicle closer to them, then buried his head in his radio. He listened to an alien sounding voice, distorted, speaking in some sort of code that Toby couldn't comprehend. The first officer still held the packages, and was staring at the name Colourways, and the addresses printed on them. The second officer replaced his radio, got out of the car and approached his colleague. He whispered to him, out of Toby's hearing, and then returned to the car. Toby knew that all was not in order, and that his uncle's paperwork was going to cause him problems.

'What's in the packets son?'

'I don't know,' said Toby, 'I just deliver.'

'Mind if we take a look?'

'They're not mine,' said Toby, 'I don't know if it's alright to open them.'

'Are they confidential then?' said the officer. 'They're not marked confidential, are they? I think we'd better take a little look, only our check on the bike has come up with the name Philip Davidson.'

'That's my uncle,' said Toby.

'You're uncle eh? We know him of old.'

'Do you?' said Toby with some surprise.

'Oh yes. Haven't seen him for some time, but in my experience a leopard changing its spots is a very rare thing indeed. I'm sure he won't mind us having a look. It'll save you a lot of time. Then you can get on your way, with a producer that is, and a summons to follow. Sorry son, but that was some speed you were doing.'

'Go ahead then,' said Toby nonchalantly, 'it's probably just artwork for the printers.'

'And you don't know what's in them, right?'

'Haven't a clue.'

The officer pealed back the sticky flap from a corner of one of the packets, and slowly pulled across the envelope as carefully as possible until it was open. While still looking at Toby, his hand went inside. He felt a bundle of card-like paper, which he half pulled out of the packet. When the officer looked down and saw the contents in his hand, he stopped pulling immediately. He took several steps back from Toby, and stared at him again. He replaced the contents in the packet, and walked towards his colleague, who was sitting with one leg out of the open door of the car, appearing to share only a fraction of his friend's enthusiasm for stopping the speeding biker. The first officer handed the half opened packet to him. Toby watched as the second officer looked at the contents, then instantly sat bolt upright. Both officers now turned to face Toby, with worrying expressions. The officer who knew his uncle approached Toby again.

'Toby Davidson, I'm arresting you for being in possession of obscene publications. You do not have to say anything, but it may harm your defence if you do not mention when questioned, something which you later rely on in court. Anything you do say may be given in evidence. Do you understand the caution?'

'What are you talking about? What obscene publications? Show me!'

Toby was led towards the car where the second officer was still holding the packet.

'Do you understand the caution?' the first officer said firmly.

'I don't know what's going on,' objected Toby. 'I want to speak to my uncle.'

'So do we son,' the officer replied. 'So do we. Now get in the car.'

Nineteen

Robert had left the house too early for Jennifer to approach him about Lucy's time off school, and the notes he had surreptitiously given to her teacher. She had heard Toby's bike start up before anyone else had woken, and then hours later the voices of Lucy and Luke, arguing as usual, before setting off for school. Today she had left this for Robert to deal with, and felt him slide from the bed trying not to wake her. She lay there motionless, allowing him to deal with their children. She just wasn't in the mood, and her questions about Lucy could wait. She knew Robert had problems of his own; something to do with work, but all she could think about was betraying his brother. She pulled the covers further over her shoulders after Robert had quietly closed the bedroom door, but she couldn't postpone the inevitable task that her brother had set.

She heard her family leave the house; all were ignorant that she was wide-awake, and the terrible job she had to do. The house was now still, and she was alone with her thoughts. She gazed towards the window, knowing that she would soon be outside, away from the sanctity of her bed, approaching Philip in a betrayal of trust. She did not know exactly how she would betray him, only that it didn't feel right. She deliberated her divided loyalties between her brother, her husband, and Philip, but in the end, there was no choice. Within minutes she was up, showered, and dressed, with an arrangement made to meet Philip for lunch. She had phoned him on the pretence that she would like him to check the mechanics she had carried out on the water pump on the Mk 2.

Philip was delighted. He watched as Natalie dried herself, and fantasised that this was Jennifer. Natalie's youth did little for him this morning and he would have given his entire fortune at that moment for her to be replaced with his brother's wife. He was impatient for lunchtime to arrive, and ordered Natalie to make coffee before she got dressed. Natalie obeyed. He envied Robert more and more, and his respect and affection for Jennifer increased each day. The more he saw her the more he loved her, and the less he saw of her the more he missed her.

Natalie brought his coffee to him in her robe; he was sitting before the French doors, staring out to the river. She knelt down, put the cup beside him, and placed one hand firmly on his knee.

'Shall I get dressed now?' she said, looking up at him.

'Do what you want,' snapped Philip, 'why do you have to ask my permission for every single thing you do?'

'Is something wrong? Is there something you want?'

'Yeah, there's something I want alright, but you can't help.'

'What do you mean?' said Natalie, hurt by his tone of voice.

'Forget it. Go and get dressed. I'll be out for an hour or so. You'll have to amuse yourself without me. Clean the flat or something. Go and get some shopping, there's money if you need it. Just do what you like.'

'It's nothing to do with Lucy is it? She had a nice time on the boat didn't she?'

'It's nothing to do with my niece and nothing to do with you. I'm sorry Natalie, I've got a few things on my mind that don't concern you. Just do your own thing for today. Is that too much to ask,' said Philip, his voice refusing to mellow.

'Sure. I'll stay in until you get back. I'll give the flat a clean. When you come home, I'll try on that outfit you ordered and you can take some photos. You know the outfit I mean?'

'I know the one you mean,' said Philip, mellowing slightly. 'Yes, o.k.'

He kissed her forehead in a fatherly manner, knowing that he had upset her; Natalie was not to blame for the way he felt. He picked up his coffee and clasped the cup with both hands. He stood up, took a few steps past the French windows and out onto the roof garden, and fixed his stare on the water. He could see two giant barges, heavily laden, with their contents hidden by grey tarpaulins. They moved slowly and majestically up river, pulled by a single tug a fraction of their size. Watching the barges on the water had soothed him a little, as the river always soothed everyone. For no particular reason that he could think of, he felt that his life was about to take a turn in a different direction. Was it Jennifer, his business, what was it? He could hardly wait for lunchtime.

Twenty

It was just after lunch when Sarah returned to the office. She was greeted by an anxious Jason Collymore, the new trainee. There had been two calls from Beconsbridge Police station and Jason Collymore was in a panic. The police had told him that Mathew's clients had been arrested at midday, and he hadn't yet done a thing about it. The inexperienced trainee had taken only a few details, and Sarah was not impressed. Mathew had always stressed that it was essential to take as many details as possible, right from the outset.

'Next to useless,' mumbled Sarah as she snatched the trainee's scribbled notes and dialled the police central control unit. Sarah spoke clearly to the operator. 'Beconsbridge Police Station please.'

'And the nature of your call?' asked the operator.

'Instructing solicitors for custody please,' said Sarah, precisely.

The custody sergeant supplied answers to Sarah's questions as best he could, but had only just begun his shift when three new prisoners were waiting to be processed. She could hear a lot of shouting in the background, and her call was cut short. She paged Mathew with the little information she had. The trainee should have been more thorough when the police had first phoned, thought Sarah; 'if he's been told once he's been told a thousand times,' she muttered. Mathew looked at his pager shortly after leaving the hospice. He preferred a paged message to a mobile phone call or text, and the police didn't make a fuss about them either, not even inside the cells. His message will have been dictated by the caller, and transcribed by a personal interceptor, with no slang or abbreviations, no numbers in place of words. It will be grammatically correct, and perfectly spelt, in proper 'Queen's English'. Mathew valued this service, which also gave him the choice of not being easily reached when it suited him; his mobile phone was rarely switched on for this very reason.

He had spent the best part of the morning with his father,

who had been completely delirious. He had listened to his ramblings for hours before George Weekes finally fell asleep. 'Josie' was the last word he heard his father say. He read his paged message in disbelief:

"Mr. Davidson in custody at Beconsbridge Police station together with one other. Phone as soon as possible. Sarah."

'Davidson,' thought Mathew. 'Which one?'

As usual, his mobile phone was low on battery. He hurried from the grounds of St. John's towards The Walnut Tree where he knew he could make a call, quietly. He picked up the phone at the bar, where only the night before he had recruited his sister to investigate Philip's activities. He called his secretary.

'Sarah? What's going on?'

'The police have two Mr. Davidsons in custody and they're going out to arrest a third. Beconsbridge custody was very busy, it was so hard to get precise information; between the police and Jason Collymore, I'm totally confused. But they said that the two they had arrested are asking for your assistance. One of them is a juvenile, I assume this is Luke. Shall I tell them you're on your way?'

'Juvenile? Yes. I'm leaving now. Cancel everything for this afternoon.'

'You have McCormack coming in at three o'clock.'

'Get him to wait - this might have something to do with him.'

'What do you mean?'

'Bernie Cullum and that logo, that's what I mean. Maybe the police have done their job, and arrested Philip for starters. Just keep McCormack there till I get back. I'll phone you.'

Mathew hailed a cab somewhere between the hospice and The Walnut Tree. He climbed in the back with his heart beating in excitement at the thought of coming face to face with Philip in custody. He could not believe his fortune, and wondered how this had happened, but he was more concerned for Luke.

The cab driver recognised him. The last time they'd met, he had earned quite a reasonable fare by driving him several times around the same block.

'Where are we going sir? I don't mind doing a block or two if you've got things to sort out.'

Mathew also recognised the driver. At least with this one he wouldn't be engaged in a conversation about Bradley General Hospital.

'Beconsbridge Police Station please, and hurry.' His tone of voice meant there was no going around blocks, no social chat. This journey was urgent.

When he arrived at the police station, Mathew was immediately recognised. An officer took him past the front desk and led him to the custody area where he was greeted by DS Morton, an experienced and mature officer, with an 'old school' attitude to policing. He was also the officer dealing with Mathew's best client, Johnnie Raybourne, who he had met only a few days previously.

'Mr. Weekes, I have two members of your family here who have been arrested on unrelated matters. One is Luke Davidson, arrested for possession of cannabis. The other is Toby Davidson, arrested for being in possession of obscene publications, possibly concerning a minor. My officers are presently out, and it is hoped they will successfully arrest a third member of your family, Philip Davidson, whose arrest is connected with Toby's. Shall we deal with Luke first? A juvenile I believe, aged fourteen.'

Mathew had a million thoughts running through his head, and for a moment he froze in front of the officer, trying to take in the information given to him. Luke - cannabis? Toby - obscene publications? He thought immediately of Jennifer and whether or not she knew about their arrests.

'The juvenile, Luke, is there an appropriate adult here for him? Have his parents been informed?' said Mathew.

'He didn't want his parents told, but eventually they will be. There's a social worker on his way if we need him, but I might consider a formal warning or a caution. See what the lad has to say for himself, and give me your views. We'll try to be reasonable; he's a nice lad, except for the cannabis of course. Do you want to speak with him now?'

Mathew nodded to the Detective Sergeant as he followed

him towards the cells.

'Does he know his brother is arrested too?' Mathew asked.

'No,' said DS Morton, 'neither of them know of the other's arrest. In my experience it's for the best, disclosing arrest details to another person is never a good idea; breaches all sorts of new rights and codes, family or not. I'll leave that to you Mr. Weekes, but I'm playing it safe. If the two offences were connected it would be a different matter, but I don't want any complications or breaches of confidentiality on my shift. Times have changed, haven't they?'

Mathew decided to take the same stance as DS Morton; he wouldn't tell Luke about Toby, or Toby about Luke. He didn't want any complications or breaches either, uncle or not.

DS Morton stopped at cell three, and after peering through the gate in the door, looked to Mathew, then turned the key.

'Here's your client Mr. Weekes. Somewhat of a pitiful sight.'

Mathew entered the cell to find Luke with his head in his hands perched uncomfortably on the edge of a blue plastic mattress. As he looked up at his uncle, Mathew saw his nephew just as he was when he was a very small child. He had an urge to pick him up and hold him as he used to. Luke's eyes were red and swollen, and his face was wet.

'I'm sorry uncle Mat - I'm sorry.'

Mathew handed Luke a bundle of tissues, which he had inadvertently placed in his pocket at the hospice.

'The police have found some cannabis on you Luke - was it yours?'

'Yes but this is all Lucy's fault. She set it up, then told Mrs. Brampton.'

'Why would Lucy do that?'

'Because I know things; about her not being at school. We argued, and I said that I would tell. I wouldn't have though - but she got in first and told Mrs. Brampton that I was smoking. I got taken to the Head and made to empty my pockets, and then the Head called the police. It wasn't really mine, I didn't ask for it, but once I had it, I wanted to know what it was like. Uncle

Mathew, please get me out of here - I want to go home.'

'This won't happen again, will it. You must know the damage it does,' said Mathew in a fatherly tone.

'Yes I do. I don't like it. It made me feel ill. I never want to go near it again. Does mum have to know?'

'One of your parents has to be told. Let's get you out of here first.'

Mathew left the cell and called to DS Morton.

'Could he take a reprimand? This is a one off.'

'It's probably the most suitable route to go down. He's not like the usual candidates is he? Seems a decent kid,' said DS Morton. 'So who's coming for him? Mum, or dad?'

'His father. Robert Davidson. Definitely not his mother.'

'Keep it from the missus eh?' said DS Morton, 'probably for the best.'

Mathew scribbled Robert's details and contact number at Graphic Solutions, and handed the note to the Detective Sergeant. He wondered what secrets Luke had been keeping for Lucy, but that could wait for another time; he had something far more serious to deal with.

'Right,' said DS Morton, 'one down, one to go; or maybe even two more to go, if we manage to pick up Philip Davidson.'

'Well if you do pick him up, I won't be acting for him,' said Mathew sharply, 'he'll want his own brief.'

'Fair enough,' said DS Morton, detecting some conflict.

Mathew was ready to speak with Toby, but first he needed as much information as possible, a full consultation with the police before seeing his client. DS Morton led Mathew to an empty interview room.

'O.k. Mr. Weekes, I'll tell you straight,' he said, 'this young man was arrested for possessing obscene publications, and we suspect they include photographs of a minor. He was stopped by traffic police for speeding. Apparently, he was really flying along. The material was found in his pannier. He tells us he was delivering to a printing firm called Colourways, having first collected the packets from Graphic Solutions, his father's employers. We're talking about twenty photographs in all; they'll be shown in interview with your client. I'm not saying anything further at the moment, except to say that we are hoping to arrest the boss of the courier firm employing Toby Davidson, Mr. Philip Davidson; another of Toby's uncles I believe,' said DS Morton as he watched Mathew try to take it all in. 'This must be a strange situation for you Mr. Weekes, all this family connection, but I need to press on. I understand Philip Davidson's courier firm is called PACE. I assume that's supposed to be some kind of joke; he's very fond of the Police and Criminal Evidence Act, and very familiar with it too as I remember. Anyway, we're also making enquiries of Colourways and Graphic Solutions, so it might be a while before our investigations are complete. Do you want a chat with your client now, while we wait to pick up Mr. Davidson senior to see what he has to say?'

Mathew found it hard to take in what he had just been told. He was anxious to speak with Toby.

'Yes. I'll see my client now,' said Mathew.

DS Morton led him to the cells once more, and this time stopped at cell number seven. Toby was sitting just as his brother had been. His head was in his hands and his eyes were red. He looked terrified as he looked up to face his uncle.

'Thank God you're here,' he said timidly. 'I don't know what's going on - I haven't done anything.'

'Well you were breaking the speed limit, so that's one thing,' said Mathew, trying to make Toby a little more at ease.

'I wish I hadn't been. I'd never have got stopped.'

'Did you know what you were carrying in the pannier?'

'No, of course not. I just deliver packets. I don't care what's in them.'

'Have you ever seen anything that you would consider obscene material being handled by anyone at all at Graphic Solutions, or Colourways? Anything a bit near the mark perhaps? What about your uncle, have you ever seen him with anything like that?'

'No. Never. I don't look at what they're doing. All I want to do is ride the Kawasaki. That's all I want to do.'

'O.k. Toby. This is what we'll do. I'll be sitting next to you when the police ask you questions. Just answer them truthfully, provided what you have just told me is the truth, and we'll take it from there. DS Morton will show you the contents of the packets found on you. I haven't seen them yet, so I don't know how bad they are; they may shock you, but stay calm and answer the questions put. If you've never seen them, or know anything about them, then that's what you must say. If you do know anything at all about them, then you must tell me now. I can't advise you unless you tell me the truth.'

'I've told you. I don't know a thing,' said Toby.

'O.k. You've got nothing to fear, just speak the truth. I'll try to get you out of here as soon as possible.'

Mathew didn't doubt his nephew. He picked up his briefcase and walked towards the cell door.

'But what about uncle Philip?' said Toby. 'Will they arrest him?'

'They're certainly trying to,' said Mathew, disguising any hint of glee, 'but it looks like your uncle Philip has got you in a whole lot of trouble.'

'Can you help him too?'

'No. He'll have his own solicitor. Don't worry about him Toby. He's caused enough problems for one day.'

DS Morton appeared by the cell door.

'We're ready now,' said Mathew.

DS Morton led them both to the interview room where there were four chairs arranged around a black oblong table. There were two plastic cups of water on the table, which had been positioned in front of two of the chairs, one for Toby, and the other for his solicitor. They sat down next to each other; the officers sat facing them both.

DS Morton, and his colleague DC Bowden, began to unwrap the tapes, ready for interview. The initial buzzing of the machinery alerted Toby to the seriousness of his situation; he had suddenly aged. The officers introduced themselves, and Toby and Mathew were asked to do the same. After a further caution, and reading the procedure on how Toby could get a copy of the tape after interview, the officers recaptured the events of the day leading to Toby's arrest. Toby confirmed all that the officers were stating; he had collected packages from the receptionist at Graphic Solutions at ten o'clock that morning. He was requested to deliver to Colourways. He admitted he had been speeding and that the officers had stopped him en route, before he made the delivery. DS Morton then produced two packets, which he described for the purposes of the tape as brown envelopes originally containing twenty photographs and marked as exhibit JM/1. He then produced a sample of photographs that were found inside the envelopes, and laid a selection of these on the desk. He referred to the individual exhibit numbers as he displayed them one by one.

'I am showing the accused a selection of photographs found in his possession today. These have been individually sealed after removal from the envelopes that I have previously referred to as exhibit JM/1. Do you recognise these photographs or the person or persons in them?'

Toby was speechless. He stared at the display before him and could not utter a sound. He looked to Mathew for support, but his solicitor was of no assistance. Mathew's heart was racing and beads of sweat appeared on his forehead. He was hot and could not breathe. His hand was visibly shaking as he lifted the white plastic cup to take a sip of water. Mathew and his client were suffering equally; both were in shock. DS Morton looked towards his colleague, DC Bowden, and back again to the accused, and his solicitor. He spoke again.

'Toby - do you recognise these photographs?'

Toby did not reply, and his solicitor was equally silent, and motionless.

'I will ask you again. Toby, do you recognise any of these photographs? Mr. Weekes - is your client refusing to answer any questions?'

The air was heavy with silence; Mathew tried to speak for his client, but he could not. He wasn't able to say what he wanted to say, neither could he question what was on display. He had to protect his client; bury any emotional reaction to the sight before him. He looked hard again at the photographs; a young girl in explicit sexual poses. In other pictures, a second young woman accompanied her. All the pictures showed the same young girl in varying degrees of undress, a variety of positions. Mathew glanced quickly at Toby; his complexion had turned a greyish white. He looked again at the images on the desk in front of them, the images of his niece, of Toby's sister. Pictures of Lucy. The police were showing them pictures of Lucy, and Mathew could not believe that this was happening. The officers were becoming visibly irate at the prolonged silence. DS Morton spoke directly to Mathew, and repeated himself again.

'Mr. Weekes. Is your client refusing to answer any questions?'

Mathew tried to think clearly. Was that Lucy? It was certainly her face, her broad smile. Her hair was in her favourite style; tufts of blonde hair leaping out in all directions from her ponytail. It was most certainly his niece. He had advised Toby to tell the truth, but this was not the time to do it. His thoughts went to Philip and his unhealthy involvement with young women. He thought of Jennifer and what this would do to her, and he thought again of his client.

'I'd like to break the interview to consult with my client,' Mathew said, at last.

'Can we ask why, Mr. Weekes?' said DS Morton.

'No, you cannot.'

'You have already consulted with your client.'

'Well I want to consult with him again. Are you denying me this?'

The officers stared at each other and leaned back heavily on their chairs. DC Bowden gave an exasperated sigh.

'How long do you require Mr. Weekes?' said DS Morton.

'As long as it takes. Please break the interview now. My client will say no more until we have consulted.'

'We could take this as being obstructive, Mr. Weekes,' said DC Bowden, the first time he had spoken. 'We have a job to do here.'

'Take it however you like,' said Mathew, as he looked straight at DS Morton for support, and a response to his detective constable's remarks.

Mathew's request was clearly suspicious. Toby was breathing fast and his forehead was now flushed, he looked like he might faint. The officers could see that not only the accused, but also his solicitor, knew something more. The photographs had clearly disturbed them both, but for the moment, Mathew was going to get his request. The last thing DS Morton wanted was a legal wrangle with a defence lawyer, particularly not on a Friday afternoon.

'Very well,' said DS Morton. 'Interview broken at thirteen forty-five.'

'Thank you,' said Mathew, with some relief.

DC Bowden reluctantly turned off the tape recorder, removed the tapes from the machinery, and began to write on some labels.

'Do you want this room for your consultation?' he said, while still labelling the tapes.

'I'd like to step outside for a bit,' replied Mathew, 'I'll be back in a minute or two.'

'Oh? We'd prefer it if you stayed on the premises,' said DC Bowden.

'That's o.k. Mr. Weekes,' interrupted the Detective Sergeant, 'more than your job is worth to go collaborating. Take five minutes.'

'I may call my office, that's all,' said Mathew, 'no one else. Of course not.'

Toby was still seated at the table. He was holding a paper cup with both hands wrapped around it, but he wasn't drinking from it.

'I'll be back in five minutes then,' Mathew said to Toby, but he didn't answer.

Mathew opened the door to the interview room and walked across the custody area. He needed more than five minutes to wrap his head around this, but five minutes was better than nothing; he was desperate for some fresh air.

'Not feeling well?' said DC Bowden as he pressed the numbered security buttons that would allow Mathew to escape.

'Perhaps we should be interviewing you as well Mr. Weekes, you being a relative. Strange situation you're in, isn't it?' said DC Bowden, inquisitively.

Mathew said nothing as DC Bowden released the door.

'Five minutes then, Mr. Weekes,' he said, as Mathew hurried away.

DS Morton had ordered a young police constable to take Toby back to his cell, where he would stay until his solicitor returned. He approached DC Bowden as soon as the solicitor had left.

'What do you think, Jim?' he said to his colleague, who was closing the security door on Mathew Weekes.

'Didn't like the look of that one bit,' replied DC Bowden, 'and he didn't look at all well.'

'Must be awkward representing family though, a bit of a shock maybe,' said DS Morton.

'I didn't like it Sarg; he knew he was his nephew before he sat down. We started the interview, showed the photos, and then they both went weird on us. No Sarg, I think you're being too generous.'

'He's a pretty straight bloke though, that Weekes fellow,' said DS Morton, 'I've had a few dealings with him in the past. Raybourne is one of his regulars; he must have the patience of a saint. But you're right. Their reactions were very suspicious. Very suspicious indeed.'

Twenty-One

Jennifer was nervous. She could think of little else other than the task her brother had set her, and how she might betray Philip.

She was easily mesmerised by the stark red warning of the traffic signals, and it took a while for her to realise that the sounding horns were those of angry motorists, directed at her. She didn't know how long she had been sitting there, gazing at the lights; the noise brought her back to reality. She looked over her right shoulder as a woman manoeuvred her Ford Fiesta alongside the Mk 2. She was shaking her head disapprovingly at Jennifer, who now realised the woman's frustration. The Jaguar had probably annoyed the woman even more; women were often hostile towards the Mk 2. This was a man's car, not to be driven by a woman with children, and especially not by a woman who stalls at traffic lights. Jennifer quickly glanced at the woman in the Ford, who continued to stare, her eyebrows raised, her head shaking disapprovingly. Jennifer turned away and looked straight ahead. At that moment, she felt that the woman knew all about her, the mission of betrayal, everything. That was why she was shaking her head, and raising her eyebrows; she knew of Jennifer's secrets, and her intention to set up her brother-in-law, all for the sake of a stranger's defence. It was inexcusable.

She pushed the gear stick into first, and balanced the clutch and throttle with enough revs to ensure she would be first away from the green light. She too had learned some aggression. She decided she would speed away, out of sight of this woman, turn the car around, and phone Philip to tell him she couldn't make lunch. Her conscience would still be in tact. But, before she knew it, she was into third gear and speeding towards a dual carriageway with little opportunity to turn back. She passed the Royal Oak, where she had agreed to meet Philip, and glanced over to its car park. She could see the ice blue XJS convertible. Philip was standing by it, and he was looking towards her; he knew the Mk 2 very well. She had no choice but to turn back at the end of the carriageway, and keep to her arrangement to meet him. She could think of no excuse to give him if she did not.

Philip was still standing by his beautiful convertible when Jennifer pulled into the Royal Oak car park. He strolled towards her as she reversed her car clumsily into a space big enough for two.

'Anything wrong? You drove straight past.'

'I overshot the driveway to the pub. I wasn't thinking. How are you?'

'Fine. Shall I check the hose now or shall we have some lunch first?'

'I think the hose is o.k. Let's eat. Let's have a drink, or we could order some food and have a drink while we're waiting. We don't have to eat if you don't want to ...'

'Calm down,' said Philip, 'what on earth is wrong with you? You look completely shaken up. Has something happened?'

'I got cut up by some woman back there, that's all. A Ford Fiesta.'

'Not like you to get wound up on the road, but then again, a Fiesta - understandable! You sure you're o.k?'

'I'm fine Philip. Just fine.'

Philip guided Jennifer to a table in the corner, close to the bar, where they settled themselves, and ordered some drinks. Jennifer found it hard to concentrate on what was on offer from the menu, so Philip made choices for them both.

'Are you worried about the kids or something? There's definitely something up with you,' said Philip, as soon as the waitress had gone.

Jennifer seized the opportunity to attempt an excuse for her strange behaviour.

'I am a bit worried,' she said softly. 'Lucy's been missing school without my knowledge, and she's getting very bold. Perhaps she's just growing up but I don't like it. I don't seem to have children any more, just adults to care for. I'm just worrying for nothing, take no notice.'

'You shouldn't worry about Lucy. She's a cute kid, and missing school isn't the crime of the century, is it. She really loves it on the boat you know - with Natalie and me. You should let her come more often; you know I take care of her. Natalie treats her like a sister.'

'I think she's spoilt enough as it is. Anyway, I don't want to spend the whole of our lunch talking about my daughter and my problems. How's your business going?' said Jennifer, wasting no time in getting the job over and done with.

'Which one?'

'How many have you got?'

'A few.'

'I've never really known much about what you do, business-wise I mean. Apart from Parcels and Courier Express, what else is going on?'

Philip never liked discussing his work with anyone. He was very surprised, and she had never enquired about his business ventures before. His face completely changed. He hated questions; he thought Jennifer would have known better.

'Why is everyone asking about my businesses lately? As I said to Mathew, I'm making no comment on any of my business affairs. I never discuss them - not with anyone - and I don't have to give any reasons at all. He's been asking me questions too. I don't have the answers, but what does that matter, he keeps on asking the questions just the same, then I end up giving him a mouthful and slamming the phone down. Now where does that get anyone? I'd hate for us to get like that. So no business questions, o.k?'

'What questions has Mathew been asking you?' said Jennifer innocently.

'I don't think we should discuss it,' said Philip, trying to steer off the subject of her brother.

'But I'd like to know. Has he been annoying you? Tell me, I may be able to help,' she pleaded.

Jennifer hoped he would open up to her, and the quicker the better. Philip looked deep into her eyes and Jennifer felt uncomfortable. She didn't like his expression at all. She had gone too far and he knew why she was there. There was a knowing, suspicious look about him, and his face saddened simultaneously. Philip might lack Mathew's intellect, but his intuition was second to none. He was nobody's fool.

'Jennifer. I hope you're not here on your brother's behalf,' he said coldly. 'I know he's your brother, but he really gets to me. I hope you haven't come to question me about a stupid logo for the benefit of your brother's client, but I suspect you have. Your husband did the job, so tell Mathew to question Robert. Not me. I don't know anything about it, nor do I know anyone by the name of Bernie Cullum. I'm really disappointed Jennifer, and sad that you've met me to question me, but I should have known; when was the last time we had lunch? I should have guessed. I was looking forward so much to us having a few hours together. I thought our friendship meant a bit more to you than that. What a fool I am. I should cancel my food, I don't feel like eating.'

'Philip, I'm sorry. I ...'

'Save it, it's not your fault. I expect that slimy brother of yours has put you up to this, loading you with all sorts of guilt feelings and sibling loyalty. He can't do the job himself so he sends his big sister. He really takes the biscuit. I'll have him for this, he's out of order.'

Jennifer had nothing to lose now; the damage was already done, so there was no point stopping. She hoped he would forgive her once she had explained. She continued, bravely, speaking quickly and without any hesitation.

'Mathew thinks that the person who ordered the logo artwork for Expressive Prints Express is Bernie Cullum. It's important for Cullum to be found or his client will never be believed. He's charged with very serious offences and could go to prison for a long time. Mathew thinks he is innocent.' There, she said it.

Philip's limit was reached. The lunch date was over before it had hardly started. He looked squarely at his sister-in-law; his expression was more serious now.

'Jennifer, you know I like you very much, and I adore your children. But your brother, I don't want to talk about him, and I don't want you to talk about him either. I don't care what he has to say about anything, or anybody. I'm not interested in him, or his client, who probably deserves everything he gets; if you can't do the time, you don't do the crime. Now eat up - I want to get out of here.'

Jennifer left the best part of her meal on the plate, but her glass was empty. She had drunk too much; a large glass of wine and little food had made her feel lightheaded. But worse, she felt sad and ashamed. Philip had never spoken to her this way; their friendship had probably ended right here. She was so angry with Mathew, and angry with herself for having agreed to do something that in her heart she knew was wrong. Far from achieving anything, the meeting with Philip had been purely destructive. She had upset him terribly.

They said goodbye briefly in the car park, without any physical exchange. No hug, no kiss on the cheek. Jennifer unlocked the Mk 2 and sat at the wheel, with the keys in her hand. She recalled how she was feeling just an hour previously; the woman in the Ford had been an omen, and she should have taken heed. She should have turned back. She looked in her rear view mirror and saw Philip's reflection. He was about to get into his car. She decided to wait until he had pulled out of his parking space, as she couldn't bear to look at him. She leaned across and opened the glove compartment, hoping to find some cigarettes. It had been some time since she had succumbed to a smoke. She pulled out an old carton, and plunged the lighter hard into the walnut dashboard. She opened the packet; there were three cigarettes. She put one to her mouth and waited for the lighter to click back out of its socket. As she lifted the glowing element to her face, she glanced again into the rear view mirror; Philip hadn't got into his car. Instead, he was standing beside his beloved Jaguar, flanked between two uniformed police officers, with another in plain clothing. All of them were guiding him towards a waiting vehicle.

Twenty-Two

'Marshall Maplin and Weekes - Good Afternoon.'

'Susan Bishop for Mathew Weekes please,' said Susan, hoping to be connected directly to Mathew.

'I'll put you through to his secretary,' said the telephonist.

This always annoyed her. It was bad enough that she hardly saw him, but it was impossible to even speak to Mathew without having to first penetrate a wall of protective females - beginning with Mavis, the switchboard operator who had been reciting 'Marshall Maplin and Weekes' for the best part of thirty years, and who knew Susan very well. Before she had a chance to say anything further, she heard the voice of Mathew's greatest protector, Sarah.

'Mathew Weekes' office,' she said.

'Sarah, it's me, Susan. Is he there?'

'I'm afraid not, but I wish he was. There's a stack of work for him to get through before the weekend, and he still has clients to see. I'm going to have to cancel some of his appointments. I just don't know when he'll be back.'

'Where is he? Do you think there's any chance of speaking to him more than once a week?'

Susan's deliberate sarcasm did not go unnoticed, but although Sarah sympathised that it must be difficult to sustain any relationship with her boss, she would not get drawn into any discussion about him. Susan's dissatisfaction, and Mathew's personal affairs, were not open to any debate with her. Sarah's role was to support her boss in a professional capacity, at the most to lend a sympathetic ear, and only then when he requested it. She would not sympathise with anyone else at Mathew's expense, not even if she thought he was at fault.

'He's at Beconsbridge Police Station dealing with two clients. I can't tell you any more than that,' she said abruptly.

'I need to speak to him Sarah. It's about his niece, Lucy. She went home from school with someone at lunchtime and she hasn't returned. From the description of the man who collected her, I don't recognise him at all. I've tried phoning Jennifer but there's no reply, and I can't find Robert either. It's probably nothing at all to worry about, but Mathew might know where Jennifer is. I think she needs to know as soon as possible, just to be safe. There's another matter too - it's to do with Luke. He was taken to the head teacher, and then the police were called. Sorry, I really shouldn't be saying all this to you. I'm just so worried, and I need to speak with Mathew.'

'Don't apologise, I know about Luke. Mathew is looking after him at Beconsbridge Police Station. That's all I can tell you. I'll ask him to call you when he gets back, though I expect you'll be home by then. I doubt if you're going to see much of him this evening by the way things are going; probably be a late one for me too. I must go now Susan - I've a million and one things to do. I wouldn't worry too much about Lucy, but I'll give him your message. I'm sorry, but I really do have to say goodbye.'

Susan was enraged at being short-changed by her lover's secretary. She was withholding information about Luke, who was for all intents and purposes her nephew. She may also know something about Lucy, but there was no chance of getting anywhere with Sarah, and she knew it. Mathew valued this protective quality in her, but Susan hated it. If there was a time when client confidentiality was not appropriate, then this was it. Sarah, however, was a stickler for the rules, and Susan would just have to make her own investigations.

'Right. Thanks for your help Sarah. Thanks a lot.'

Sarah replaced the receiver calmly and professionally. It immediately rang again.

'It's me,' said Mathew. 'I'm still at the police station dealing with Toby. Luke has been warned and he's on his way back home now. I'm going back in for Toby's second interview and I might be some time. I'm bang in the middle of something and I don't know what to do. If Jennifer phones, you must tell her nothing, I'll square it all with her later, when I know what's going on myself. I might have some trouble getting Toby out until they've picked up Philip Davidson. The police are also going to make some enquiries at Graphic Solutions, Robert's place, so whatever you do, don't say a word to Jennifer. The whole thing stinks and if I ever had to contemplate divided loyalties I wouldn't have imagined it would be this bad.'

'You're not making that much sense Mathew. What on earth has Toby been arrested for?'

'You wouldn't believe it - I don't believe it. He's been found with some photographs, but it's more complicated than I can explain; it's terrible, I'm really shaken up. I'm not sure if I should be dealing with this at all; it's too close to home, but I can't leave him. Anyway, I'd better get back in there. Get McCormack to come back later. Cancel all my other appointments. If Susan phones, tell her I'll ring her, but don't tell her anything either - she speaks to Jennifer quite a lot. This is going to destroy my sister.'

'I won't say a word to anyone, but Susan has already phoned. She knew about Luke; the police came to the school. You go and deal with your nephew, I'm sure you'll represent him very well. Just try to relax and keep a clear head; deep breathing is good. You'll be o.k.'

The line went dead. Sarah rang down to the receptionist, who confirmed that McCormack had arrived early for his appointment, and was waiting in reception. She would apologise to him, and get him to return at four o'clock. McCormack was unlikely to complain, he never did. Sarah proceeded to systematically telephone each client to cancel Mathew's appointments, offering genuine apologies to all of them in turn. She was puzzled, and concerned, by Mathew's phone call. She could not imagine what his two young nephews had been up to, and the seriousness of the allegations against Toby that would mean he could be denied bail. Mathew said it depended on the arrest of Philip Davidson; she was well aware of Mathew's dislike for him, and that he may have information that could help with the McCormack case. If anything positive emerged from the afternoon's events, it would be Mathew's pleasure at seeing Philip Davidson in a police cell. But why on earth were the police going to Robert's place of work? She felt a sudden and overwhelming sympathy for Jennifer. Two sons arrested in one afternoon.

She walked into Mathew's office and placed the file of

McCormack back on his desk, ready for his return; all the correspondence, conference notes, attendance and telephone notes, were all typed and completely up to date. She glanced to the side cabinet where Jennifer and her three children were displayed in a solid silver frame; what she would give to have children like these, or any children at all. Nature had not been kind to Sarah; after twenty years of marriage, nothing had happened. Her husband refused to take tests, and that was the end of Sarah's chance of motherhood. But she was not unfulfilled; her days were busy, interesting and rewarding, filled with the activities of the job she loved.

She took a closer look at the photograph, Jennifer looked stunning, and each child was hugging, leaning, or draping around her. It was a happy picture, with Luke and Lucy appearing to collapse with laughter. Toby was displaying his heart-melting smile, and she could understand Mathew's fondness for them all. Another photograph stood next to the one of his sister, of Mathew and Susan, which was now several years old. The picture looked like any other loving couple, but to Sarah, it didn't generate the same affection, or maybe she just refused to see it. As Sarah looked at the image of Susan, she felt a sharp reminder of their earlier conversation. Susan had been concerned for Lucy, but she had dismissed her. She should have mentioned this to Mathew while he was on the phone, but with all the concern about Toby's arrest, it had slipped her mind.

Twenty-Three

DS Morton had allowed Mathew to take a short break before returning to Toby Davidson's interview, but DC Bowden was not happy that the solicitor had left the confines of the police station, and he watched him as he hurried past the front desk and towards the main doors leading to the street. Mathew Weekes looked panicked; something was not right with him.

As soon as Mathew got outside, he phoned his secretary. He gave Sarah few details, but left her with strict instructions to say nothing to anyone, particularly Jennifer. He was relieved to be standing on the pavement, away from Beconsbridge Police Station; he didn't want to be overheard. The interview room had been stuffy and overwhelming; he was very conscious of the air entering his lungs, helping to clear his head. His client was waiting, still locked in the confines of the police station, desperate for him to return and make everything right. Mathew had never felt so disturbed, not even listening to his father's ramblings was as bad as this and his mind was in turmoil. He tried to gather his thoughts; consider his position as Toby's solicitor, nothing more. But he wasn't finding it easy.

He took refuge in a bus shelter, trying to get to grips with what he had just seen, what he should do. He sat under the plastic covering along with ordinary people; people who were not tearing apart inside. He didn't want his emotions to wrench a single speck of professionalism from his grasp, but it was dangerous for him to continue acting for Toby; a blatant conflict of interest, as clear as day. He knew he should remove himself from the whole affair, but he also had a duty to Jennifer, quite outside of legalities and confidentiality. The photographs had depicted his client's sister, and his own niece. What was he supposed to do? His first thoughts were that he couldn't carry on. He should abandon Toby and let someone impartial take care of him. He must tell Jennifer about the photographs of Lucy, she had a right to know. But Toby had rights too; another solicitor would have no problem staying quiet. If Jennifer was told at this very moment, Lucy's identity, and age, would most definitely be revealed; there was no doubt about that. For now, the police do not know the girl in the pictures, but what would be his position if they discovered she was his niece? Could he be accused of perverting the course of justice regarding a minor? He spoke to Lucy only yesterday; could she be in danger? Was he putting Lucy at risk for the sake of her brother's position? Or, should he risk Toby's position for the sake of his sister? His whole career was on the line. He wanted very much to tell the police, and he most certainly wanted the person responsible to be captured, but disclosing this information now would not be in Toby's best interests; it would only make things worse. If he was to remain acting for Toby, his position as his lawyer meant that he must stay quiet. But what of Jennifer, what would she want? Would she agree with his logic - surely she wouldn't want two children at risk for the sake of one.

He knew the police were suspicious of him, particularly DC Bowden; his behaviour in interview must have looked strange, but he couldn't bring himself to hand his nephew to another lawyer, not to someone who would care little about him, and removing himself at this point would make DC Bowden even more suspicious than he already was.

He concentrated hard on Toby's position as a client, not a nephew. If they were going to charge him, the police had choices, but whichever way they went, it was as serious as it could get. Mathew struggled hard to recall the law concerning obscene publications, and those involving a minor. He had not dealt with a case like this; his knowledge was limited to what he could remember from recent case decisions in journals. He didn't like this area of law, and he had no expertise in it. He didn't feel capable of the job he'd taken on, and he began to panic.

He sat in the shelter, trying to separate the routes the police might take. He began by defining the photographs found on Toby. To prevent a charge involving a minor, he would need to convince the police that the girl in the photographs is over sixteen; at least he will remind the police that they have no evidence to confirm she is under that age. They don't know the girl, and just because she looks young, isn't enough; but if he argues this point, he will be deliberately misleading the police; he knows exactly how old she is. She's thirteen. She's his niece, Lucy Davidson. He was about to lie to the police in order to argue her age; he could be struck off, never to work again, even arrested. Was he prepared to take the risk?

If the argument about the girl's age was successful, then there could be no charges for offences concerning a minor; the police would remain ignorant of her true age so long as they did not discover her identity, and while this was the case, Toby had a chance. Mathew would not, under any circumstances, disclose Lucy's identity to the police, despite the risks, despite the lies.

At least he was getting somewhere; an action plan was slowly emerging. He vaguely remembered reading a case involving obscene pictures of a child whose identity was never discovered for the whole duration of the trial. There was a young girl, abused, photographed and exploited; yet no one knew her name, and she was never found. It was a horrific case; one jury member had to be dismissed because she was so distraught. In the absence of identity, the question of the girl's age was left for the jury to decide. There had been a lot of legal wrangling over the prosecution argument as to whether it was correct to leave a jury to decide the girl's age from simply looking at a photograph, or whether expert paediatric evidence should have been called. The case went to appeal where it was judged to be proper, meaning that a jury was as well placed as any expert to assess whether a person depicted in a photograph was under sixteen; expert evidence would be no more reliable.

Mathew hoped that in Toby's case it would never get that far, but if a judge has ruled that ordinary jurors can decide on a person's age simply by sight, then so can he. He thought that Lucy looked much older than her thirteen years, but whether he could convince the police that she might be over sixteen was still doubtful. If the police accepted that Toby knew nothing of what was in the panniers, of course, all this would be academic, but that was not a foregone conclusion. The police were already suspicious of Toby; he was Philip's nephew, they share the same name, he works in the family business, is treated more favourably than other courier riders. He was in a good position to share everything with his uncle, with whom he has a close and amicable relationship. There is every chance that the police will make something of this, and suspect that Toby knew exactly what he was carrying; that he played a big part in this nasty business. The other issue was whether Toby knew the pictures were of a child; as Mathew could recall, both these factors had to be established to secure a conviction, not just one of them. He would have to know what was in his possession, and know they were images of a child. He hoped he got his facts right. If he succeeded on the issue of age, there was still the charge of carrying obscene publications of adults; are the pictures obscene, did Toby have prior knowledge of what he was carrying in his panniers, and did he intend to gain through publication or distribution? The words 'publication or distribution' sat heavily in Mathew's mind. Toby was on his way to deliver to Colourways whose job it was to do just that - to 'publish and distribute'. Graphic Solutions to Colourways was a regular run for Toby, specially selected for him, perhaps, by Philip Davidson, not out of favouritism for his nephew, but because he was deliberately entrusted to the care of the illicit packages, with Toby's full knowledge of what was in them.

Then there was Philip's involvement; this was tricky. He might identify the photographs when they are shown to him. He could give the police Lucy's identity and true age in an instant, although he could not see what Philip would gain by doing so, except to lay the blame squarely on Toby. Would he do this? Mathew certainly wouldn't put it past him. There was one thing he was sure of; he would not be representing Philip Davidson, not at any price.

Mathew churned the facts over and over again in his mind. Divided loyalties, conflict of interest, personal involvement, and the route the police would be taking to get Toby charged. He tried to plan his procedure for his return to Beconsbridge Police Station. He wanted a clear and precise idea of the performance he was about to give, but his thoughts were still muddled. He pictured the best scenario of all; he was determined to secure freedom for his nephew, without any charge. He'll take his chances. He'll deliberately withhold information from the police, in cohorts with his client, knowing that a child is at risk, knowing the child's identity, and all too aware that his client knows her too. There was no other choice.

He took deep breaths as Sarah had advised, and coolly numbered his procedures in his head. He went over them until he got the order of priority right. One, the pictures are not of a child. Two, the pictures are not obscene. Three, they are only provocative photos of adults. Four, Toby didn't know what he was carrying. More importantly, there was no intention of gaining from publication, or distribution. Provided he was successful with these representations, in particular Toby's ignorance, the police may be minded not to charge him at all. This would be the perfect outcome, and would give the family time to find out more. But what on earth had Lucy got involved with? Who had encouraged her to do it?

He was now thinking more positively, with a clear action plan. But he was still about to risk his whole career.

He looked up to where a bus had pulled alongside the shelter, and saw several faces staring down at him. All were strangers, all with their own problems, but he would have bet anything that none of them would have wanted to swap places with him. The faces continued to stare, and Mathew stared back blankly. As he got up, the driver of the bus re-opened the doors. Mathew waved negatively and the doors slammed shut again. He walked towards the police station, continuously heeding his secretary's advice on deep breathing. The faces on the bus still followed him as he crossed the road. 'One step at a time,' he thought, 'one step at a time.'

His legal arguments were fixed in his head, 'One, two, three, four. Not a child. A jury would decide. Toby doesn't know her. We don't know her. No gain from publication ...'

He arrived at the entrance to Beconsbridge Police Station and pushed speedily at the doors. He was keen to get on with this while everything was fresh in his mind, but would have felt far more confident if only he knew what Philip was going to divulge. If Philip revealed Lucy's age, Mathew's legal arguments would be exposed for what they were: complete fabrications. His career would be in ruins. He would never work again.

DS Morton was at the front desk, and called to a uniformed officer.

'Toby Davidson's solicitor is back,' he said, 'take him through to the custody area. I expect he wants another consultation. Isn't that right Mr. Weekes?'

Mathew said nothing to DS Morton. He followed the officer through to the custody area where he saw something that lifted his spirits. It was Philip Davidson standing in front of the Custody Sergeant, giving his full name and address, like any other client. Just like McCormack. Just like Johnnie Raybourne. The sight pleased him enormously. He then heard another familiar voice; it was Dominic Sabastas-Grant, standing behind him, waiting for his client to be booked in. He had that familiar cynical look and grinding tone in his voice.

'What's this I hear Weekesie? Keep it in the family eh? Three Davidsons in one afternoon - can't be bad. So short of clients that you call in next of kin?' said Sabastas-Grant, grinning widely as he spoke. 'You take the little boys and I'll take care of Mr. Davidson here. I doubt very much whether my client is eligible for legal aid. Cash only I expect, and lots of it. How about yours?'

Sabastas Grant had that false and unashamed smirk that Mathew remembered so well from earlier days. He was almost as obnoxious as Philip Davidson. They deserved each other, Mathew thought, as he looked over to where Philip was being led to the cells.

The custody officer looked towards both solicitors. He raised his eyebrows and tilted his head down like a disapproving head teacher, peering over his spectacles at two mischievous pupils.

'Ready for a consultation Mr. Sabastas-Grant? And you Mr. Weekes? I can only assume that you are discussing matters that are not concerned with either of your clients, or the reasons why you are here. You know the rules. This way gentlemen.'

As the two solicitors followed him towards the cells, Sabastas-Grant whispered to Mathew so quietly that it was barely audible. Mathew was worried that the custody officer would notice; it wasn't proper to consult before interview, and both solicitors could be dismissed because of it.

'It's got to be a no comment Weeksie,' whispered Sabastas-Grant, 'I don't care what this bloke's done - he's not saying anything. Trust me. I haven't got the time. I've got a dinner date for seven.' Sabastas-Grant retained a fixed smirk as he spoke. Mathew was certain that he saw him wink an eye.

The custody sergeant turned one key, then a next, leading the solicitors to their respective clients. Mathew was grateful for the remark from Sabastas-Grant, despite the smirk and the wink. He almost liked him for it. He decided there and then that if Philip was saying nothing, he would prepare a statement for Toby and hand this to the police, instead of him being interviewed; there will be no further questioning of his client today. This would also give him time to check up on the law. If Philip Davidson was going to keep his mouth shut, it would be less likely that Toby would be charged. Nevertheless, the arguments were still firmly fixed in his head. He greeted his nephew a little more confidently than he had done earlier.

'How are you Toby?'

'Scared.'

'I'm going to try to get you out of here as soon as possible,' said Mathew, 'but listen to me carefully. To say I'm in an awkward position is putting it mildly. I'm really sticking my neck out, in fact, it's illegal, and it's dangerous for us both. Your uncle Philip has now been arrested and his solicitor has told me that he won't be answering any questions. Your mother and father don't know anything, and I'll say nothing until I've had a word with Lucy and found out what's been going on. It's all going to come out the bag one way or the other, but not right now, it will jeopardise your position. If Philip stays quiet, and your parents stay out of it, Lucy's identity won't be revealed while you're here, and there's a better chance of getting you out. I don't know how I'm managing to keep this from my sister, but I will, at least for the time being while I'm representing you. Just try to forget I'm your uncle for the next few hours, and that the photos are of Lucy. If the police find out who she is, we're done for. My advice is to answer no further questions; the police have no evidence against you other than you were carrying the packages on your bike. Courier riders are not expected to know the contents of the parcels they carry. The fact that you didn't know what you were carrying is most important. I just hope the police believe you, bearing in mind your relationship with Philip and the frequency of your runs to Colourways. Instead of giving an interview, we can write a short statement instead. If you answer questions, the police will ask you about Philip, and your dad's place of work, and Colourways, and a whole lot more. You'll get in a complete mess answering questions and trying to protect Philip at the same time, which I fear is what you'll try to do, so best to avoid going down that road. Graphic Solutions will be investigated anyway, as this is where the packages originated, so you might have to stay here until those investigations are complete. If the police do things correctly, they shouldn't tell Robert you're here, but that's a chance we'll have to take. Am I making sense?'

Toby did not seem to take in the legalities of the situation, nor did he fully grasp the procedures Mathew had planned for him. He was certainly unaware of the gravity of the professional risks Mathew was taking.

'Why would Lucy do that?' asked Toby. 'Why would she have photos taken like that, and who was that woman with her?'

'I don't know Toby. I just don't know. I'll talk to Lucy, you can be sure of that, I'm her uncle, and I want to find out too. But right now, we have to think carefully. We'd better just let the police do their own investigations, and hope that Lucy is not identified. So long as you understand what I'm doing here, this isn't at all legal, Toby. But I don't think we have any choice. Are you listening to me, Toby?'

'I think so,' said Toby vaguely, 'I'm not to say anything about Lucy.'

'That's right,' said Mathew, 'nothing at all. We'll deal with it in the family; the police need never know a thing. I think your father will have his own methods of sorting this out, and if I know Robert, he won't need the help of the police. The only person who can give the game away is Philip, and if his solicitor is right, he won't be saying anything. Shall we go ahead?'

'O.k.' said Toby, understanding only a fraction of what his uncle was saying.

Mathew prepared a statement for Toby, and handed it to DS Morton, who had been waiting, and hoping, for a full interview. DS Morton read the statement; he looked concerned, and disappointed.

'This boy knows more than he's letting on,' said DS Morton, looking straight at Mathew, 'aren't you going to let him talk?'

'My client has given a statement, which speaks for itself. If you're going to charge him on the evidence you have, which is very little in my book, then please do so. The decision is entirely yours.'

Mathew stared straight ahead, motionless; his breathing was under control. He was nearly there. DS Morton took Mathew and Toby back to the interview room where he read the statement out loud.

DS Morton was not at all happy.

'You're going to have to give me five minutes on this. You can wait in here with your client,' said DS Morton as he closed the door of the interview room behind him.

Philip Davidson and his solicitor had come to the end of their interview, and DC Bowden, together with a colleague, DC Wells, were standing by the custody desk.

'What's he said Jim?' asked DS Morton as he approached.

'Nothing. Nothing at all,' replied DC Bowden.

'Any statement from him?'

'No, nothing. He gave a no comment, didn't respond to one single question, we're just wondering what to do with him. What did the boy say?'

'He's given a statement, a bit strange since he was ready for an interview the first time around,' said DS Morton. 'We might have to let them both go.'

135

'Shouldn't have let the brief cut us off. We should have persisted with Toby Davidson,' said DC Bowden, 'we might have got something out of him.'

'Possibly, but I didn't fancy being accused of oppression, he's got some balls that Weekes fellow, I've had a lot of dealings with him. I didn't want to push our luck,' said DS Morton. 'I'll bail the Davidson lad now, to another date, it's not cut and dry with him is it. We don't even know if the girl is a minor.'

'It's your call,' said DC Bowden, 'but all we've done today is capture offenders and let them go. A few hours ago we had three Davidsons in custody – pretty soon we'll have none, and no charges made. What have we got to show for a day's work by a dozen officers? A summons for a speeding biker.'

'Don't worry,' said DS Morton, 'they'll both be coming back. I haven't finished with Toby and Philip Davidson just yet, nor with their solicitors.'

'I'll keep Philip Davidson for a bit longer, let him sweat for a bit, then I'll bail him,' said DC Bowden, 'anyway, we don't want them leaving together do we. His brief asked if he could have a word with you before you consider any charges, off the record he said.'

'Did he indeed. This could be interesting. I'll sort Toby Davidson, then we can have a chat with Sabastas-Grant.'

DS Morton reluctantly agreed to bail Toby, pending the police investigations on the identity of the child and the origins of the photographs. Toby wasn't off the hook, and the Sergeant applied some stringent conditions to his bail; he was forbidden to communicate with Philip Davidson, or to return to the family home, and neither could he continue working for Parcels and Courier Express, at least not until the investigations were concluded. Toby was taken to the custody sergeant and bailed for four weeks; when he next returns to Beconsbridge he may be charged. In the meantime, he was to expect a Summons for speeding; this was the least of his worries. Mathew had wanted to buy some time, and this had been achieved. Four weeks was long enough for him to discover the truth, and find out who it was who had seduced his niece to produce the images he had seen.

Toby and Mathew were leaving the custody area just as Sabastas-Grant was coming out from an interview room, and approaching DS Morton. Mathew caught another knowing glance from his rival that confirmed his client had said nothing; but it didn't look as though Philip Davidson was going to be as quickly released as Sabastas-Grant had hoped.

Mathew had achieved all he could, and was satisfied he had done his best for Toby. Both of his nephews were now out of police custody and Robert had been informed of Luke's arrest. Mathew was certain he was not going to be the one to tell Jennifer anything; that was for Robert to do. The legal restrictions placed on him gave him some relief from this dilemma, though he might not have a legal career to worry about by the end of the day. In time, Jennifer will learn of the work he had done, and she will be grateful, he thought.

The only bonus in the afternoon's events was that Philip Davidson was still in custody. Mathew could not dispel any of his suspicions, he had an uncomfortable feeling that Philip knew all about the photographs of Lucy; perhaps making a fortune shipping them off to all corners of the world. He tried hard to stop himself jumping to conclusions. Just because he hated Philip's lifestyle, it did not mean that he was photographing his niece and getting rich at the same time, anyone could have placed the orders, and arranged delivery. Mathew thought of his many conversations with Susan; how she always assumed that Johnnie Raybourne was guilty, no matter what. This was exactly how he was thinking about his brother-in-law, but as hard as he tried to remain impartial, he could not dismiss these uneasy thoughts.

Mathew's big dilemma was Jennifer. He had informed one parent about Luke, enough so far as his legal position was concerned, but his family obligations had been sidestepped; he'd done nothing about the photographs, and nothing about Lucy, deciding to wait for the results of the police enquiries to see what turned up. Hopefully, Robert would discover all the day's events in no time; then a family discussion would be inevitable, and Robert could then resolve these matters with his daughter in his own way, in a family setting. Courtrooms, police proceedings, and Lucy giving evidence, is not what anybody would ask for. Robert would neither want, nor need police assistance to resolve the mess that Lucy had got herself into. Mathew began to feel more confident that the decisions he had made today had been the right ones, illegal as they were.

He left Toby outside the police station where arrangements were made for him to collect his bike. It was agreed that nothing would be said to his parents, at least not for now; apart from anything else, his legal position required it. Thankfully, Toby wanted it that way. He was to remain at Rachaels flat and lay low, stay away from Philip, and disconnect the land line, just in case he tried to contact him through Rachel. Toby was surprised, but Mathew reminded him of his bail conditions; no contact with Philip Davidson.

'Don't take any chances, Toby. He'll rope you into a conversation and before you know it you'll have breached your bail,' said Mathew.

'What shall I tell mum?' asked Toby. 'She'll be really worried if I'm not home for four weeks.'

'Can't help you there, but you'll think of something,' said Mathew, knowing that his sister will probably know everything within the next day or so.

Mathew gave his nephew a quick hug around his shoulders and watched him walk towards the officer who would take him to recover the Kawasaki.

Mathew's day was not yet over; McCormack would be waiting for him.

Twenty-Four

Mathew entered the reception of Marshall Maplin and Weekes. He barely had a chance to put two steps beyond the front door before a highly excited Martin McCormack leapt to his feet and approached him.

'I've seen him! I've seen him Mr. Weekes! I saw him earlier when I was walking about waiting for you. I've seen him, but I lost him.'

'Calm down; let me get to my office and I'll see you in a moment.'

'But I've seen him. I've seen Bernie Cullum. He got into a blue Jag - an XJS. I didn't get the number 'cos it was off in a flash. Before he got in the motor, he was talking to a black guy. I think it was Spike. He's around, Mr. Weekes. We've got to find him. He's right on our doorstep.'

At that point Sarah appeared. She looked disapprovingly at McCormack.

'Mr. McCormack, please take a seat. Let Mr. Weekes get to his office,' she said firmly. 'It doesn't help to pounce on him as soon as he's through the door. He'll see you in a moment. Now please sit down.'

McCormack obeyed as any sensible person would. Sarah walked ahead of Mathew, leaving McCormack seated on the edge of a chair, with the heel of his foot tapping and his leg bouncing excitedly. When Mathew reached his office, he slumped into his chair. He gazed at the photograph of Jennifer and the children, and Sarah watched him.

'It's a lovely photograph that one,' said Sarah. 'Did everything go alright at the police station?'

'I got my nephews out, but I can't believe what I've done. I think this will be the end of me. It's all going to come out. There's no stopping it. I've probably blown away my whole career.'

'Is there anything you want me to do? Shall I get McCormack out of the way?'

'A coffee. A large coffee. Give me ten minutes and then send him up. He reckons he's seen Bernie Cullum. This should be interesting.'

As Sarah left the office, the telephone rang at Mathew's desk. Unusually, the caller had not been intercepted by his secretary, and instead was announced by Mavis. Mathew was taken a little by surprise.

'Jennifer Davidson for you Mr. Weekes. Will you take the call?'

'Yes... er...'

Mathew tried quickly to prepare himself on what to say to his sister. He decided equally as quickly to say absolutely nothing.

'Jennifer. You ok?'

'No, no I'm not. I've been trying to get hold of you, and Robert, and I didn't know what to do. I'm in a call box and I've been walking about for ages. I won't forgive you Mathew, making me meet Philip about that stupid letterhead. I won't forgive you because now he's been arrested. The police came and took him from the pub car park. I didn't even go to help him. I just let them take him; I've betrayed him, and it's all your fault.'

'Jennifer, don't worry about Philip. He can look after himself. If he's been arrested then it won't be for nothing.'

'Mathew! Don't you care at all? This has gone far enough. You're turning into a callous pig and I don't know you. Did you get the police onto him because of that case? You don't seem like my brother any more. You've lost your heart and you've lost your soul. Philip has been arrested and all you can say is not to worry.'

'Jennifer, listen to me. It wasn't me who got him arrested, but I was at the police station this afternoon. I saw him get brought in.'

'What?'

'He was fine, honest. He's got a solicitor whose right up his street. He's in good hands, don't worry about him. Did you find out anything about Bernie Cullum?'

'How dare you ask that! No, I did not! I've had an awful day and I wanted to go and see dad, but now I'm too upset. You're so insensitive; I don't know what's happening to you. I don't know how Susan can stand it, I really don't. You pay more attention to your stupid clients than you do your own family.'

'I'm sorry Jen, honest I am. Please don't be angry with me. Philip Davidson does not deserve your affection. Believe me. He's into some nasty business. I wish I could tell you more, but I can't. Trust me Jen. Please. You'll know all about it soon enough. Then you'll change your mind about him. Guaranteed.'

Mathew was left with a dialling tone and his sister was gone. He had betrayed her, just as she had been made to betray Philip. He saw the photograph of himself with Susan and wanted to be with her there and then, he needed her right now. She would talk him through the problems of his day and would come up with some solutions, he was certain of that. She would stay calm and think it all through, piece by piece. That's what made her a good teacher; line-by-line she would listen and observe, until the whole story would appear, uncluttered and manageable. He could never love anyone the way he loved her, but he just hadn't had time to show it.

Sarah appeared at the door, with McCormack close behind her. He was still very excited. Sarah placed a coffee in front of Mathew and retreated quickly.

'Take a seat,' said Mathew, 'so what's all this about Bernie Cullum?'

'I spotted him driving off down the road at lunchtime. He was in a blue Jag convertible. The guy he spoke to, who I'm sure was Spike, got into a saloon, an XJ6, another tidy motor. I saw him in it earlier on, when he had a kid in the back; I'm sure it was Spike driving the XJ6. They're all up to something Mr. Weekes.'

'So, let me get this right. Earlier today, you say you saw Spike in a Jaguar saloon with a child in the back. A few hours later, you say you saw Cullum talking to Spike by the Royal Oak, and before you could approach him Cullum sped off in the blue convertible.'

'Yeah. That's right Mr. Weekes. It shifts you know, an XJS - it shifts fast.'

'I don't doubt it. I don't doubt that at all. You say Spike had a child with him the first time you saw him today.'

'Yeah. I'm sure that was Spike. Cullum and Spike had something going on but I never got to the bottom of it. I told you before that Spike owed Cullum a favour. He was well under his thumb. But I've never seen the kid before, didn't know Spike had kids, and in any case this kid was white.'

'So, Cullum gets away in his Jag at great speed? Tell me, why didn't you have a word with Spike, or did he speed off as well?'

'Because you told me not to Mr. Weekes. You said if I spoke to any of them I'd breach my bail and get banged up until the trial.'

'You're right, I did. Forgive me; I've had a very exhausting day. Did you get the registration number?'

'No. But there can't be many motors like that around here Mr. Weekes. It's an XJS convertible. Metallic light blue, dream machine.'

'And where was this?'

'Just before the Royal Oak Pub. I was heading along that way for a quick pint - I was just going to have one, while I was waiting for you. Then I saw him. He had a few seconds talk with the black guy, he was a ringer for Spike, and the next I saw was him pulling around in a U-turn. Then he sped straight past me. I'd swear it was him. It was the motor that took my eye, but when I looked closer, it was definitely him. Then he was gone in a flash. I was so taken aback I didn't think about the number. I thought of going towards the Royal Oak to look for Spike, but because of what you said Mr. Weekes, about keeping away from them all, well I thought I'd tell you first.'

McCormack waited for Mathew to respond. He wanted his solicitor to tell him that he'd somehow find Cullum, track him down, get him arrested, get him to court, make him confess that all the dealings were down to him. McCormack waited patiently for an answer from Mathew, who was having difficulty concentrating on his client, while trying to make some comprehensible notes on a pad. McCormack's eyes wandered about the office. He was curious to know if his solicitor had read all the books in the room, and he gazed in awe at their volume. His eyes then rested on the photograph of Jennifer and her children, in the solid silver frame. He leaned closer across the desk towards Mathew, staring to the side of him at the photograph on the cabinet.

'That's the kid!' McCormack screeched. 'That's her - that's the kid! Who's that kid? That was the one in the back of the saloon with Spike. On my life that's her Mr. Weekes.'

Mathew looked at McCormack in disbelief. He picked up the photograph of Jennifer and her children and calmly placed it face up on the desk, in front of his client. He pointed his finger at the glass covering the picture of his family, and glided it over the photograph carefully and deliberately. With a weary, and slightly condescending tone, he looked at McCormack, then back to the photo, and spelt out the group depicted in it, one by one.

'That's Lucy,' said Mathew, coolly, 'she's my niece.' He pointed to Jennifer. 'This is my sister, Jennifer.' Lastly, he pointed to Toby and Luke. 'These are my nephews, that's Toby, and that's Luke. I think you must be very much mistaken.'

But McCormack persisted.

'I'm telling you Mr. Weekes, that's the kid in the car with Spike. Why doesn't anyone ever believe me? Just because I can't read good and I'm no use with numbers doesn't mean I haven't got eyes. That kid was in the car with Spike. Please believe me Mr. Weekes. Please believe me.'

McCormack looked long and hard at Mathew, and his eyes were pleading with him not to be doubted any longer. McCormack looked desperate; there was not a second to be wasted in finding Cullum to prove his innocence of all the accusations; for the real culprit to be found. All pressure was on Mathew, as he looked deep into McCormack's expression. With a sudden horror, he shuddered at the thought that McCormack, and his story, could be perfectly credible. His suspicions returned immediately to his brother-in-law; Bernie Cullum, alias Philip Davidson, lover of Jaguars, driving a blue XJS convertible, with Lucy sitting in an XJ6 saloon, driven by Spike, on Philip's instructions. What on earth was going on? Didn't Philip meet Jennifer at lunchtime? Was there time for him to do this and meet Spike? Jennifer said he was arrested as he left the pub. She said she saw him arrested. Maybe he picked up Lucy, met Spike, dropped Lucy off at his flat, or the boat, and then met Jennifer for lunch. Philip was so slippery, Mathew thought, he could work his day around anything, and still his left hand wouldn't know what the right was doing. He looked down again at the photograph as he spoke to his anxious client.

'It's not that I don't believe you; it's just that the whole day's events have run away with themselves. It's left me in a bit of a daze. Now I think my niece is kidnapped, or something even worse. I'm sorry if you don't expect your solicitor to sometimes be stuck for an answer. I'm sorry if you don't think your solicitor should have feelings, emotions, and problems of his own; or even a life. Things seem to be hitting very close to home; I don't know which way to turn, or how to help you, or my sister, my nephews, my niece, my dying father - and this woman most of all.'

Mathew turned to the side cabinet, and lifted up the picture of him and Susan and placed this also on his desk, next to the family photograph, so that his client could see her clearly. He continued to spill his emotions in McCormack's direction.

'Do you see this woman?' he said to McCormack, as he tapped the glass that covered the photo, his eyes watering uncontrollably. 'Can you see her? This woman deserves my love and attention, and she gets neither most of the time. Do you know that I have spent more time with you, given you more attention, more thought, even more care, than this woman here. Do you even know her name? Well let me tell you something, she most certainly knows yours.'

Mathew picked up the photograph and brought it closer to his chest so that his client could now barely see it. His tears were clearly visible. McCormack had never seen a brief behave like this. It was quite a shock to witness it. He'd certainly had some stressful interviews in his time, and some had nearly come to blows, but he'd never seen a brief crack, not like this, not right here in front of him. This had to be a first.

McCormack could feel a lump in the back of his throat that he hadn't felt since he was a child. It was true that he didn't know the name of the woman in the photo, and he had never given the private life of his solicitor a moment's thought. He had certainly not thought of solicitors having real problems at home, not like McCormack's family, because the money they earned would have solved everything. If there was plenty of money for food and rent, then what on earth was there to grumble about?

For the first time in his life, he could feel equilibrium with a man of law who was educated, wealthy, and very smart. McCormack's feelings of inferiority were replaced by a sense of identity with his solicitor, coupled with an instinctive desire to protect him, and care for him. For the first time ever, McCormack felt needed, he felt useful, and he wasn't in the least afraid. He would look after Mathew Weekes as best he could. He'd be proud to.

McCormack was overwhelmed by this role reversal. This was not his solicitor, but a comrade, a friend in trouble. He hadn't realised how close he had become. To be of any use at all he would need to take control.

'Mr. Weekes, are you alright?' he said softly. 'I'll find Cullum. And I'll find Spike. And if they've got your niece, I'll find her and get her back safe. Don't you worry Mr. Weekes - I don't want you to get yourself all worked up. Why don't you get on home to your good woman? She looks very nice. What did you say her name was?'

'Susan. That's Susan. You'd like her. I love her.'

Mathew felt a clicking in his head. It was loud and causing him pain. He closed his eyes and saw the brightest lights he'd ever seen. They were mostly white, with jagged edges. Others were white with hollow tunnels in the middle and he was forced to travel down them. He felt some tightness across his chest, and he put his head into his cupped hands. He gave in completely, listening carefully to the warnings his body was giving him.

'I'll get your secretary. You don't look at all right Mr. Weekes. I'll go and find her. You just sit tight. I'll sort things out for you, don't you worry. I'll sort the bastards out.'

Twenty-Five

Mathew refused any help, despite the efforts of Sarah and Martin McCormack. He left Marshall Maplin & Weekes almost immediately after McCormack had gone. He had made light of his ailments, but the pain was still tight across his chest, and his sight was blurred.

'Let me call Jennifer,' pleaded Sarah as she followed him to the main reception doors. 'Please Mathew, you look awful,' but Mathew pushed open the doors and stood for a few moments on the stone steps of Marshall, Maplin & Weekes. He didn't answer Sarah, and began to walk, uneasily. He felt old, incapable of deciding on the best course of action for anyone.

As he walked slowly along the pavements, he listed people in his head for whom he thought he had responsibility, and tried to sort them in order of priority. As he did so, none of it made sense any more. Everyone seemed to have the same importance, but this could not be so. He put his sister first, then replaced her with Susan, putting Jennifer in second place. He replaced both Susan and Jennifer with Toby, whose interests must come first because he was a client. He then thought of Martin McCormack, who was already an existing client long before any of this stuff had happened, but he switched priority again because Toby was family. Then there was Lucy, his niece, caught up in a nasty family saga, and in need of protection. The only thing he was certain of was that he had no responsibilities for Philip Davidson, and if he could put him out of operation for several years, he would be very satisfied. Despite the effect this might have on Jennifer and Toby, they will thank him in the long run for unveiling Philip Davidson for what he truly is.

In all his attempts to unravel his loyalties, he had forgotten his father. He wandered the city streets for some time before feeling able to hail a taxi to take him to St. John's.

It was an all too familiar scene when he arrived. He approached his father's bedside and sat quietly until his father opened his eyes. To his amazement, his father did not speak immediately about Josie, but looked at Mathew with a fatherly concern that had come too late by several years.

'You've got a lot to deal with haven't you son. Don't take it all on your shoulders. Jennifer's a grown woman; she'll make her own decisions. She confided in me you know. Those were dark secrets. I think she thought I was too far gone to understand, and she was pouring her heart out. I think she thought I couldn't hear her. These things happen don't they? She loves Robert, he'll understand. It did her good to get it off her chest. Poor Jennifer.'

Mathew had no idea what his father was talking about. He watched as he shut his eyes again, and Mathew sat and took his hand. He had no intentions of leaving his father before knowing what he meant. A nurse appeared by the bedside and lifted the notes from the end of the bed. She took the old man's wrist and held it for a moment. She felt his forehead and gently pulled down the lower lid of his eye with her middle finger. She glided her hand softly across his forehead, upwards to his hairline, smoothing back the little hair he had. If George could feel anything at all, he would have felt her compassion, her devotion to an old man who had little time left to grieve. She scribbled something in the notes and replaced them at the foot of the bed. She turned to Mathew and smiled serenely before walking away from them both.

Mathew leaned back in his chair and closed his eyes too. Still holding his father's hand, he pondered on his words concerning Jennifer. He sat patiently with his eyes closed, until his father spoke again.

'I tried to save her son. I wasted precious moments when she slipped. I should have gone in the water to where my Josie was drowning. I could have saved her. All her clothes were all astray when they pulled her to the quayside. My Josie - you be careful son. You tell Robert to take care of his wife and that little girl. No one will save her.'

'Dad! Please don't keep on about it. It's too long ago. Please dad. Tell me about Jennifer coming to see you. What's wrong with Jennifer? Why was she upset? When did she come to see you? Dad?'

His father's eyes closed again as the nurse approached Mathew.

'He needs to get some rest now,' said the nurse, as she re-arranged George Weekes' pillow and bed covers. 'He's very weak. He's been most upset about your sister, but I can't get to the bottom of it. I know it's not my business, but I think it's time to spare him the details of any family quarrels right now. He deserves his last days to be as peaceful as possible, don't you agree?'

Mathew couldn't bear to hear the nurse use the phrase 'last days'. He had somehow got used to his father dying, as if he would always be dying for many years to come. Mathew did not want to leave his side. He held his father's hand tighter still and looked back at the nurse tearfully. She placed her hand gently on Mathew's shoulder, convincing him that his father was comfortable, in no pain. Seeing that Mathew was so obviously distressed, she took a visitor's chair from a spare cubicle and sat down by the bed next to him. She recalled several events concerning his father; a few stories made Mathew smile, giving him some small comfort. It was soon apparent that the nurse knew a lot about him, and his family. In particular, she knew about Josie; she told Mathew of the many times she would sit with George, and allow him to relive his married life with the woman he loved. He had told her of his joy at the birth of Mathew, and his sister, and his liking for gambling on horses. On many occasions, George had shared the names of his favourite runners with the nurse, some names had made her laugh, others were very curious, she said. George liked nothing better than talking horses, their distances, trainers, riders, and racing events that had excited him in the past. She had also heard a hundred times his recollection of Josie drowning, how she had gone under the boat, and how he had waited for her to come up the other side. The nurse told Mathew what he already knew, that his father had not wanted to forget that day as a way of punishing himself for failing to save Josie's life. But now there was more than this that bothered the old man; there was something else he had been struggling with for several weeks, the nurse said. His mumblings now included 'secrets', and he would ask the nurses whether he had given any secrets away in his sleep; it disturbed George a lot to think that he might have done. Occasionally he would talk about Jennifer and Lucy, but it was mostly incoherent; nothing that the nurses could properly understand, and George wouldn't confide in anyone about what it was that was troubling him. Mathew listened carefully to the nurse as she recalled a specific incident not that long ago when his father had first mentioned this particular worry. He had been half asleep when he had done so; on that occasion, it was in front of a visitor who became very disturbed at what George was saying, according to the young nurse who was on duty. The visitor tried to get George to say more; almost shouting at him to repeat himself, but his father was incapable of doing so. The young nurse eventually asked the visitor to leave.

Mathew let go of George's hand, and thanked the nurse for the care she had shown. He hadn't fully appreciated how much the nursing staff knew about his father, or the patience and time devoted to him. There was little point in waiting for him to wake; he would never pressurise his father to find out more. The nurse was right, his father's last days should be as peaceful as possible, but he was still very curious about the visitor who had been asked to leave.

Mathew stood outside the hospice and stared at the passing traffic. His head was spinning and the pains in his chest were still present. His thoughts were clouded and muddled and he was dangerously close to breaking down completely. He concentrated on each vehicle, looking inside at every driver and passenger, trying to imagine their ordinary daily activities, trying to return to some normality. He struggled to regain some stability while his world was slowly crumbling in on him. He found a haven in his favourite form - a passing taxi. He clambered inside, and slumped on the black leather seats. He needed to get home, to Susan.

Twenty-Six

DS Morton was not happy with the events of the day. He hadn't wanted a statement; he had wanted to re-interview Toby Davidson. He had a feeling that the boy knew more, and he didn't trust his brief one bit. Their reactions to the pictures shown in interview had disturbed him a lot. On the other hand, Philip Davidson had shown no reaction at all to the photographs, save for a small shrug of the shoulders to denote that he couldn't see what all the fuss was about. Philip Davidson had decided not to say anything, which puzzled DS Morton, and he couldn't understand why his brief had not submitted any statement, or said anything at all in support of his client. It was true that his solicitor had baffled him with his knowledge of the law, but DS Morton was of the opinion that Mr. Sabastas-Grant was more interested in his Friday night than he was in his client. He would like to have kept hold of Philip Davidson a lot longer, but the weekend was looming and DS Morton also had a Friday night to look forward to. There was nothing worse than crowded cells at the weekend. But all was not lost, and there was plenty of time to ask more questions at a later date. Philip Davidson was a businessman with a lot to be getting on with. It was safe to let him go, for now. DS Morton was confident that he wasn't going anywhere.

DS Morton was looking forward to his officers returning from Graphic Solutions and Colourways; there was little evidence at the moment to link Philip Davidson with any direct involvement with the publications.

He sat and pondered the evidence that he already had; twenty photographs of a young girl, some with another slightly older female. Was the girl a minor? Who knows. Were they obscene? Debateable. Were they likely to offend a person of reasonable mind? What's reasonable, he asked himself. He'd been in the business so long he just didn't know any more. What else did he have; Toby, the courier rider, found with the packets in his possession, and Philip Davidson, the boss of the courier firm that he had called PACE. The man disliked the police and was happy to provoke them, that was for sure, but he'd looked up Philip Davidson's record, and this type of crime didn't seem to match with his past history of offences. He considered Philip Davidson to be mischievous, not entirely honest, but there were no crimes against the person, nothing violent, nothing particularly sinister. Most of his convictions were bank frauds, dishonest car dealings and the like. He was a flashy womaniser, but he couldn't come to terms with his involvement in offensive child photography. On the other hand, DS Morton had been caught out in the past by being over generous in his belief of a prisoner, and he knew that the younger officers, particularly DC Bowden, considered him too much of a soft touch. He didn't want to be taken for a ride, but Philip Davidson was a tricky one; soft touch or not, he would have to reserve his judgement for another day.

He read Toby Davidson's statement again, which his solicitor had given to him. Toby Davidson describes how he collected a sealed package from the receptionist at Graphic Solutions. He did not know what was in the package. He states that he had done this same run several times. If the police had not stopped him for speeding, he would have left the package in the reception area at Colourways where he would have obtained a signature on his delivery sheet. He knew nothing about the photographs and could not comment on the involvement of the courier firm for which he works, nor could he comment on the activities of Graphic Solutions or Colourways. It was a simple short statement that gave nothing away.

He looked at his watch. He saw one of his investigating officers trying to push the door with his shoulder, his arms laden with bundles of paperwork.

'Look what we've got boss,' said the officer, with some excitement. 'The entire job sheets from Colourways. It's going to take some time to go through them all, but we can match them with the order sheets from Graphic Solutions. Somewhere in here is the order from the artists, Graphic Solutions, and their instructions to Colourways to print. Colourways seem to be straight printers, but you never know. We're trying to trace the boss, but not much luck so far. According to one of the lads there, he hardly ever showed his face, maybe once every few months. They know him as Mr. Cullum. Mr. Bernie Cullum. Who have you sent to Graphic Solutions?'

'Jim Bowden and a PC,' said DS Morton, as he helped the officer to arrange the paperwork in bundles on the desk. 'Let me know when DC Bowden gets back and we can start work on this straight away. There's going to be a lot to wrap our heads around; if it carries on like this I won't be fit for retirement.

Twenty-Seven

Jim Bowden pulled his identity card from inside his jacket and held it up to the face of the young receptionist at Graphic Solutions.

'Jim Bowden - Beconsbridge CID. I want to speak to someone in charge of your orders going for outside printing.'

'In which department?' asked the receptionist politely.

'How many departments do you have?'

'About fifteen sir.'

'About fifteen?' said DC Bowden with some surprise. 'Well do you have a photography department?'

'Yes sir. We have about twelve sections within the photography department. Is it to do with television, board advertising, the music industry, National Heritage, fashion and design....'

'Don't get clever luv,' said DC Bowden abruptly, 'just let me speak with one person from one of the photography departments, any bloody department, right now - please.'

The receptionist caught sight of Robert Davidson, who had only just returned from signing papers at Beconsbridge Police Station, to secure his young son's release. He was crossing the reception area.

'Mr. Davidson!' called the nervous receptionist. 'Could you please help. These gentlemen are from...'

'I'm Jim Bowden from Beconsbridge CID,' interrupted DC Bowden, 'could my colleague and I have a word in private please sir.'

Robert didn't know if he should enquire about Philip. Sabastas-Grant had telephoned him on Philip's instructions with a simple message that he had been arrested, the solicitor would say no more, except that his client would like him to pick up the XJS, which was stuck in the car park of The Royal Oak pub; the keys had been entrusted to the pub manager, who Philip knew well. Robert had obliged, but that was as far as he wanted to get involved; he'd be better off saying nothing to these officers, as Philip's solicitor had already advised.

'Come this way,' said Robert, as he led the officers through a side door, leading to a stock room.

'So, another Mr. Davidson. We've come across a few of those today,' said DC Bowden, while looking at the boxes of stock piled high around them.

'What do you mean, a few? Oh, my son Luke you mean. I'll deal with him tonight. He's had a warning for the cannabis. It won't happen again. I'm very cross with him. Very.'

DC Bowden knew that the man he was talking to was related to the courier rider, Toby Davidson. This was his father. Mr. Davidson either didn't want to mention that his eldest son had been arrested as well, or maybe he didn't yet know. DS Morton was a stickler for the rules on that sort of thing, and if DC Bowden enlightened him, all hell could break loose, and possibly scupper the investigations that had now got underway; not his place to disclose the arrest of Toby Davidson, an adult, nothing to be gained by it either at this stage of the investigation. He'll stay quiet, he thought; just to be on the safe side.

'Could I have your full name sir?'

'Robert Davidson.'

'Robert Davidson,' thought DC Bowden. His relationship with the courier rider was definitely confirmed. This was Toby Davidson's father, and Luke's father; he had been to Beconsbridge to collect him. Does that mean Philip Davidson was his brother? He'd have to find out, this might be interesting.

'And your position in this company?' said DC Bowden, casually.

'I'm a graphic designer.'

'What does that involve specifically?'

'Graphic design.'

'Could you elaborate please sir,' said DC Bowden, impatient to get some straight answers.

'Well, how long have you got?' said Robert. 'The job is very varied. At the moment, I'm doing work for National Heritage. I'm drawing castles actually. You can take a look if you like,' said Robert, keeping his demeanour as casual as possible.

'Maybe later sir,' replied DC Bowden. Castles were the last things he wanted to be looking at. 'Are you a relative of Philip

Davidson?' asked DC Bowden directly, regardless of any breach of code or rights to privacy. If he had his way, the Human Rights Act would be scrapped tomorrow.

'Yes. He's my brother,' said Robert. 'What's going on?'

'He was arrested earlier in relation to some obscene material, and it may involve a person under sixteen.'

'My brother's been arrested? Never.'

'I'm afraid he has, sir, he's the boss of the courier firm that had charge of the package,' said DC Bowden, now convinced that this guy knew nothing about Toby Davidson's arrest either. Somehow, DS Morton had managed to keep the two Davidson boys apart, and the father was only informed about the juvenile. For all his criticism of DS Morton, and his meticulous methods of keeping to the rulebook, DC Bowden had to hand it to him; it was a smart thing to do. He could still learn a lot from an old chap like the Sergeant. 'The pictures were found on a courier rider in his employment,' DC Bowden continued, 'we understand that the package containing the material was collected from here to be delivered to Colourways, a printing firm.'

'Obscene material? Do you mean photographs? Collected from this company? You have to be joking. Were they collected today?' said Robert, very surprised.

'Since you've asked, yes, they were photographs, and they were collected today. Fortunately, the delivery wasn't completed. The courier was stopped for speeding when the contents of his pannier were discovered,' said DC Bowden, waiting for Robert Davidson to enquire about which courier had been arrested, but he did not; perhaps there were dozens of couriers employed by PACE, thought DC Bowden, but even so, he expected him to ask something about the courier, it might be his son. DC Bowden continued with his enquiries. 'Could you please assist, and show us how the orders for delivery to printers are made?'

'Follow me, I'll show you the order books.' Robert led the officers to another room, where various order books were kept. He located the outgoing sheets for the day, without difficulty. There was one delivery to Colourways, which clearly showed that it should have been collected by a PACE courier some time during the morning. Robert pointed to the entry, which in turn was cross-referenced to a docketed job sheet. Robert referred to another book and found the relating job sheet. It was hand-written to say that the relevant package contained " twenty photographs requiring enhancement as appropriate and immediate delivery to Colourways on completion. Invoice at usual rate."

DC Bowden read the remarks with interest.

'Who has requested this job, and who completed it?'

'The job appears to be for someone called Cullum. I've never met him. I can't tell from the sheet who did the re-touching.' Robert pointed to a specific area on the job sheet. 'They're supposed to put their name in that box there, but they haven't; it happens a lot. A memo went out only recently about this; if the artwork isn't up to scratch, you can't find the culprit. That's how they get away with sloppy work. If I had my way, they'd be made to fill in their details on the docket and cross-reference it to their salary code: no code, no pay. Then they'd fill them in every time.'

'I see,' said DC Bowden, detecting some animosity between the graphic artist and the boys in the 'touch up' department. Robert continued to explain.

'This one could have been done by any one of about thirty workers in photo enhancement. Some use the old style airbrushing but we do have advanced computer equipment, scanners, and special software if the original photograph isn't good enough to take it. Why don't you get in touch with Colourways and see if they can help? We could narrow it down a bit if you can find out which method of enhancement was used. Nasty business all that; can't believe that someone in this company has got away with doing stuff like that.'

'Does your brother have access to any of the equipment here?'

'What do you mean? You can't think my brother has anything to do with this. He wouldn't know where to begin. He's just the courier firm. It's obvious to me that Mr. Cullum is the person you're looking for. I hope you find him.'

'We will. Don't go anywhere Mr. Davidson. We may need

to speak to you again. In the meantime, I have authority to seize certain items and equipment from this establishment. We'll start with the computers. How many are there in this building?'

'There's hundreds of them. All the departments have them.'

'Well, we'd better make a start then hadn't we. Just the hard drives will do for now.' DC Bowden turned to the police constable who had accompanied him. 'Call in some bodies. There's a lot of shifting to be done.'

'Do you have to remove them all?' asked Robert.

'I'm afraid we do Mr. Davidson. This may have been going on for some time. We'll also make a thorough search of the photography department and remove items as we think fit. Your receptionist tells me there are a dozen different sections, is that right sir?'

'Yes,' said Robert nervously, 'about twelve, I think.'

'And printing?' asked DC Bowden.

'Just one department. We don't do much printing on the premises; we don't have the space. Colourways is our main contractor. Well, you know that already.'

'Yes, we do sir,' said DC Bowden with an air of aloofness. 'The printing department will also be given a thorough going over. Do you have a problem with that?'

'No,' said Robert sheepishly. 'I'll inform the managers. I'm sure there'll be no problem at all.'

Twenty-Eight

Spike didn't like doing this one little bit. Cullum had been serious about getting the girl out of the way. This thirteen year old could land them all in jail with just a few wrong words, he had told him. And Spike believed him. The only bonus to Spike was that on this mission he got to drive the saloon. When he got to the school at lunchtime, there were so many children fitting Lucy's description he was afraid he would capture the wrong one. He was forced to ask a couple of kids in the playground, and felt ridiculous. One young lad pointed to her, then it was up to him to snatch her. There were few adults at the school at lunchtime, but he was so conspicuous he could hardly believe that no one approached him. A couple of people looked over, but that was all. Someone was bound to question why an ageing black man was asking around for Lucy Davidson, blonde hair, blue eyes, definitely not his child. Cullum had made it clear that if this kid felt like spilling beans, then everyone was going to be in it right up to their necks. Including him. Spike was still indebted to Cullum; he wondered if he would ever get him off his back. He had plenty of stuff on him that had never been revealed. Spike had no choice. He was now well into his fifties, uneducated, and virtually unemployable. He detested Cullum for his hold on him, but he still had nobody else.

Lucy was sitting wide-eyed in the middle of the back seats of the midnight blue saloon. She looked lost in the mass of cream leather that surrounded her; like a princess, sitting amongst the luxury of one of the finest motorcars ever manufactured. If he hadn't known better, a first glance at Lucy would give the impression that she was thoroughly enjoying the chauffeur driven ride.

'You o.k. in the back there?' said Spike, as if he cared. 'It's not much further.'

'Where's my dad?'

'He's going to meet us. Your dad's got a surprise for you and asked me to pick you up. That's all.'

'Why didn't he pick me up himself? I don't even know you.'

'I told you - it's a surprise.'

Lucy suddenly became unsure of this man. She had never seen him before and he wasn't talking much, not at all friendly for someone who knows her father. She decided to get out of the car there and then. Spike stopped at the traffic lights and looked at Lucy in the rear view mirror. He saw her reach across towards the right hand door and heard a click as she tried in vain to open it.

'Do you know this sort of Jag Lucy?' Spike said casually. 'It's got central locking and childproof locks. In fact, you couldn't even open the window unless I opened it for you. Just sit back and relax. Nothing to worry about; just a few miles more.'

'My dad isn't meeting us is he? Where are you taking me?'

'Can I ask you something Lucy?' said Spike, changing the subject, 'Why did you do it? Nice kid like you having photographs done like that. Why did you have them done? I've seen them you know. We've all seen them.'

Lucy's eyes were filling with water, and she became terrified of what would happen next. At the same time, she didn't want this journey to end. She remembered all the talks that had been given in school about speaking to strangers, walking home alone, getting into cars, and yet here she was. She'd been asked to get in the car by a man she'd never seen in her life, and she just did it. He said her father had a surprise and had sent him to pick her up. She wasn't to worry about missing any lessons; her father would square it with the school. It was going to be a nice surprise, he had said. She made no fuss, asked few questions, and just got in, but this man did seem to know an awful lot about her, and her family. Maybe he was her dad's friend after all. She was very confused, but she didn't like him one bit. She thought about school, her friends, and her brothers. Susan had talked about safety when meeting strangers, and had once told a story of a girl who was abducted and kept in a flat for three days. It was thought that she only stayed alive because she used her head and didn't panic. She won her abductor's confidence by talking to him persistently. Eventually the girl was left alone for a very short time while her kidnapper went to stock up on food. The girl had seized that moment and screamed from the window to a passer-by.

Lucy tried to continue the conversation with Spike with an air of confidence, but she didn't like his interest in the photographs, they weren't intended for him. There should be a law about old men looking at pictures of models.

'I want to be a model,' she said, proudly. 'Lots of girls think about being models. There's nothing wrong with it is there. My uncle said that sometimes you have to be adventurous to get the things you like.'

'Your uncle? Are you saying your uncle got you to do those photos?'

Lucy wanted to change the subject. She didn't want to talk about the photos any more; it was making her feel very uncomfortable. Her father would sort things out with this man, and she felt a little easier when she began to recognise her surroundings. This was the route to uncle Philip's boat.

'My uncle's got a boat not far from here. It's called Sea Lavender and it's a sloop. It's all timber, and quite old. All the family have days out on it; my mum, dad, and even my brothers sometimes. If my uncle isn't using it then I just come with my dad. Dad sometimes says he doesn't know which he prefers, driving a fast Jaguar, or sailing a yacht when it's really windy. Do you go sailing?' Lucy asked, trying hard to change the subject and win his confidence.

'Sailing? I prefer a Jag myself,' said Spike. 'Funny you're uncle's got a boat around here, because that's exactly where we are heading. To the moorings at Highbrook Creek.'

Lucy felt less scared now. It could be that her father was meeting them at the creek after all; she had been there with him many times. Perhaps uncle Philip would be there too, and maybe Natalie. Perhaps there really was a surprise waiting for her at Highbrook Creek. She could be panicking for nothing.

Spike on the other hand was a little disturbed by the coincidences. Bernie Cullum had told him to snatch the kid and take her to Highbrook Creek. He'd told him the name of the boat, but he'd forgotten it. He remembered its description and the place where it was moored, but had completely forgotten the name. Was it Sea Lavender? He was curious. Did Cullum know the kid's uncle had a boat at Highbrook Creek where they all played happy families? Spike thought this was a bit too close for comfort and feared that Cullum had not done his homework thoroughly enough on the kid's family background. A worrying thought went through his head as he could see patches of water shimmering on the muddy flats ahead; was Cullum that stupid not to check the kid's family set-up? Was he heading for an un-expected union with this kid's uncle, or father, and who knows who else, or worse still, was Cullum himself this kid's uncle? He didn't like Cullum, and he didn't trust him. He felt trapped. Driving the midnight blue saloon was not at all compensating for the task he had been given. He didn't want to know any an-swers right now, but he liked this latest mission less and less as he got closer to the creek. He couldn't wait to ditch the kid.

Twenty-Nine

The house was unusually quiet when Luke returned home. There was no food cooking, no music blasting from his sister's room, and his father and mother were nowhere to be seen. He grabbed a cold piece of cooked chicken from the fridge, and walked into the lounge, but he didn't feel much like eating. He turned on the television to try to take his mind off the afternoon's events at Beconsbridge Police Station. He wasn't quite sure what he was watching, but at least it put some noise into the house. He hadn't realised how much space there was in the place when there was nobody in it. He made a decision there and then never to smoke anything ever again. He felt very ashamed, but worse than this, his sister was now his biggest enemy. He decided he would tell his mother as soon as she got home; he could never keep it a secret, especially not with Lucy around, she would only end up blackmailing him to do something or another. He wanted it all out in the open, and he thought about the words he would say to break it to her gently. He tried many phrases and approaches in his head, but there was no getting away from it; she was going to go crazy. Maybe he'd leave it up to his father who had, according to Mathew, been surprisingly cool about his arrest.

While he was contemplating his confession, and almost delighting in thinking about whether or not his father's earlier tolerance was down to him being a cannabis smoker himself, the doorbell rang once. He went to the front window to try to see who it was, but could only see part of the man standing there, and could not see his face at all. He went to the door and opened it slightly. There stood a tall thin man, desperately in need of a shave.

'Hello son. Is your dad in?'

'Who are you?'

'I need to speak to your dad. Is he in?'

'No.'

'This his car? The Jag convertible?'

'No, not really. It belongs to my uncle. I don't know why

it's here.'

'I need to speak to your uncle then. I'm trying to make him an offer on it. He won't be happy if I don't get in touch with him. I've got a good deal set up. He wouldn't want to miss out.'

'I don't know where my uncle is. He's a businessman.'

'Businessman eh? Then he'll want to speak with me then won't he, because that's what I'm here for; business. What sort of places does he go to at this time of day? He'll be disappointed to have missed me. I can try and track him down.'

'Don't know really. I could phone his girlfriend if you like.'

'Yeah. You do that and I'll just wait here for a bit. Thanks son.'

Luke shut the door on McCormack and stood in the hall-way looking through the address book for his uncle Philip's number at the penthouse. After a few minutes, he returned to McCormack who was pacing up and down on the gravel driveway.

'His girlfriend hasn't heard from him all afternoon. She said that sometimes he goes down to his boat on Fridays, to check the moorings before the weekend. A lot of people get down there on a Saturday so he makes sure it's secure. It's at Highbrook Creek - do you know it? The boat's a Bermudan sloop called Sea Lavender.'

'Thanks. I'll find it.'

Toby finished his chicken and watched the remainder of a documentary, with little idea as to what it was about. He heard a key go in the door, and his father greeted him without any mention at all of the day's events. Luke hoped to keep it that way.

Robert had many other more important things on his mind, not least the recent developments concerning his colleague, Mark Daniels. Robert was again late leaving Graphic Solutions, and most of his week had been taken up with keeping watch on Daniels' movements. He had seen him sharing lunch with senior management on more than one occasion and no matter how early Robert had arrived for work in the morning, Daniels was always at his desk before him. It would be perfect for Robert if he could lead the police to suspect Daniels in their recent investigations. There was one morning in particular when Daniels was caught unaware of Roberts presence. He was placing a bundle of transparencies into a large brown envelope, but on seeing Robert arrive, he had quickly placed the envelope with its contents into the bottom drawer of his desk, and closed it quickly. Robert waited for his opportunity to remove the envelope and discover the contents, but Daniels did not move from his desk for the rest of the morning. He had even asked a passing secretary to bring him a coffee. Come lunchtime, Robert held out as long as possible, until finally Daniels had to leave his desk on an invitation to join the Directors for lunch. Robert was excited at the prospect of discovering Daniels' sideline, hidden in his desk. When he got possession of it, he would have no hesitation in placing it before the Directors. With Daniels out of the way he approached his desk and leaned over to pull the drawer open, but it was locked tight. He pulled at the top drawer, which was also locked. He was determined not to waste the opportunity and went to an adjoining office where all the security keys were kept. As it was lunchtime the Department Manager was elsewhere, and Robert began to search through the wall-rack for any key that looked as though it would fit Daniels' desk. He found nothing resembling a desk drawer key and began looking obsessively in the Manager's various boxes and drawers surrounding her desk. He eventually came across a small bunch of about eight keys tied together with a cardboard tag indicating that they operated the locks to desks 1 to 8 in rooms 2 and 3. For all the years that Robert had been employed by Graphic Solutions, he had no idea his office was numbered, let alone his desk. He grabbed the whole bunch of keys and got out of the Manager's room minutes before she returned holding a plastic carton containing a sandwich, and a polystyrene cup. He walked briskly back towards Daniels' desk and frantically tried each key, but without success. The Director's lunch must have been abandoned because just as Robert was about to give up on the exercise, Daniels re-appeared, also holding a plastic covered sandwich, and a cup. He was just in time to see Robert still fumbling at his desk, wearing an astonished and embarrassed expression. Daniels put his lunch down abruptly, thudding the desk with his fist as he did so. Robert calmly walked away, but it was too late. Daniels shouted after him as loudly as he could.

'I don't know what your beef is Davidson, but stay the fuck away from my stuff. What are you up to, you fucking nutter!'

Robert was forced to make a quick exit from his office to avoid any further confrontation. He caught a glimpse of the Department Manager holding a half eaten sandwich as she looked round her door at the sound of Daniels' voice. When Robert returned from lunch, and for the duration of the whole afternoon, nothing at all was said to him, not by the Department Manager, nor by Daniels. He continued working throughout the rest of the day, embarrassed, and with poor concentration.

He still had the Manager's keys, and he would now have to replace them without being seen. Robert thought that the best way to do this would be to return late one night; he'd be less likely to be spotted. His plan to expose Daniels was becoming an obsession, but the keys were a burden and he could be dis-covered at any time. Now that the police were ransacking the whole establishment, the keys will be wanted. He needed to put them back, and quickly.

He acknowledged Luke as he entered the house. He didn't want to talk about his arrest, the cannabis, or anything. Luke was just another small problem out of the many problems and anxieties that he had.

'Is your mother not home yet?' said Robert to Luke, 'I think it's best we say nothing about the cannabis or your arrest, but don't let this happen again. Toby's gone to Natalie's for the weekend and Lucy left a message to say she's gone to Fiona's straight from school, so your mother and I can hopefully get some peace and quiet. Might be best if you stay out of the way - amuse yourself upstairs for the evening.'

Robert walked away disinterested in any response Luke was about to give him. He headed for his study where he unloaded various materials from his bag and placed them on the desk. Luke had to talk much louder to get his father's attention.

'Why is uncle Philip's car outside? Someone came round

who wants to buy it. He wanted to know where he was so I directed him to Highbrook Creek. He wanted to do some business with him.'

Robert returned to the lounge quickly. He stood glaring at Luke.

'What did you say?' shouted Robert.

'Some man knocked on the door asking about the car. I told him it was uncle Philip's but that I didn't know where he was. I spoke to Natalie who said he was probably at the creek. I think the man's gone down there to look for him.'

Robert was not sure if his brother had been released. It was unlikely he would go to the creek straight from the police station, but he couldn't take any chances. Robert knew that whoever was knocking at the door was more interested in the owner of the car than the car itself. If he hadn't been held up at work with detective constables, he would have met this man himself. He wasn't at all unhappy about missing him.

'Did this man give his name?'

'No. I didn't ask.'

'Well what did he look like?'

Before Luke could give his father a descriptive account of the visitor, he heard his mother's car approaching the drive.

'It's your mother. Go to your room. I think it's for the best right now.' said Robert sternly.

Luke was happy to oblige, and took himself upstairs. His father had given him good advice to stay out of the way, and Luke welcomed the opportunity to hibernate and forget about the day he'd had.

Robert heard the sound of Jennifer's Mk 2 on the gravel, and then the heavy thudding of the driver's door. She appeared exhausted as she entered the hallway.

'What's Philip's car doing here?' she immediately said to her husband, 'do you know he's been arrested?'

Robert raised his eyebrows, giving a vague confirmation to his wife. He didn't know how much she knew.

'I met him lunchtime. It was awful Robert. It was all Mathew's idea that I met him but I really wish I hadn't gone. I tried to get some information about that logo because Mathew thought Philip would open up to me, instead of which he got really angry about it. When he left the pub and got to the car park, the police arrested him.'

'So, one of Mathew's great ideas,' said Robert. 'He shouldn't have asked you. He shouldn't have got you involved, I asked him not to talk to you about any of it.'

'Why is his car outside? Have they let him go?' asked Jennifer.

'His brief phoned me and asked me to pick it up for him. I'm going to see if he's been released. I'm going down to Beconsbridge Police Station. Wait here.'

'Why don't you just phone them? Phone Mathew, he might know something, especially if it's to do with his client.'

'No, I'm going down there. I want to know what's going on.'

'Where's Lucy?'

'She phoned work to say she's at Fiona's straight from school. Toby said he was staying at Rachel's, and Luke's upstairs, best not to disturb him.'

'What's Philip been up to?'

'I don't know the full story but I'm going to find out. Don't answer the door to anyone.'

'What? Robert, what is going on?'

'Philip's firm were delivering some obscene pictures to the printers, some photos of a kid or something. The police have arrested Philip for questioning. That's all I know. That's all his brief would tell me.'

Robert walked back towards his study and picked up his jacket. He looked in his bag, and to where he had left his materials. Jennifer followed him, questioning him constantly about Philip and the photographs, and who it was who might come knocking on the door. Robert was nervously shuffling papers, trying to tidy his desk before leaving for the police station, when Jennifer noticed a bundle of colour photographs. All were of women in various shots. Full-length, head and shoulders, fully clothed, partly clothed, and almost naked.

'What are these?'

'Photographs. What do you think they are?'

'What are you doing with them?'

'Improving them. I take out freckles and spots, elongate legs, enlarge eyes, shorten noses, and give them hair you can see your face in. It's what I do. It's a break from drawing castles.'

Jennifer felt uneasy, again. She didn't like Robert spending his time creating perfect women out of imperfect ones to the satisfaction of his own eye. It gave her a sudden rush of insecurity, but that was nothing new, she had them all the time. It didn't take much to make her feel inadequate; a bad mother, a bad wife. As she turned away from the pictures, Robert was already out of the front door and starting up Philip's XJS Jaguar convertible.

Jennifer stood by the street door, unable to get Robert's attention, and watched as the XJS roared away. She went to the lounge and almost removed a plate of chicken bones, which Luke had abandoned on the coffee table. Instead, she made a conscious and deliberate decision to leave it. She slumped on the sofa and closed her eyes. All she could see now were pictures of women who were about to become more perfect. Then she thought of the pictures that had caused Philip to be arrested. She wondered what they were like, and whether or not her brother-in-law was capable of being involved in pictures of children, he was always reluctant to talk about his businesses. But the idea was unthinkable, unimaginable. With her eyes closed and the house almost empty, she enjoyed the peace that she only occasionally experienced on visits to St. John's. She thought of her father and his ramblings of Josie, and how he had wasted his years deliberately devoting his waking moments to the morbid memory of her drowning.

As she lay still on the sofa, she drifted into sleep. She was gliding almost silently in her Mk 2. Her father was in the back of the car. He had pulled the walnut picnic shelf down in front of him, which was attached to the back of the front passenger seat. He had placed a flask on top, full of tea. He was still talking of Josie and how she slipped under the boat; how he foolishly waited for her to come up the other side, but for once, this didn't bother Jennifer at all. Her foot was hard on the throttle and the Jag was driving itself to the coast. The sky was a vivid blue; she had directed the quarter light chrome window so that the warm breeze was maximised, and directed straight to her neck and shoulders. The sun was ahead and uncatchable, and the ocean was just around the corner. She still heard her father calling for Josie, wishing he had jumped in the water and ignored the advice of the others on the quayside. But Jennifer was smiling, her hair was blowing, and she didn't have a care in the world. She heard a telephone ringing from the back of the car, but her father didn't answer it; she called to him to do so. As her voice became louder, she woke abruptly to find the cold reality of her empty lounge, Luke's left-over pieces of chicken, and the relentless calling of her own telephone from the coffee table.

She picked up the receiver, angry at being taken away from the glorious sunny day with the promise of the ocean. She greeted the caller abruptly. A female voice replied.

'Jennifer?'

'Hello Susan, I'm sorry I sound so miserable. I think I was asleep.'

'That's o.k. You've had a pretty awful day by all accounts. I tried to drag it out of Sarah but I only got part of the story. You know what she's like. I thought I'd give you a call before Mathew gets home just to see if I can help in any way. Did you find out where Lucy went?'

'What do you mean?'

'Didn't Mathew tell you? I asked him to tell you that Lucy went home again from school this afternoon, but since then I've found out a bit more. She's been missing so much school that at first it didn't seem out of the ordinary. She got collected at lunchtime by a man who no one has seen before. It was a black guy driving a Jag saloon; I think someone said it was a dark blue XJ6. I asked Sarah to speak to Mathew about it because I couldn't get hold of you, or Robert. I was really worried.'

'Mathew hasn't told me anything. What man? Robert didn't say she'd left school at lunchtime. He told me she'd gone to Fiona's.'

'Well I expect he's been very concerned about Luke and Philip; if he hasn't said anything, it's all probably ok. Maybe it was a friend of Fiona's family; what a day it's been for you all. Do you want me to come over - just to sit with you or something?'

'Susan. I don't know what you're talking about. What do you mean concerned for Luke? What do you mean Lucy has been taken out of school? What man in a Jag?'

'Oh God,' said Susan regrettably. 'Hasn't anyone told you? Oh my God. Me and my mouth. Oh Jennifer, I'm so sorry. I thought Mathew would have phoned you straight away about Luke. Didn't the school phone either?'

Jennifer closed her eyes again as Susan was forced to tell as much as she knew about Luke's arrest at school, Philip's arrest as the boss of the courier firm, and Lucy.

'I'm sure Robert just doesn't want to worry you,' said Susan.

'Worry me!' screamed Jennifer.

'I mean, what with your dad so ill and all the stuff between Philip and Mathew,' said Susan, nervously. 'Jennifer, I don't know what to say, but it's too much of a coincidence for all this to be happening in one day. Let me come over.'

Jennifer looked up to see Luke standing sheepishly by the doorway.

'It's o.k. Susan. I'll find out what's happening. I'll let you know,' she said as she replaced the receiver.

'Luke! What's going on?'

'I'm sorry, really I am. Dad didn't want you to know about me getting in trouble.'

'Well there's quite a few things I'm not to know about lately. Where is your sister?'

'I don't know. She told Mrs Brampton that I had some cannabis because she thought I'd tell about the photos, but I wasn't going to.'

'What photos?'

'With uncle Philip. She skips school to get pictures taken because he's told her she could be a model and earn a load of money. I think she's stupid.'

'She does what?' screamed Jennifer at her son. 'You had better tell me everything.'

'Uncle Philip organises it but I don't know where she goes. Probably his flat, or maybe the boat. She's told some kids in school about it so that's how I got to know. She was really mad that I'd found out, so she got some kids to give me some dope, and then she had something to blackmail me with. Once they'd given me one bit, they kept on giving it to me. I didn't really want it, but they'd put it in my bag.'

'Oh, Luke. You should have told me,' said Jennifer.

'I was afraid of what dad would do. He wouldn't have believed me, he never does, and Lucy would have denied it all. He believes everything she says. I think uncle Philip is horrible and I hope dad gets really cross with him. Someone came to the house about Philip's car, and dad was asking all sorts of questions about him. Do you think that's where dad has gone? To find that man?'

Jennifer put out her arms and pulled her son towards her on the sofa. She hugged him tightly while a multitude of terrible thoughts went through her head. She wished her dream had not been broken. Nothing added up without a sinister conclusion. Try as she did to remain calm, she soon began to panic. She had no idea who had collected her daughter from school; was it a drug dealer, someone she'd got to know who could supply cannabis at the drop of a hat to school kids, and who on earth had come to the door looking for Philip? She wished Robert had not gone out so quickly. He was probably in as much of a hurry to find Philip as he was to find the caller to the house. How much did Robert know? Does he know about the photographs Philip has been taking of his daughter, his precious Lucy? Robert will go berserk, what will he do when he finds Philip. She thought of going after Robert, to find him at the police station, but instead she ran to the study for the address book and ordered Luke to Lucy's room to find as many names and numbers as he could. Between them both, they found the numbers of almost two-dozen friends where it was possible Lucy could have gone.

First, she phoned Fiona.

'Everyone thought it was a family car,' Fiona said, 'Lucy seemed quite happy to get in it; it was a Jag you know. A dark blue saloon, that's why we didn't take much notice.'

'Stay in the house,' Jennifer said to Luke, 'don't you dare move,' she said as she slammed the receiver down on Fiona. She didn't need to phone anyone else. She pulled a photograph of Lucy from the frame on the wall, and clasping the picture in her hand, she ran up the gravel path to the waiting Mk 2. It started on the button. With the photograph of Lucy staring upwards from the passenger seat, she plunged the gear stick straight into second and headed for Beconsbridge Police Station to report a missing child.

Thirty

Robert was torn between finding his brother and finding the visitor to the house. So far as he was concerned, he had a lot of reckoning to do with both of them. If he planned his moves wisely, he may just be able to confront them both together. Philip was not stupid, and by now would have guessed he was looking for him; did his brother expect him to stay ignorant forever?

As Robert sped in Philip's convertible, his eyes filled with tears of rage. Everything was coming to a head, and pretty soon it would all be out in the open. Philip had some serious explaining to do, but Robert wasn't going to feel like listening. He feared his own mood, but relished the thought of reaching a final explosion; it was well overdue.

As he drove, he pictured Jennifer at home with Luke, and thought of all the secrets that had dwelled for years within his loving family. He had doted on Lucy when Jennifer had found it difficult to bond with her, and he had been a perfect father. He would have given his life for Lucy. His memories took him further back, and Jennifer's devotion to her young brother after Josie's death. Without Robert's support, she would never have coped. His love for Jennifer was still as strong as it was then, but now, in his madness, he needed to put love and all rational feelings aside.

He turned into the forecourt of Beconsbridge Police Station and took several deep breaths before getting out of the car. He ran up the few steps, entered the foyer of the police station, and rang the bell at the front desk. A young woman police officer immediately appeared. Philip Davidson was with his solicitor, she told him, and he wouldn't be ready to leave the police station for several hours, if at all. He could make further enquiries about him later that evening, but for the moment, she could tell him nothing about his arrest.

Robert returned to the Jaguar convertible. He was enraged that his brother was unapproachable, and protected by the law. He thought of waiting in the forecourt, but the officer had told him that he might not be released at all. He would use the time to tell Natalie a few home truths about Philip, and in his rage, he had no qualms about doing so. He decided to go straight to Philip's penthouse and speak to her, tell her all he knew. He would enjoy watching her reaction to the revelations. His hatred for Philip was almost unbearable, he had to do something, and he had to do it right now. An evil had grown inside him, out of the deceit of others; people whom he had trusted and loved. He was excited that it would soon all be over and the whole story would be told. He was looking forward to the reactions.

If Robert had remained at Beconsbridge Police Station just a few minutes more, he would have seen his brother leaving, accompanied by a smug solicitor who had secured his release on unconditional bail.

As he drove towards Philip's penthouse, Robert gave a moment's thought to old man Weekes. He had been very fond of Jennifer's father. Had it not been for him, he would be none the wiser, but then perhaps it would have been better in the long run if he had never known. He would have remained in his loving relationship with his three children; stayed close to Philip, and to Mathew, and continued in the job he loved. He could have stayed in blissful ignorance, and would never have become the person he was now. He knew he was suffering some form of insanity, but what person wouldn't be, knowing what he knows. He wondered if he truly was insane. Did the mentally disturbed know they were mad; he knew he was. He had lived with it for some time, for too long, and he truly was a monster now. He wanted to discuss this with Mathew; could he be defended by pleading diminished responsibility, even though he was fully conscious of his madness, and his intended actions; both were out of his control.

No one was at the penthouse when Robert arrived. He left the Jaguar where Philip had asked, and took a long stroll by the river. He walked for half a mile along the river's edge before turning into the main carriageway, which would lead him eventually to The Royal Oak where his wife had lunched with Philip that same day. He felt the presence of them both as he entered the bar, and his uncontrollable rage continued to build up inside him. After two swift shorts, he asked the barman to call him a cab. He had people to find and business to attend to, and he was very impatient to get started.

Thirty-One

The job sheets and order sheets between Graphic Solutions and Colourways covered a multitude of subjects and tasks. DC Bowden supervised scrutinising the mountain of paperwork, mostly by standing over the police constables who had been hand picked by him for the laborious work. They were looking primarily for any orders to Colourways from a Mr. Cullum. He had already seen one order from Mr. Cullum at Graphic Solutions for photo enhancement, and then delivery to Colourways to print. What he wanted now was a link to the courier, or the courier boss. Occasionally, DS Morton would appear to see how things were progressing, and it was at these moments when DC Bowden would be seen seriously handling a batch of paperwork as if the missing clue was about to manifest itself in his fingertips. When DS Morton was safely out of sight and through the next door to his office, the Detective Constable would return the very same paperwork to its rightful owners, the constables. DC Bowden recalled very well the tedious tasks he would be set by his superiors when he was a police constable, and it was only because he had performed those jobs meticulously that he had gained his promotion to the rank of detective. He was not about to deny any police constable the benefit of his own experiences.

'Come on lads, you've been at it for bloody hours. You must have found something,' he shouted in an authoritative tone. 'There's no use looking for the words "obscene publication", it'll be a bit more obscure than that. It won't be handed to you on a plate, so look for it. In those stacks of what you might see as worthless bits of paper, is the link between that kid in the photos, that arty farty place Graphic Solutions, Jack the Lad "PACE" Davidson, and the duckers and divers at Colourways. So get a bloody move on.'

DC Bowden reluctantly picked up a bundle of order forms and sat with his officers at the end of the table, more to pass the time than anything else. It also had the effect of easing the pain of watching the constables slowly lift and read the flimsy sheets one by one.

After reading several hundred orders, DC Bowden stood up abruptly. He read a particular order out loud, as if it was to have a special meaning to the five police constables who were still wading through batches of the same in silence.

'Listen to this! "Two hundred and Fifty A4 letterhead as per attached draft headed with design logo where fixed. Wide Latin 18 Font for company name Expressive Prints Express" and what's more, it's an order from our man Cullum!'

The officers looked at him expressionless as DC Bowden flew from the room to take his findings to the Sergeant. As he knocked on the door, he entered almost immediately. He could hardly contain his excitement. DS Morton was leaning across his desk with a sorrowful expression. Sitting opposite, and with their backs to DC Bowden, was a woman police constable, and a young woman who was clearly distressed. The WPC was comforting her, and on the table was a photograph of a young girl.

'A quick word please Sarg?' said DC Bowden.

'Not now Bowden,' said DS Morton sharply.

'It's to do with those order sheets Sarg. I've found something.'

DS Morton gave a deep sigh and raised his eyebrows in his usual fashion. He apologised to the woman, and promised to arrange some tea. As soon as he got outside of the room, he faced DC Bowden squarely.

'That distressed young woman is the mother of the child in the photographs,' said DS Morton, exasperated. 'The child's name is Lucy Davidson, a thirteen year old who has been missing since lunchtime. I have only just disclosed to that young woman that I can identify her missing daughter because of the indecent photographs in police possession. How do you think that must feel? I have also had the unfortunate task of telling her that those photographs were about to be delivered by her son Toby. She also knows that her brother-in-law has been arrested because of the photographs, and not in relation to something else; she wouldn't say any more on that, and I didn't want to push her, but it could be that Philip Davidson has done more than we suspect. But it doesn't stop there; it has come to light that Toby's solicitor, Mathew Weekes, is in fact this young woman's brother.'

'Blimey Sarg,' said DC Bowden.

'That's about as far as we got in this horrible family saga, when you burst open the door. I really don't think you could have chosen a worse possible moment to interrupt. Whatever you've found had better be good,' said DS Morton, agitated.

'You really will want to see this Sarg,' said DC Bowden confidently.

He handed his Sergeant the order slip. While DS Morton was reading it, DC Bowden reminded him of the name Expressive Prints Express, referred to in the order for a letter-head. It was one of the bogus companies they had tried to trace earlier in the year in connection with a fraud case; due to go to trial very soon. DC Bowden also reminded his Sergeant of the other companies, such as Masterprints, that had been fraudulently set up by McCormack, Mfgwe Olebedogayani, (otherwise known as Spike), David Black, and a few others. The Sergeant was always impressed by the DC's memory for names and past cases that he often had trouble in remembering himself. He listened to him attentively. DC Bowden continued to refresh DS Morton's memory, recalling that so far as he could remember, McCormack had put forward the name of Cullum as the person in charge of the lot, but that others who were accused had said that Cullum and McCormack were the same person, and the prosecution had tended to believe this at the time. DC Bowden continued to elaborate.

'So, we have Cullum on the order sheet from Graphic Solutions to Colourways in connection with the photo enhancement, and Cullum on this order for a letterhead and logo for Expressive Prints Express. Another thing Sarg,' DC Bowden continued, 'the brief for McCormack is Weekes, and two of the co-defendants, Spike and Dave Black, are using Sabastas-Grant. Is it a coincidence Sarg that they also represented Toby and Philip Davidson in interview? It's like a double-act. This is all connected somehow, the fraud, the photos, the missing kid, the families. It's a tangled web, and Cullum and the solicitors are bang in the middle of it.'

'This is a mess, Jim. A complete mess. This Cullum has got to be found. His name was mentioned at Colourways as being the boss. If these order sheets are anything to go by, he's a definite link between the cases,' said DS Morton.

'Do you think the solicitors are up to something? All a bit close if you ask me,' said DC Bowden.

'Forget the briefs for now. See if Weekes withdraws his services. If not we'll take it further, but I don't want to shake anything up that might put the kid in jeopardy. It certainly smacks of conflict, or something much worse. Those pictures were of Weekes' niece. How could he stay quiet? We may just have to take him in. On the other hand, he might lead us to the girl, and to Cullum. Keep your eye on those briefs. Both of them.'

'Shall I pick up Philip Davidson? The kid was his niece too. What about Toby Davidson? That was his sister for heaven's sake. What about McCormack?' asked DC Bowden, excitedly.

'On what further evidence?' said DS Morton. 'No point getting the courier picked up, horrible though it is to think he didn't say a word, and you can forget McCormack. We can't investigate him in connection with the kid just on this piece of paper, and it doesn't prove he's Cullum, or that he's involved with the child. We've already got him facing several counts on the frauds. If McCormack turns out to be Cullum it will all come out at the trial, there's nothing new to arrest him on. We can't go rounding people up just like that. My concern is finding the girl, and we've got to find her by tonight. I'm not convinced at all that McCormack is our man. He's just not smart enough to have got away with it for so long. My money is on this Cullum character, but who is he? If it's not McCormack, what about someone from Graphic Solutions, they produce pictures don't they, and letterheads. You were down there, what did you make of them?'

'Don't ask me Sarg, they all looked weird to me, except for the receptionist,' said DC Bowden, 'can't stand artists. Not my type. Doubt if they've got the intelligence for something like this,' said DC Bowden. 'What do you think?'

'My top suspect is the courier boss, Philip Davidson. The mother said he'd been taking photos of her daughter for modelling work, without her knowledge, and missing school because of it. But she's known him for twenty-five years, and is adamant he wouldn't have taken those pictures, and him kidnapping the child was unthinkable. But you never know in this game. I think we'll keep an eye on Philip Davidson's movements. If the kid's in danger then we can't take chances, and if we bring him in again we might never find her. On top of that, we've got Sabastas-Grant to think of, he'll be clocking up the custody times if nothing else. Philip Davidson is likely to be our man, but we can't clinch it Jim. Not yet.'

'So, what next Sarg?' asked DC Bowden.

'I'm going to send the mother home for now, and circulate the photo of the girl,' said DS Morton, 'let me know if her father turns up. You met him earlier, Robert Davidson, the artist. It'll be all out the bag as soon as his wife gets home. I'd like to see his reaction when he finds out what his eldest son was carrying in his pannier. There's no reason to keep it confidential any longer if he's the girl's father, and now we know her identity we can tell him the lot. Looks like he'll have his own suspicions about his brother Philip. Get to Philip Davidson's penthouse, but lay low, and whatever you do don't let him see you, and don't pick him up. If he leaves he could be on his way to Highbrook Creek, according to the girl's mother, so let me know his movements. I'm going to organise a search down there, but the place is vast; with the marshes and the tides to watch, I'll need some professionals. I'm not having my officers walking on toe paths that could disappear under water at the blink of an eye. I've seen it myself, one minute you're on dry land, the next your wheels are three feet under. We need some special equipment, divers, the lot. I don't want to be morbid, or jump the gun, but I'm doing this the old-fashioned way, and it's going to be done right. Just watch Davidson's comings and goings for now, but don't approach him, and for God's sake don't take a uniformed officer with you.'

DC Bowden returned to where the officers were still ploughing through the orders and dockets, and his announcement that they could take a short break was very welcome. He made his way to the control room to circulate Lucy's description to all units, together with a further description of a dark coloured Jaguar saloon, registration unknown.

He secured the presence of a colleague, DC Wells, to accompany him to Philip Davidson's penthouse where they would watch and wait for any sign of movement. He would like to have done a lot more, and was disappointed in his Sergeant for sticking to the rules. He knew McCormack had previous, and lots of it. He had served time for possessing obscene literature. He had worked at Colourways, and helped set up Expressive Prints Express and Masterprints. There were too many coincidences so far as DC Bowden was concerned; McCormack and Cullum could still be the same person. His Sergeant had not persuaded him that McCormack did not have the ability or luck to avoid disclosure of his identity up until now, nor did he think he was beyond the capability of kidnapping a child. He thought McCormack was capable of both; his illiteracy and pathetic demeanour didn't cut any ice with DC Bowden, he could see straight through his act. Kidnapping a child was a natural progression for someone like McCormack. He was no different to the hundreds of other offenders he'd met; start by taking cars, end up taking lives. It was a natural criminal path; all criminals progressed in one direction or another, like any other profession or trade. Simultaneously, DC Bowden had an intense dislike for Philip Davidson, and he couldn't rule him out of any equation either. He was going to find it hard to resist questioning him again, now that the identity of the kid in the photos was known. As DC Bowden and DC Wells headed for the penthouse as their Sergeant had instructed, DC Bowden was half hoping that Philip Davidson would not show up. This would avoid any temptation of him giving Philip Davidson what he deserved. It wasn't worth putting his job on the line, but he'd find it hard to restrain himself.

The WPC was still talking to Jennifer when DS Morton re-entered the room; she helped Jennifer to her feet. The police had a lot of enquiries to make, a lot of leads to follow up, and it was probably best that she went home and waited for some news of her daughter, the Sergeant explained to Jennifer.

'We'll need to come to your home,' said the WPC, 'to take a look through Lucy's things, and any home computers. If you can give me a list of her friends, we'll check with them again, just in case they know something. You will be contacted immediately we have any news, we'll do all we can to find Lucy as quickly as possible. Please stay at home in case she tries to make contact, and call me if you hear, or remember, anything at all, no matter how trivial it may seem.' The WPC put her arm on Jennifer's shoulder. 'Are you sure you won't let us drive you?'

'No,' said Jennifer, 'thank you. My son and my husband will be at home waiting for me. I'll be fine,' Jennifer said.

Jennifer walked slowly from the main doors of the police station and the WPC watched as she headed towards the car park. Jennifer opened the door of the Mk 2 and slumped into the leather comfort of her Jaguar. She felt dazed, as if she was still dreaming. She turned the key and pressed the starter button. Without much thought, she pushed the gear stick clumsily into first, grating the gears noisily. She instantly thought of Philip; nobody could like first gear on a Mk 2.

She stayed focused on Philip as she drove home; she felt she had again betrayed him, as she had done earlier, at Mathew's request. Everyone seemed to be using her, not telling her the truth, not telling her anything. She felt her family was falling apart, and she had no one. Robert had not been honest with her, even though this may have been to protect her. Mathew had not told her about the arrest of her two sons, nor of the obscene pictures of her daughter, his own niece. Lucy had been taking time off school and Toby had been about to deliver pictures of his sister through his uncle's courier firm. Despite all that had gone on, everyone had chosen to stay quiet. Now she trusted no one, no one at all.

Thirty-Two

Sabastas-Grant was happy to drive his client home, along-side the luxurious penthouse suites overlooking the Thames. He was content in the knowledge that he had impressed Philip Davidson at Beconsbridge Police Station, and would undoubtedly be defending him in the not too distant future, after a large cash advance.

He had stopped the police from charging his client, by convincing DS Morton, in a private conversation, that the Sergeant may be embarrassed by his lack of knowledge of the relevant Acts involving obscene publications; the police had better be sure of which Section of which Act they were going to be proceeding with, and be up to date with the amendments made in recent times. The solicitor was adamant that whichever path they took, and on the evidence they had at the moment, it would be thrown out before it even got off the ground.

Sabastas-Grant thought he had sounded very convincing; confusing the Detective Sergeant by his own understanding of the law. Limited though his knowledge was, it luckily exceeded that of DS Morton, and Sabastas-Grant thought he had excelled himself, giving an impressive and knowledgeable performance. The solicitor had emphasised that firstly, no pictures whatsoever had been found on his client. Although DS Morton argued that they were found on his employee, Toby Davidson, perhaps as his agent, the Sergeant could not follow it through; there was nothing to show that Philip Davidson was distributing the pictures for gain. Secondly, Sabastas-Grant argued that the Sergeant had no proof of the age of the person in the photographs, as he didn't know who she was; he should therefore be cautious about charging his client with possessing photographs of a child, until he could prove that it was in fact a child. Finally, Sabastas-Grant had challenged the Sergeant's knowledge of computer-generated pornography. He had put it to him that in addition to the photographs not being of a child, they may not even have been produced from images of real people. He reminded the Detective Sergeant from where the photographs were originally collected,

and that Graphic Solutions had highly sophisticated computers; perfectly capable of producing convincingly genuine images
of people, bearing no resemblance at all to any living person.
Such equipment could fabricate pictures produced entirely from
scratch, out of nothing but the imagination of the user and his
skills in the use of computer generated art. Sabastas-Grant continued to baffle the Sergeant, who clearly felt out of his depth
in this field. On the other hand, and fortunately for Philip
Davidson, the solicitor had only recently been forced to update
himself on the subject. By sheer luck, Sabastas-Grant was well
aware of recent decisions concerning obscene data stored or copied by computers. In particular, he had been forced to read up
on possession of computerised images of children that were capable of conversion into a photograph. He had tried to defend a
client on the grounds that computer data did not comprise a real
photograph, but he had failed miserably when the Judge decided
that a computer disk, or anything stored on the computer, was
capable of producing an indecent image, and therefore capable
of producing a print for distribution and gain. This particular
client was imprisoned for three years for having indecent photographs of a child, having an obscene article for publication
for gain, and for distributing indecent photographs available for
downloading through the Internet.

DS Morton had not recently researched the law as thoroughly as Sabastas-Grant had done. By the end of his conversation with the solicitor, he was totally baffled by his options of
possible offences, so much so that he was nervous of charging
Philip Davidson at all. The Sergeant had contemplated bringing
more than one charge, so that at least one of the alternatives
would stick, but eventually conceded to the request of Sabastas-
Grant to bail him; this would give him time to get the charges
absolutely right. In the meantime, he would gather more evidence, compare the fingerprints from the photographs with
those of Toby, and Philip Davidson, and seek further advice on
the law. He particularly needed updating on the laws of computerised images; it had left DS Morton completely bewildered.

The solicitor had quite enjoyed the ride to docklands with

his client and was not at all put out, since he had a dinner engagement at nearby Tower Bridge. At the same time he could get to see exactly how rich his client was, remembering only too well that he would not be applying for legal aid. Sabastas-Grant knew he was good for his fee when Philip said goodbye and strolled across the pink stoned pathways leading to a cluster of newly converted residences, alight with fake gas lamps. The reflections from the river gave the whole area a feeling of light and well-being. There was a definite sense of wealth. Sabastas-Grant sat and observed the area for a few minutes after Philip had disappeared, and thought how good it would be to return to this place after a day in the office, a marvellous place to retreat. He would make enquiries through his estate agent friends at dinner tonight.

DC Bowden and DC Wells sat patiently. They watched Sabastas-Grant and Philip Davidson as they said goodbye to each other. Their unmarked saloon did not look too out of place, and they had a good view of Davidson's penthouse. They watched him walk away from his solicitor and pause by his blue Jaguar convertible, which had been parked underneath the property where normal homes would have a bay window.

'How did that motor get there?' said DC Bowden, 'we left it at the Royal Oak.'

'He's got a lot of mates,' said DC Wells, 'someone's stuck their neck out for him.'

'Makes me sick.'

They saw Phillip Davidson look briefly inside the car, presumably checking it over, and then he disappeared along a short pathway. A few minutes later DC Bowden and his companion watched in delight as Philip Davidson appeared by a huge glass window one floor up, telephone in hand, lounge lights full on, gazing towards the water, and completely unaware of their presence.

DC Bowden looked at his companion; from the look on his face, he was feeling the same as he did.

'He's a flash bastard,' said DC Bowden. 'How did he get to own a place like this? I tell you what, I don't think I'm going to be able to sit here all night just watching him.'

'I know what you mean,' said DC Wells, 'but don't go jumping in there. Didn't the Sarg tell you not to approach him?'

'The Sarg wouldn't have to know. Not unless I got a result.'

'Leave me out of it if you're going in. We're here to eye-ball. Nothing else.'

DC Bowden heeded his companion's words. They watched Philip disappear from the window, and then return shortly afterwards, holding a glass and a lit cigarette. He was no longer speaking on the telephone, but simply gazing out over the river, sipping his drink. The officers could only observe. They had no idea of Philip's thoughts.

He was re-living the episode in the police station, the pictures of Lucy, and how Jennifer would react; if only he had captured her heart when he had the chance. He thought he had come so close, but if he had succeeded, he would have lost his brother's friendship forever. It was a regular habit of his to gaze at the water, drink in hand, and recall that one night with Jennifer. He thought about it almost every day, though more than fourteen years had since passed. Old man Weekes had taken a turn for the worse when Robert and Mathew were away skiing, leaving Jennifer to care for young Toby and baby Luke. She had been exhausted from the day's events, and was tearful. She thought her father was going to die. She needed some help, and Philip was there. He had not intended it to happen, and she certainly had not. Philip could not regret a single moment, but Jennifer had instantly told him her regrets, her deep shame; a big mistake. From that day, she had never referred to it again; neither had he. He was glad they had managed to remain close in-laws, and that he could spoil her on occasions without any embarrassment. He wondered if his affection for Lucy was a substitute for his love for Jennifer, a way of getting close to her. Although Lucy did not immediately resemble her, she was still a very beautiful girl. He thought again of the photographs shown to him at Beconsbridge Police Station, and the pain it would cause Jennifer if she ever discovered them. He wanted to go to her as he had done that one time before, but on this occasion, and on the advice of Sabastas-Grant, it was the very last thing he should do.

He finished his Scotch and walked away from the window to pour himself another. As he did so, he heard a key turning in the door. Natalie rushed at Philip and wrapped her arms around him from behind, as he was half way through pouring his drink from the decanter.

DC Bowden and his companion had seen Natalie get out of the black cab a few minutes earlier, but could not have imagined that the same young girl was hurrying home to embrace their suspect.

They watched in amazement from their vantage point as she greeted Philip Davidson with enviable affection, causing the DC to become even more determined to spoil his night.

'I don't believe it,' said DC Bowden. 'What does she see in him?'

'Search me,' said DC Wells, 'but he's doing alright on it.'

'Yeah? Not for long.'

The officers kept up their observation, but could not hear their suspect's conversation with the young woman. They could only watch as Philip turned to embrace Natalie.

'I think there are some would-be burglars downstairs,' said Natalie excitedly. 'They're sitting in a car under the tree, just opposite, but they'd have a hard job getting in here wouldn't they? Go take a look.'

Philip walked towards the window as Natalie continued to talk.

'By the way, young Luke phoned here today.'

'Luke?'

'Some bloke apparently called at the house for you. He said he was interested in the blue XJS. Why was it at Robert's? Anyway, I said I didn't know where you were so I suggested he tried the boat being as it's Friday and that sometimes you check it over for the weekend. Can you see those guys in the car?'

Philip moved quickly away from the window and put his face uncomfortably close to Natalie's.

'Haven't I got enough problems you stupid bitch! I've been

188

at Beconsbridge Police Station for most of the day, I've now got two gorillas sitting outside my place watching my every move, and just to put the cherry on the cake you go and send some head-case down to the creek to go over my boat! Get out of here! Go and pack some things and disappear for a few days. I don't care where you go, just get away from me before I do something I'm going to regret.'

'What do you mean?' said Natalie tearfully, 'what have I done?'

'Just about everything,' snapped Philip, 'now, please, just disappear and give me a break.'

Philip cautiously returned to the window, and caught one last sight of the two officers before pulling the cord to the blinds. They fell immediately, blocking any further observation of him. He couldn't decide whether to get down to the moorings or go straight to Robert's home to find out more from Luke. All he knew was that he had to get out, and the quicker the better. His first decision was to have 'one for the road' and as he headed again for the drinks cabinet, he glimpsed the back of Natalie hurrying out of the door. He felt slightly relieved that at least something was happening that he'd asked for.

DC Bowden was not happy; his unobstructed view of Davidson had come to an end.

'He's clocked us and pulled the fucking blinds down! I'm going up.'

'I wouldn't do that if I were you,' said DC Wells, 'you're asking for trouble.'

'Well I'm not you, am I. You stay here, but if there's any word of this gets out then I'll know where it came from.'

DC Wells did nothing as his colleague slammed the car door and ran quickly across the pink paving, past the convertible, and along a short path. He turned left at the end and disappeared from sight.

It was just after Natalie had left, that the intercom buzzer went off. Philip assumed Natalie had forgotten something, most probably her key. He pressed the door release impatiently, expecting to see Natalie back again. To his horror, there stood DC

Bowden in his open doorway.

'DC Bowden - Beconsbridge CID. We met earlier. Mind if I have a look around?'

'Yes I do. Where's your warrant.'

'Well in that case can I just ask you a few questions Mr. Davidson, only it's come to light that the photos you looked at today were in fact photos of your young niece. You never said a word, did you? You got anything to say about that?'

'No. Nothing. Now go.'

'Do you like taking photos of young girls Mr. Davidson?' DC Wells continued. 'You sat in interview like butter wouldn't melt, quite happy to be looking at those pictures, and you said nothing. Now why would you do that.'

'Get out of here. You've got no right to be here and I'm saying nothing, so get out. I'm getting my brief.'

'I think you'll find he's got a dinner date Mr. Davidson,' said DC Bowden as he persisted with his line of fire. He was thoroughly enjoying the opportunity to express his complete hatred for men who commit this sort of crime. The opportunities didn't come along very often, not like they used to; he might never have the chance again.

'How could you take photographs like that of your own niece? Is this how you get your money, dealing in stuff like that. How do you sleep at night.'

DC Bowden was pleased at the effect his words were having on Davidson and took great delight watching beads of sweat appear on his flushed complexion. This was a nervous reaction if ever he saw one. He continued with the confrontation. He was enjoying himself far too much to stop now.

'The girl who just left; she looked a bit young too. Is this how you earned your fortune? Exploiting young girls?'

'You don't know what the fuck you're talking about,' said Philip, enraged.

'No? Don't I? Well the kid's mother does. She knows what I'm talking about. We only know you're a keen photographer of children because the kid's mother told us. Your sister-in-law has shopped you Mr. Davidson, and who could blame her.'

DC Bowden only just managed to restrain himself from speaking about Lucy's disappearance. He couldn't be certain that Philip Davidson knew the kid was missing, but if he did, the DC had a feeling that he would lead them to her. He really didn't want to mess that up. At the same time, he wanted his suspect to know that he was hot on his trail. He wanted him to panic so that in doing so he would inevitably make the one mistake that would prove his guilt. They always did. DC Bowden was happy to leave Philip Davidson physically shaken.

'I'll catch up with you eventually Davidson,' said DC Bowden, 'I promise you that. Enjoy your penthouse luxury while you can. You might not be seeing it again for a very long time.'

'You've got it all wrong, Bowden,' said Philip, his voice shaking uncontrollably, 'it's all wrong. Get out of here. You've no right to be here. You're going to hear from my brief about this.'

'Good. I look forward to that. And I hope he takes you for every penny you've got.'

While DC Bowden had been engaged with their suspect, his colleague had decided to follow Natalie to the corner of the cul-de-sac; she had turned right, and walked smartly along the high road that ran alongside the Thames. She came to a halt at the taxi rank and pulled her mobile phone from her shoulder bag; one large holdall was rested on the ground by her feet. DC Wells saw her make several calls, and he was still watching her by the time DC Bowden emerged from his encounter with Philip Davidson. He saw that the saloon was now parked at the end of the cul-de-sac, and walked towards it.

'How did it go?' said DC Wells.

'Fine. Just fine,' said DC Bowden as he got in the car. 'Managed to get his blood pressure up, that'll do for now. You been watching the girl?'

'Thought I might as well. She might throw up some clues.'

'Let's go and talk to her, before she disappears,' said DC Bowden.

'You're really pushing it tonight, what's got into you?' said

DC Wells.

'People like Philip Davidson, that's what. I want to nab the sicko.'

'But we've got nothing on this girl.'

'Just pull alongside her, I'll do the talking. Go on. Just do it,' said DC Bowden, anxiously.

Natalie had just finished another call. She was trying to fix herself up with some short notice accommodation and it looked as though she may have succeeded; she put her phone back inside her shoulder bag, picked up her holdall, and walked towards the first waiting cab in the queue. DC Bowden jumped out of the saloon and approached her before she reached the taxi. DC Wells straightened up his parking, then hurried to join his colleague; why not, he thought, it was his idea to follow her.

'I'm DC Bowden from Beconsbridge Police, this is my colleague, DC Wells,' said DC Bowden to Natalie.

'What do you want?'

'Mind telling us where you're going?' said DC Bowden.

'What's it to you?' said Natalie.

'We saw you leave Philip Davidson's place.'

'What if I did?'

'No need to get narked, we just want a chat,' said DC Bowden as he got closer to Natalie and stared into her face, 'we're only asking where you're going.'

As Natalie was forced to look at his face, she had a flashback. Her life had been hard before meeting Philip; meeting him had been the best thing to have happened. He was kind, he was generous, and she didn't have to dance any more; privately or otherwise. He said he'd look after her, and he had. Although he had his moods, she couldn't fault him, it was just that his businesses were stressful; he was entitled to his bad moments, and she knew he would be back. She was part of his new venture; he'd definitely be back. There was too much to lose. She had left the penthouse with plenty of cash, Philip had made sure of it; he was so generous. These two guys, they were going to get nothing out of her. Whatever trouble Philip was in, she wasn't going to make it worse. The officer was still staring at her, asking her where she was going, but she wasn't going to tell him anything. Then she recognised the face that had taken her mind back to her days at the club.

'I know you,' said Natalie, 'I know you from The Cinnamon Bar.'

'You what?' said DC Wells. 'You know him from the Cinnamon Bar?'

'She don't know me,' said DC Bowden, 'never seen her in my life.'

Natalie looked into DC Bowden's eyes, and said softly, 'I beg to differ.' She paused, and then said, '... Jim.'

DC Wells gave a half chuckle, 'I don't believe this,' he said, 'you dark horse.'

'It was one night, a one-off event. Ages ago,' said DC Bowden, uncomfortably.

'Yeah, right,' said Natalie sarcastically, 'so, shall we have a chat then Jim, or should I say, DC Bowden. I tell you what, when I get settled somewhere I'll ring you at home and leave my contact number with your wife, I'm sure she'll want the details.' Natalie looked at DC Wells, who was still finding it amusing. 'You should get your friend out of here before I call the police myself,' she said, as she walked towards the taxi driver's door to give directions, 'this is harassment, isn't it ... Jim?'

'Where to luv?' said the driver.

'I'll tell you when these two have gone,' she said, indicating to the two officers who hadn't quite yet given up.

'You bothering this lady?' said the driver.

'We're police officers,' said DC Bowden.

'Well do your policing,' the driver replied, 'do what you have to, then let me get on with my fare.'

'Yeah. Do what you have to ... Jim,' said Natalie teasingly, as she ignored the two men, climbed into the back of the taxi, and slammed the door closed. She leaned forward, whispered her directions into the driver's neck, and waved cheekily to DC Bowden and DC Wells as the taxi moved slowly away from the rank. The officers just watched.

'Well, well, well,' said DC Wells, 'The Cinnamon Bar eh?'

'Drop it. We never stopped her, we never spoke to her, this never happened. O.k.?'

'Fine by me,' said DC Wells, not wanting to embarrass him any more than he had been.

'Let's get back to the penthouse,' said DC Bowden, changing the subject, 'we don't want to mess that up, do we.'

Thirty-Three

Immediately after the DC had left, Philip poured himself another Scotch. DC Bowden had had his fun, off the record, and would probably now be tired of watching for his next movement. He kept the blind pulled down and flicked on the TV, both to calm himself, and give the police officers the impression that he was in for the night. His desire to see Jennifer was now overwhelming him. He could think of nothing else. He was not sure how he would explain his role in the recent events, or how he would be able to convince her of his innocence, but he knew he had to face her. He wouldn't even try an explanation by telephone.

He reflected on his representation by Sabastas-Grant, whether he'd been given the best advice, which was to say nothing. He had told Sabastas-Grant the identity of the child in the photographs; he also confided his affection for the child's mother. Both revelations received an emotionless response from the solicitor, and Philip put this down to his experience and professionalism; it was perfectly correct that his solicitor should give no indication of his own thoughts or opinions. However, in turn, Sabastas-Grant had expressed his own opinion of Mathew Weekes, more on a personal level than professionally, and Philip was very happy to know that his solicitor's feelings for his rival were on a par with his.

Philip was finding it impossible to stay away from Jennifer any longer. He pulled the edge of the blind back slowly until he could see where DC Bowden and his colleague had been waiting. Their saloon had gone, but he could not be certain they were completely out of the area. If the police followed him to Jennifer, the possible implications were many. If Jennifer was hostile towards him, as she was likely to be, then he would be seen as intimidating her. He could not know exactly what events had taken place with her at Beconsbridge Police Station, and he only had the word of DC Bowden that Jennifer had said anything at all. He wasn't sure what she had discovered; maybe she had been at the police station with Toby, and then got to see the photos, or maybe Mathew had kept her out of the way.

He distrusted all police officers, and DC Bowden was no exception; he could have been bluffing about Jennifer's accusations. DC Bowden may have just been playing out a hunch to watch for his reaction, after all, he could have simply arrested him there and then, but he did not. Sabastas-Grant had said that Toby was likely to make no comment at all, because of the situation that Mathew Weekes was in. If this was the case, then the police still had no knowledge of Lucy, but there was no guarantee, it was always possible that Toby had identified his sister, or maybe Mathew had. Knowing Mathew's intense dislike for him, and the recent furore regarding the logo for Expressive Prints Express, his brother-in-law had the perfect opportunity to inform the police of his own suspicions, not just to protect his client, but to see him ruined for good. He wanted to phone Toby there and then, to see what he had said, he knew he would be at his girlfriend's for the weekend, and he had her number. Philip considered the risk of breaching bail, and weighed this up against the amount of money he was paying Sabastas-Grant to discover anything relevant. He thought better of it. Speaking to Toby was not the way to find out what he needed to know, he would have to talk to Jennifer.

Philip swigged the last large mouthful of Scotch and went to the hall lobby to a rack of keys. He had made his decision. He juggled around with several sets until deciding on the ring holding a small leaping cat, made from solid silver. It held two single keys. He pulled his sheepskin jacket from the hall cupboard, and was still putting it on as he fled from the penthouse, leaving the television and lights just as they were. He made his way along the back route of the complex, away from the river, and so far as he knew, he had not been followed. He walked at a brisk pace, almost running, and then doubled back on his journey, until he came to a set of six garage doors painted alternate pink and midnight blue. He looked over his shoulder once and pointed a key fob at a pink door, which instantly gave a quiet humming sound. The door curled upwards and over to reveal Philip's greatest love - a 1961 E Type Series 1 three-point-eight

Jaguar. It was finished in British racing green and was in flawless condition. It was a car that Philip rarely used, but had won him many first place prizes in shows all over the country. Philip's superstition of green cars, and their connection with bad luck, stopped here. The car was remarkable; it had brought him nothing but pleasure and good fortune, and good fortune was certainly what he needed right now. The E-Type was not about to let him down.

The car started immediately, roaring loudly in the confines of the garage space, eager to take Philip to his destination. Philip drove it out of the garage, stopping just beyond the pink doors. He again pointed the key fob and the doors again hummed gently, moving over and downwards until they clicked shut and the humming stopped. Before long, Philip was on the dual carriageway, happy in the knowledge that the police would be keeping watch on his blue XJS convertible; he would soon be on the motorway, heading towards Essex. With the mood he was in, their saloon wouldn't have a chance of catching him, even if the DC and his companion had spotted him leaving. Regardless of his experiences that day, his encounters with the police, his row with Natalie, his thoughts for Jennifer, everything changed for him inside this car. It was a thrill to drive his prized possession. Even if the feeling was to be short lived, right now he could handle anything thrown his way. Now the speedometer was reading eighty-five mph, and climbing fast; despite her age, the E Type had barely begun to show her owner her full potential. Philip smiled, as the passing traffic became a blur, but he wasn't in the mood for risk taking; the last thing he wanted was to be snapped by a camera. He became calmer, and slowed the car down; he felt luck was on his side.

While Philip headed for the M11 motorway, which would lead him to Jennifer, DC Wells drove the unmarked saloon back to Philip's penthouse. DC Bowden and DC Wells said nothing more about their encounters with Natalie; it was best forgotten, for both of them. They found a new vantage point, one where their suspect would have difficulty spotting them.

'The Jag's still there, the TV's still on,' said DC Wells, 'looks like he hasn't moved.'

'Wouldn't have had time,' said DC Bowden, 'we've only been gone a minute. It's going to be a long night,' he said as he pulled a fast food leaflet from his pocket. 'Fancy a curry?'

'If you're getting a take-away delivered to the car, you can call control yourself,' said DC Wells, 'I've done enough under-handed police work for one day.'

Thirty-Four

When Mathew arrived at the flat Susan hardly recognised him. He looked exhausted, and appeared to have the look of his elderly father about him. His eyes were bloodshot and his face looked pale and bloated. If she didn't know him better, she would have thought he had downed several pints since lunchtime. As he walked towards her, she could feel his despair. He said nothing at all. Susan placed her arms around his shoulders without letting go of the damp tea towel she was holding. It draped down his back and remained there while Mathew buried his head on her shoulder and collapsed, still standing in his overcoat.

She helped him unbutton his coat, and led him to the settee where she sat him down. He slipped backwards with his head rested on the cushions, and closed his eyes. She held his hand gently.

'There's a lot of trouble,' said Mathew, quietly, 'I've really messed up today. A lot of people are relying on me to help them, and I can't do it. I just can't do it.'

'Yes you can,' said Susan gently, 'take it easy, calm down.'

'All the kids are in trouble. All of them.'

'I know Luke was arrested,' said Susan, 'the police were at school. I had a hard time getting anything out of Sarah, but I got there in the end. She said Philip was in trouble too, but wouldn't tell me any more.'

'It's worse than that. Much worse. Toby was arrested as well, while he was working. The police stopped him on his bike, and he was carrying photographs of a young girl. They were in his pannier. It turns out the girl was Lucy. I should have said something to the police, but I didn't, and neither did Toby. On my advice, he kept quiet.'

'Photos of Lucy? I don't understand,' said Susan. 'Did Toby see them? Do you mean bad photos?'

'Bad enough. Philip's got something to do with it; I know he has. What am I going to say to Jennifer?'

'Why did you stay quiet?'

'His legal position, I thought it was for the best. I'm not so sure now.'

'Oh God, this is awful; it all ties up. I tried to speak to you about Lucy. Are you ready for this?' said Susan gently.

'Ready for what?'

'She was taken out of school at lunchtime today. I tried to check it out with Robert, but he was so pre occupied, he couldn't talk to me. But he didn't seem concerned, maybe because he lets her have so much time off school anyway. Oh, Mathew. It's all falling horribly into place. I think you should speak to your sister. Why don't you phone her and see if Lucy is home.'

'Lucy missing? Taken from school? Oh Christ!'

'Jennifer had no idea until I told her; I told her about Luke too. Nobody had even phoned her. She must be at her wits end.'

'It was up to Robert to tell her about Luke, not me, but he's the least of her problems. She knows nothing about Toby, he didn't want her to know, and legally it was the best course of action for him, or so I thought. He's hoping it'll all blow over, but it's not going to, is it. And now Lucy is missing; we won't be able to keep this quiet. This will hurt Jennifer so much. I'm scared to phone her. McCormack was positive he saw Lucy this afternoon with one of his co-defendants.'

'How on earth does your client know Lucy?' asked Susan.

'He saw a photo of her in my office; he was convinced it was her. He said he saw Lucy in the back of a Jag driven by one of his co-defendants. He's been desperately trying to trace someone called Cullum who he says is involved in the scam, and now he thinks he's seen him, talking to the same co-defendant who was driving Lucy. It's all getting too much for me. I think I'm losing it.'

'Phone Jennifer. Do it now and see what's going on.'

'Have you got that note excusing Lucy from school?'

Susan went to her bag, and among all the exercise books and various pieces of paperwork that she was supposed to be catching up on, she found the note concerning Lucy. She handed it to Mathew. It was signed R. Davidson, and it excused Lucy because of family problems. Mathew looked at the note carefully. He wondered if the letter 'R' was a badly written 'P'. He asked Susan to take a closer look but she wouldn't give an opinion.

'It could be either,' she said diplomatically, 'but it makes no difference, anyone could have written it. Even Lucy herself.'

'I've got a feeling that Philip wrote and signed this note. Do you think it's his writing?'

'I don't know Philip's handwriting,' said Susan, sensibly, 'and neither do you.'

'But it's all coming together now. It's all coming together,' said Mathew, 'what an idiot I've been; that's why he stayed quiet, said nothing to the police about the photos.'

Mathew's pager began to buzz. He slowly pulled it from his belt loop, and pressed a small button. The screen lit up and he read the message.

"Weeksie. The police have resumed their search for Bernie Cullum. They've found his order sheets for the photographs, and for a letterhead for Expressive Prints Express. Ring any bells? The police are connecting our fraud case to these obscene publications. Thought you'd like to know. We need to have a chat. Always ready to oblige, you can thank me later. Dominic Sabastas-Grant."

'You've always had your doubts about Philip,' said Susan, as Mathew read his pager, 'but don't go jumping to conclusions without any evidence,' she said, knowing the extent of Mathew's obsession with Philip, and trying to get him to see that his accusations might be going too far.

'Evidence? How much more does anybody want?' said Mathew as he clipped his pager back onto his belt, 'I'll give you bloody evidence.'

Susan was afraid. She could only watch as Mathew reached to the side of the settee and picked up the telephone to call his sister. She could just about hear Jennifer's distressed voice as she answered her brother's call.

'Jennifer. I'm going to sort this out for you,' said Mathew, his voice trembling and broken. 'I'm so sorry about everything, especially what I'm about to tell you.'

'Don't bother Mathew, I already know.'

Mathew listened in horror as his sister screamed her knowledge of events at him. She knew about Luke because he had only just told her. She knew about Philip because she saw him arrested. She knew about Toby and Lucy because the police had told her that they recognised her missing child from the indecent photos Toby had been carrying.

'Lucy is missing, do you hear me? Missing!' Jennifer screamed. 'I went to the police with her photograph, and they'd already seen plenty of photographs; dozens I'm told, and in my son's possession. Where is she Mathew? Where the hell is my daughter? Why has no one told me anything? If it wasn't for Susan I still wouldn't know. I demand to know what's been going on.'

'I'll tell you what's been going on shall I,' said Mathew, his voice becoming suddenly harsher, and angrier, as he was about to unfold the whole terrible story as he saw it.

'Your wonderful brother-in-law runs a courier firm from which he delivers obscene pictures to printing firms. He runs off hundreds of copies, sells them to perverts, and gets bloody rich. Before he gets them printed, he gets Robert's place to enhance them, make them perfect, a bit more attractive to his market. Then he uses your son to deliver them, and it looks like he uses your daughter as his subject matter. He has a hand in the printing firm, and easy access to the expertise at Graphic Solutions. Don't tell me he knows nothing about that line of work, he knows enough. With me so far? In addition, I have found out from Martin McCormack that the person he was looking for has now turned up, quite out of the blue, talking to a man he knows as Spike. He saw Spike with Lucy earlier today, sitting in the back of a Jaguar saloon. He recognised Lucy from the photo in my office. The guy he's been looking for, Bernie Cullum, was seen driving a blue XJS convertible, and how many of those have you seen around? It's got to be Philip. Shall I go on?'

'I can't take all this in,' said Jennifer, weeping.

'Well you're going to have to,' continued Mathew harshly. 'The order that was put in at Graphic Solutions for the photos to be enhanced was in the name of Bernie Cullum; this guy is also known at Colourways, the printers at the end of the line, and the police have also recovered some order sheets from there in the same name. It's all too much of a coincidence, and Philip has to be the link between the lot. The real clinch is the letterhead for Expressive Prints Express. When I came round to see Robert about it, first of all he would say nothing to me, then he said it was for one of Philip's associates, I suppose to protect him. But it was Philip who wanted the letterheads all the time. McCormack is accused of setting up Expressive Prints Express, a non-existent company. McCormack says that Bernie Cullum was the man who set up this company, together with dozens of other companies that never existed. Well, now I believe him, and I know who Cullum is; Philip Davidson is Bernie Cullum, and I'm going to nail him. Use your loaf Jennifer. It all adds up. If Lucy is missing you can bet your life that Philip knows where she is. He's got her out of the way, to keep the police from asking questions.'

'Mathew this can't be true. Not Philip. So help me if this is true I'll kill him. I'll kill him! Those trips out with Lucy on the boat, Luke told me he took photos of her; she set Luke up with the dope to keep him quiet. If Philip's done this to my daughter, I won't be responsible for what I might do. What did Toby say? Does he know anything? I want to speak to Toby; Rachael's phone is just ringing and ringing.'

'Toby didn't want you to know, he was shattered, and if we'd told you straight away, if you'd been there, you wouldn't have stayed quiet. Lucy's age would have come out, and Toby would have been in greater danger of being charged, or at least held a lot longer. Avoiding any charges was the best thing I could do for Toby, no matter how I got there. All I focused on was Toby; he was my client. He's not quite home and dry, he's only bailed, but in four weeks we can find out a lot, starting with Philip. Toby has disconnected Rachael's phone, on my say so; I didn't want Philip getting to him. I did my best for him Jen, that's all I could do. Getting him charged wouldn't have helped Lucy, would it? I didn't know how the police were going to run with it. I did my best.'

Mathew could hear Jennifer crying. It was the first time in many years.

'Where's Robert?' asked Mathew. 'Is Robert with you? Please don't cry. Are you alone in the house?'

Jennifer answered her brother in short bursts, in between her sobbing.

'Luke's here with me. Robert's gone to the police station after Philip. Do you think Robert will do something? Someone was here looking for the owner of the convertible. Luke directed him to the creek. Do you think he's got something to do with it?'

'I've got a good idea who that could be. Stay where you are in the house. Promise me you'll stay where you are. It'll be o.k. I'll find Lucy, wherever she is. Trust me, I'll find her.'

Mathew stood up, and grabbed his coat.

'Where are you going? Don't go out now, you look terrible,' said Susan, trying to hold on to his arm.

'I've got to,' he said, 'I can't just sit here. Jennifer has reported Lucy missing. Her identity is out in the open now, and I'm done for. The police know her age, and that she's my niece. I'm finished.'

He left Susan standing in the lounge. The front door closed and Mathew was gone, heading for Highbrook Creek.

Thirty-Five

Philip pulled up cautiously. He knew nothing had followed him. He had his words prepared, and rehearsed them over and over again as he strolled up the gravel path to Jennifer's front door. Only the Mk 2 was visible outside the house, and Philip was confident Jennifer was alone. He looked through the porch window before ringing the doorbell.

Jennifer leapt to her feet, hoping that whoever it was would be bringing news of her daughter. She opened the door to Philip, and fell towards him, shouting and screaming violently. Her head was almost buried in his neck while she pounded his shoulders and chest with her clenched fists. Philip had not anticipated this. His rehearsed lines were both wasted and forgotten. He held her wrists in an effort to avoid any further blows, but Jennifer continued to struggle. She wanted to hurt him; she managed a few loose strikes to his jaw before Philip grabbed her wrists again.

'Jennifer let me explain. Please let me explain.'

'I'll kill you. You sick bastard. I'll kill you.'

Jennifer was weakened by her attempts to injure him, and she collapsed, exhausted, with her head against Philip's chest. She sobbed uncontrollably. Philip held her head close to him while his mouth rested sensitively on the crown of her head. He could feel her thick dark hair as he spoke.

'There's been a terrible mistake Jennifer. You must believe me. I took some photos of Lucy on the boat, I admit that, and I should have told you, but I didn't take those photos. How could you think I'd take photos like that? Ask Natalie. Phone her. I took some pictures because I thought she had a future in modelling. It's a new venture I'm trying to get going. I know it was wrong not to tell you, and we were going to as soon as it got off the ground. Lucy was worried that you wouldn't let her do it. Robert was o.k. about it, I'd already squared it with him; his only worry was Lucy taking time off school. I've taken a couple of hundred shots, Natalie helped her with her clothes and make up and I thought she looked a bit older than she really is.

But I promise you, those photographs I saw - they're not mine. Something's been done to them, but not by me. Jennifer, are you listening to me?'

Jennifer lifted her head slightly and pulled away from Philip. She walked into the lounge. Philip followed her slowly.

'I don't believe you. No one has told me the truth about anything. I won't trust anybody ever again,' said Jennifer, sobbing uncontrollably.

'I'm telling you those pictures are not my doing,' said Philip, wishing he could wrap his arms around her and comfort her. 'I took them to Graphic Solutions,' he continued, carefully, 'and I wanted them enhanced a bit. I asked for a few to be blown up, and some to be fused so that they had a hazy look about them, you know, like they do for wedding photos. There are a lot of teenage magazines out there that would love photos like that. They'd use them quite legitimately; fashion, make-up, music, and just teenage stuff. But they wouldn't touch the ones I saw. Mine were innocent pictures; I don't know what happened to them after I dropped them off. I filled in the order form and gave them in at the front desk. Someone's got hold of them and turned them into something else, but it's not Lucy's body, it's only her face.'

'How the hell do you know that? How do you know my daughter's body? You're lying to me,' screamed Jennifer, 'Mathew was right about you all along. I should never have been so gullible. You can sweet talk your way out of anything. Robert's out looking for you and you'd better be prepared for when he finds you. You're sick Philip. Really sick. Get out of here before I call the police. Get out!'

'Jennifer, please listen. You have to believe me. I want to help. Graphic Solutions have computerised procedures they use all the time. Ask Robert the sort of equipment they've got there. I've seen the results, and sometimes they're incredible, but I haven't a clue how they do it. They can put anyone's face onto another body. It was Lucy's face, and the background was showing Highbrook Creek, and parts of the boat; I assume they're the pictures I took. If they are my photographs then they're not really pictures of Lucy are they? It's just her face and outline, the rest has been done by computer.'

'I don't care what it's been done by,' said Jennifer, still screaming, 'all I know is those pictures showed my daughter naked and posing explicitly. The police said that they had other pictures of her, with an older girl; I suppose one of your girl-friends. They were so offensive, they said, that they wouldn't even show me. You disgust me. You took those photographs and I know you're lying to save yourself. All I want right now is for Lucy to come home. The police can catch up with you later. If you know where she is you'd better tell me now.'

'Are you saying Lucy is missing?'

'Oh, I see. You're going to play the whole game. You know bloody well she's missing. You're hiding her somewhere so that the police can't get to her first. If you know nothing about it then how did Toby get hold of those pictures? You're his boss aren't you? Who gave him the order to collect them?'

'I don't know Jennifer. I really don't know. Graphic Solutions to Colourways is a regular run. The police would have checked the order by now, so maybe they have a name or something to go on, but I don't know about Lucy being missing. The police didn't tell me she was missing. I wouldn't do anything to hurt Lucy would I? I love the kid.'

'Well the police have found some order sheets, and they're from Bernie Cullum. That's you, isn't it?' shouted Jennifer.

'Bernie Cullum? That's the guy Mathew was going on about. Of course it's not me, I've never heard of him.'

Jennifer wanted to believe him, but something wouldn't let her. She couldn't think straight, and her dark secrets were sur-facing again. She was tempted to purge them there and then, they had been buried for so long she would welcome the release; she could take this opportunity to scream it all in Philip's direc-tion, let him take this burden from her. He deserved it. But her brother's words were still in her head; she couldn't allow herself to trust him. Philip made a move towards her and wanted to hold her again as he had done a few moments before. He could even take the pain of her blows just to be able to feel close to her.

Jennifer walked briskly to the door and opened it wide. Her eyes were glazed and tearful.

'I'd like you to go,' she said, a little calmer than she had been. 'I'm leaving everything to the police and when they bring Lucy home, I'll know the truth. Until then, I've got no proof of what you've done. All I know is that I don't believe a single word you've said. Now get out of my house.'

'You'd better go,' said Luke, who had now appeared at the top of the stairs and was looking down at his mother and Philip. 'I know what you've been doing, and so does everyone. You'd better do as she says and get out of our house.'

Thirty-Six

She was cold and exhausted. The blindfold was tight and itching her face, and the cloth around her mouth was hurting. She could just about feel the wooden surface if she stretched her fingertips. She tried hard to free them from the ropes tied at her wrists behind her back, but she could not. She could remember the walk from the Jaguar, but the black guy had blindfolded her eyes long before she reached the dinghy. Out of fear, she had put up no resistance. She had felt, and heard, the small boat moving, but for how long they rowed, she did not know. She was helped from the boat onto the soft muddy ground that squelched beneath her feet with every pace, before her captor brought her to a halt. There was a noise of a padlock clicking open, and then the door that creaked a little as it swung backwards against its wooden frame. Silently, she was taken by her arm and led to where she was now seated. She heard the padlock noise again, and then Lucy was totally alone. Spike had told her that he was only doing the job he had been asked to do, and had no intentions of harming her. If he had his way, he told her, he wouldn't have anything at all to do with kids.

'If I don't get back to collect you, then someone else will,' promised Spike, as he left her trembling on the bench in the boatman's hut. 'Just stay quiet, do as you're told, and you'll be alright.'

But Lucy wasn't alright; she had been tied, blindfolded, and abandoned. Her feet were bound at her ankles and tied tightly to a permanent fixture so that she was prevented from standing or moving at all. She could do nothing but wait. She tried to scream, but the gag in her mouth stopped all but the faintest whimper. Her throat burned so much that she could not utter another sound, not even to save her life. She wouldn't have imagined that she would long for her captor to return, but now she did.

She drifted in and out of dazed confusion and she assumed that by now it must be getting dark. She was afraid that no one would come back for her and no one would ever be able to find her. She listened hard, but there were no recognisable noises. She knew she was at the creek but she couldn't hear the sound of water, or the familiar noise of rigging clanging against the masts. She was in total silence. She recalled what her captor had said about the photographs, but she didn't know how he had seen them or why she was being kept at this place. She knew that it had been wrong to keep what she had done from her mother, and believed that all that was happening to her now was entirely her own fault. If only she had listened to her brother. If only she hadn't told Mrs. Brampton about him, she felt ashamed for getting him arrested. If only he was with her now. If only. She should have tried to be a nicer person but she had enjoyed the vanity, the attention, and the promises of a future that involved nothing more than showing off. She should never have done any of it, and now she was feeling both shame and fear at the trouble she was in; ignorant of how serious it all was. The black guy hadn't told her a thing, but she knew she must have been hurting someone, probably the people she loved the most. This was the punishment for her vanity, but it was hard to believe that anything she had done could justify this. Her tears would have fallen fast down her cheeks had they not been absorbed and diverted by the tightness of the cloth across her eyes.

Some time passed before she heard the noise of the padlock again. She heard the footsteps coming towards her and a man's voice telling her that he was taking her for a walk; a short walk. He untied the cord around her ankles and stood her up. He loosened the gag at her mouth, and the cords around her wrists, though not enough to free her hands completely. She thought she knew the man, but his voice was not immediately recognisable. It was almost as if it was deliberately disguised.

'Uncle Philip? Philip is that you?' Lucy yelled. 'Uncle Mathew? Dad? What's going on; please tell me. Who are you? Please speak to me.'

'You don't know when to shut up do you. You were told to be quiet. You had your chance.'

The man took another piece of cloth and tied it so tight around Lucy's mouth that most of it was inside. It was an instant success at keeping her totally silent.

'I'm not your dad, and I'm not your uncle. I'm nothing to you. Now move.'

The man clasped her elbow and led her out of the hut. She walked just a short way before descending some stone steps. She walked again along a stoned pathway. She then felt herself be lifted into the air and passed from one set of arms to another. She could feel the movement of a boat, a big boat, big enough to be able to walk along the deck for several paces before descending again into a cabin where she now sat, on a fabric covered bench. Nothing more was said, and the two men returned to the deck and waited.

McCormack had found the creek with no great difficulty. It was now getting dark, but with the description of the boat given to him by the kid in the house, it should be easy to find. There were several boats lining the quayside, and McCormack didn't know a sloop from a gaff-rigged ketch. He made his way on foot across muddy ground. He descended some stone steps to the quayside and moved quietly alongside each yacht, looking for their names; the kid had said to look for Sea Lavender. He saw the silhouettes of two men sitting on a deck of one of the boats, which he reckoned was at least thirty feet long. This could be it. He stood still and tried to focus on the men. He edged back slightly and felt the inside pocket of his anorak. The gun was still there. He pulled it out, repositioned it in his outside pocket, and kept it in place with his right hand firmly gripping at the handle. One man was standing now, and pacing the foredeck. McCormack moved towards the boat until he could hear the men talking and could see them a little more clearly. He felt his heart racing; it was thudding loudly beneath his coat as the outline of Cullum and Spike became clearer.

McCormack was steady on his feet and as quiet as a mouse. All those years experience of break-ins and burglaries were paying off at last. Every step made him painfully conscious of each and every sound of his own movements. He could hear the loudness of his own breath. He waited until Cullum paced towards the foredeck. Quickly, and as light as a feather, he landed on the aft.

He crept along the deck with his body bent double. He moved between the cabin and the guide rope, and the timber was quiet beneath his feet. Suddenly, he could see the kid through the porthole of the cabin. She was sitting with her head bent down, blindfolded, her hands behind her back. He could see the cloth tied firmly and deeply in her mouth. The sight of Lucy sickened him. McCormack continued forward towards the two men, softly, without a breath of noise. He pulled the gun from his pocket with his right hand. He stretched his gunned hand out in front of him, and his left hand followed. As he stood almost upright, both arms were now outstretched; his legs bent slightly, the gun held steady with both hands. Cullum was still standing, looking out at the marshes. He suddenly swung around, together with Spike, and faced McCormack, who shouted directly at them both.

'Cullum you bastard! Don't you move.'

'Ah, McCormack, we've been expecting you,' said Cullum, as he made a move towards McCormack, then stopped instantly on hearing the noise of the gun's mechanism as MacCormack got ready to use it.

'I'm warning you Cullum. Don't you move a fucking inch,' said McCormack, 'I'll use this if I have to. Spike - get the girl out of there.'

Spike looked nervously towards Cullum, as if asking for permission to do so.

'I said get that kid out of there, Spike. Get her out now!' McCormack shrieked.

Spike gingerly approached the entrance to the cabin and McCormack watched as he slowly descended. Spike grabbed Lucy by her arm and returned on deck with her close behind him, still tied, still gagged. McCormack reached out and grabbed Lucy instantly, clasping her to him. Lucy was disorientated and scared, and tried in vain to make a sound; there was a slightly muffled moan, but little more. With one hand, McCormack tried to undo the rope that was binding her hands, but only succeeded in slackening it a little. He wasn't going to get Spike to do it; the kid wasn't going anywhere near either of them ever again. He held her tightly.

'Steady love, you'll be o.k. I've got you. Don't be scared. Stay close to me. I'll get you out of here.'

McCormack ordered Spike to stand next to Cullum, and he kept the gun pointed at them both. Lucy's back was firm against McCormack's stomach; both his outstretched arms encircled her, while gripping the pointed gun. McCormack could hear the distant sound of a car, or maybe two cars, but he dared not be distracted, or take his eyes off the two men for a second. McCormack glared at Cullum; there was pure hatred in Cullum's eyes.

'What are you doing with this kid?' said McCormack. 'You hoping for ransom money or something? Don't you know when to stop? You make me sick. This is just a kid. Whatever we've got going on, we don't need this. Let her go; you've got enough to get sorted. You're going to get me off all this stuff Cullum; I'm not taking the rap for any more of your shit. I did time for you, now it's pay back; I've had enough. What gives with this kid? You gonna tell me?'

'I'll tell you alright,' said Cullum, 'I'll tell you McCormack. People like you, and Spike here, you're two of a kind. No talents, no knowledge, no personality. You care for no one and no one cares for you. You use people to get what you want because you have no talents of your own. You may as well be dead. But me? Well, I'm one of those used people. I've been had over like you'd never imagine. And this kid here? She's nothing. Why should I care? I'm not her father. I'm not her anything; she's nothing to me. Do you hear? Nothing. She earned me some money and that's the least I deserve. You talk about payback; it's payback time for me now. I produced some pictures and printed thousands; not just for the money, but for revenge. You wouldn't understand. You're both too dead and dumb to even try to explain. I was making a fortune, now it's time to stop; they're on to me and I'm ruined. But I don't care any more; my beautiful life has been a sham all along. They know all about the companies; it's only a matter of time before I'm banged up. Spike and me were planning one last go at it before making enough to never have to work again, then I would have disappeared, leaving a trail of revenge and devastation behind me. That would have been the end of it, but you and your solicitor; you wouldn't let it go would you? Well if I'm going, then she goes too, and so do you. So, go ahead and kill me McCormack. Go ahead. I've got nothing to live for. This kid has been my ruin. My total destruction.'

Cullum's speech left McCormack slightly bewildered, and unguarded. He had never heard Cullum speak like this; it was all too emotional, not the Cullum he knew. Cullum took the opportunity to leap towards McCormack, grabbing at his wrists and forcing McCormack's arms, and gun, upwards. A shot fired into the air. Lucy tried to shriek as Cullum kicked her away from McCormack's grasp, but as he did so, she stumbled to the edge of the boat. She hit the guide ropes with force. They were not enough to protect her, and she tumbled overboard, falling deep into the black water.

Another shot fired into the air, and while Cullum took a stronger grip on his opponent, Spike took the opportunity to leap from the deck, run full speed along the quayside, and disappear into the darkness. McCormack and Cullum continued to struggle. McCormack still had hold of the gun while Cullum pressed hard at his wrists, until McCormack felt both hands go numb; eventually losing his grip. The gun fell, and skidded away from them both, sliding towards the edge of the deck. McCormack could hear someone shouting in the distance. He instantly recognised the voice that he knew well, the voice of his solicitor. Cullum and McCormack grappled with each other until they fell to the deck and rolled from one side to the other, each one equally determined to gain control, until Cullum was finally in reach of the gun. He stretched his fingers out wide and touched the edge of the gun's handle. He pulled it towards him, holding it tightly in his grasp, pushing McCormack backwards with a sharp knee to his chest. Both men rolled further from each other, tumbling across the deck, but Cullum still held the gun. When he had regained his balance, he stood upright; McCormack did the same, and the two men stood still, facing each other.

Mathew witnessed the affray from a distance, while running towards them as quickly as he could; now, out of breath, he reached the boat.

'McCormack!' Mathew shouted from the quayside, 'what are you doing? Stop this!'

'Find your niece; get in the water,' McCormack shouted, breathlessly. 'This is Cullum, I've found him,' he panted, not taking his eyes off Cullum, or the gun, for a second. 'Your niece,' he said, 'find her.'

'Cullum?' Mathew said in astonishment. 'What do you mean?'

Cullum aimed the gun at McCormack. There was another shot, and McCormack was quiet. The boat tilted completely as Mathew leapt clumsily and heavily from the quayside on to the deck. McCormack was bleeding profusely, and with the sudden sway of the boat caused by Mathew's weight, he stumbled carelessly to the edge of the boat, hit the rails, and fell immediately over them into the pitch-dark water, just as Lucy had done. Mathew watched him falling, clutching the upper part of his wounded chest; the splash of his body on the water caused the boat to sway even more.

As Mathew ran to the side of the boat, he saw McCormack disappear into the blackness; and then sensed the gun was now pointed at him. He turned to face it.

'He called you Cullum. You're Cullum? Tell me for God's sake!' shouted Mathew. 'Put the gun down and let me get him out of the water. What's going on? This is murder. Let me help him before he drowns. Where's Lucy? What have you done?'

Cullum stood still, with the gun pointing straight at Mathew. He had no intentions of letting him get to his client, who he hoped was slowly drowning. If he kept Mathew standing there on the deck for just a few minutes more while McCormack remained under water, either drowning or bleeding to death, then he knew he would be safe. There would be no one else willing, or able, to identify him.

McCormack stayed close to the boat. He had sunk towards the keel when he hit the water, and was able to feel his way along the length of the hull until he was far enough away from the two men for it to be safe to surface. He lifted his head above the water line, taking large gasps of air into his lungs. He repeatedly ducked under, staying under the water until he could hold his breath no longer, looking for the child who had gone before him. But he couldn't see her in the pitch-black mud. Her only chance was that she'd got to the quayside, or found the protection of a neighbouring boat; there was nothing more he could do. He now focused on the safety of his solicitor. Knowing Cullum as he did, he knew he was capable of anything. McCormack was bleeding badly and he pressed hard on the wound in his chest to try to stem the flow; he used all his efforts to stay afloat while edging his way towards the aft, in the hope that he could once more get on deck.

He tried not to breathe too heavily as he struggled to climb aboard, refusing to surrender to his pain. He pulled at the fender; a black rubber tyre that hung on a rope, which was half emerged in the water. He slowly eased his way onto it, and levered himself up, back onto the deck. As he crept again along the deck, he left a trail of blood, mixed with the river water, dripping from his soaked anorak. He was unarmed, and he was wounded, but he had very little to lose. His hatred for Cullum spurred him on with an undeterred will to get to him. Cullum had ruined his life; he was a child molester, a murderer, and now Mathew Weekes was staring death in the face.

He was only slightly relieved when he could hear the two men talking; hopefully this would give him some extra time to save his solicitor. As McCormack approached them, clutching at his wound, he could hear Mathew Weekes pleading with Cullum; but he wasn't pleading for his own life. He could hear his solicitor demanding explanations, and the whereabouts of his niece, Lucy.

'He's mistaken isn't he,' he heard his solicitor say. 'McCormack has it all wrong. Tell me you're not Cullum. Where's Lucy? For God's sake, this is crazy!'

'Crazy?' said Cullum, 'I'll tell you about crazy. Where is that brother of mine? I thought he'd be here by now with the woman of his dreams, in search of their lost child. Do you hear what I'm saying Mathew! What have they done to me? How bad have they made me?'

'What do you mean? What's wrong with you?' Mathew said. 'Who's done what to you? Tell me,' Mathew pleaded.

'He's caused my suffering and now he'll know just how it feels to lose a daughter. I want to see his face when he feels the same pain that drove me to this insanity. They say revenge is best when it's cold; I've been calculating his suffering for some time, you wouldn't believe how long this has taken.'

'Put the gun down,' said Mathew, 'you're not well. Let me help you; whatever it is - we can sort it out.'

'Sort it out!' yelled Cullum, 'how can you sort it out. They lied to me. Years of love and devotion, and they tricked me. They ridiculed my love for all that time. I never dreamed that I could feel such hatred or do the things that I have done. How my love for her turned to hate, real hate. It had to be demolished, extinguished. The images had to be destroyed. She was mine. Those beautiful years that I cradled her as my flesh and blood. I stole the photographs and abused them with the same abuse they have all shown me. They all knew, even your father. Can no one see that it's me who's been abused? Do you not think it obscene? She used me, but her beauty was not mine. I had to make her image be seen for what it really is. Ugly. The daughter of obscenity. I was only showing the truth, just the truth. Like father, like daughter. Obscene. Ugly. Just the truth Mathew, just the truth.'

Cullum was beyond repair; he had gone completely mad. McCormack listened to him pitifully portray his own self-destruction, as if he longed to escape from the hell he was in. As he broke down before him, McCormack took advantage of Cullum's crazed weakness. McCormack moved swiftly across the top of the cabin and ducked beneath the boom; still dripping, and still in pain. He leapt from the top of the cabin onto the deck and grabbed Cullum from behind. His left arm went immediately around his throat, and with the other, he pulled his gunned hand behind his back, and upwards, until Cullum was forced to release his grip on the weapon. McCormack grasped the gun, spun Cullum around towards him, and fired a single shot deep into his chest.

Robert fell to the deck, motionless. His eyes were open and he lay frozen still, staring up towards his assailant.

'I loved her as my own - Philip's child,' gasped Robert. 'They lied to me.' There was a gurgling sound coming from his throat. Then he was silent, his eyes still gazing at McCormack.

McCormack stooped over the man now lying at his feet; trying hard to make some sense of his words. He turned to his solicitor for help.

'What's he saying, Mr. Weekes? Oh my God. Is he dead? I killed him; I had to, Mr. Weekes. I had to do it. He was out of his mind, he would have shot you.'

'I'm sorry,' said Mathew, barely able to speak at all, 'so sorry.'

He stepped away from Robert; his blood was flowing fast across the deck, seeping into the grooves between each plank. Robert's head turned involuntarily towards Mathew, as the boat swayed. His open eyes seemed to watch him as Mathew walked slowly to the side of the boat and stepped from the deck in a trance, stumbling onto the quayside. The boat gave a gentle tilt as McCormack followed after him. Bleeding heavily from the wound in his chest, McCormack slumped to the stone ground, creating a small pool of blood around him on the quayside. Mathew knelt beside him; in a daze, he reached for his mobile phone inside his coat, the phone he rarely used. He dialled the emergency services. As a voice responded to his call for help, a shape in the water distracted him. He saw it slipping outwards, from beneath the hull of the sloop, and now it was lying afloat between the fender and the quayside. He watched in horror. He could not speak a word. The voice on the receiver was persistent, repetitive.

'Emergency. Which service? Emergency ... please respond caller.'

Mathew's eyes were fixed on the water, and the unbearable sight before him. He could not speak; he could hardly breathe.

McCormack reached up to Mathew and took hold of the phone; his voice was so weak it was barely audible.

'Ambulance … ambulance, and police. One shot dead … one wounded … one drowned.'

Mathew continued to stare at the water, unable to move. He could hear again that cracking in his head and the same flashing lights that he had seen before, with the tunnel beckoning him to travel down it. Feeling his father's presence by his side, he moved closer to the edge of the quay where he could see Lucy afloat, lying quiet and still in the dark water. She had been forced to breathe the darkness deep into her lungs, just as his mother had done. He hadn't jumped in to save her. He suddenly recalled McCormack's warning, "find your niece, get in the water …", but he hadn't listened, and he hadn't been thinking. How would he ever be able to forgive himself? He had waited those precious moments while she slipped out from beneath the boat, and came to the surface. And now she had - and she was gone.

He reached down to Lucy, and pulled her lifeless young body to the water's edge. She had been his sister's secret all along; Philip's child, of which he too was ignorant. It was the secret she had confided in their father, and he had broken her trust by his semi-conscious ramblings to Robert, the mystery visitor at his father's bedside. Now Robert had reaped his ultimate revenge. As much as Mathew had always longed to witness Philip's de-spair, he did not want this. Not for anything in the world.

McCormack cried openly at the sight before them. He crawled nearer to the quayside edge, manoeuvring himself so that one arm, then the other, painfully reached down the quay-side wall, towards Lucy. With all the strength he could muster, he helped his solicitor lift his niece from the water, grabbing at her clothing, until Lucy was pulled free of the fender. Together they hauled her up, resting her body gently on the quayside. McCormack collapsed, face down, his arm still resting gently across Lucy. Her blindfold had gone, and her hands were free, but still there was the cloth around her mouth that Robert had tied so tightly.

Lucy's eyes stared up at Mathew. They were the biggest and

deepest he had ever seen; the expression on her face, the fear, the lost trust, the betrayed innocence, would be a lasting image that was never going to leave him, as it had never left his father. Now he could begin to understand his father's pain.

The flashing lights were still present in his head, and the tunnel still beckoned him. He could hear his father's voice; it was so clear, as if he was standing there beside him.

'She did slide out - and she was gone. I should have saved her, but I wasn't thinking. That's what killed her. She trusted me, and I failed her bad. And there she was, my Josie, laying between the quayside and the fender.'

THE END

ISBN 141209530-1

9 781412 095303